A Place Among People

Born in 1935, Rodney Hall has published twenty-three books, including three novels and many volumes of poetry. He was the first writer to be awarded a Creative Arts Fellowship at the Australian National University. He has held two Senior Fellowships from the Literature Board of the Australia Council and has been abroad six times as a visiting Australian artist, to India, Malaysia and Europe. His latest novel, *Just Relations,* was hailed by the *Saturday Review* in New York as "immediately establishing its author's place among the best writers of his time".

Rodney Hall is married and lives with his wife and three daughters on a headland on the south coast of New South Wales.

Rodney Hall

A Place Among People

University of Queensland Press

ST LUCIA ● LONDON ● NEW YORK

First published 1975 by University of Queensland Press
Box 42, St Lucia, Queensland, Australia
Reprinted 1984

Printed in Australia by Dominion Press—Hedges & Bell

Distributed in the U.S.A. and Canada by University of Queensland Press,
5 South Union Street, Lawrence, Mass. 01843 U.S.A.

Cataloguing in Publication Data

National Library of Australia

Hall, Rodney, 1935—
    A place among people/ [by] Rodney Hall. —
    St Lucia, Q.: University of Queensland Press,
    1975.
    I. Title.

    A823.3

ISBN 0 7022 0963 5

With my wife and three daughters, I now live in a place of such beauty (on the far south coast of New South Wales) that this dedication is a public thanks to all those who helped us find and buy the property:
Wal and Nada Taylor, Geoffrey Lehmann, Tom Shapcott, John and Wendy Blay, David Malouf, my mother, and Mrs V. A. Herde

I wish to express my gratitude to the Commonwealth Literary Fund for a six-month fellowship in 1970 during which time I completed the first draft of this book; and to the Literature Board of the Australian Council for the Arts for the three-year fellowship.

1

Mosquitoes were already coming in off the bay, spreading out, hot for blood. Although it was past five in the afternoon the sun still blazed in its passage with explosive control, the air still glittered with salt. Resting his back against a split-log wall sat a man, rather overdressed in jacket, long trousers and shoes. He was like a child's drawing of a man, with circular face, a knob of a nose, staring eyes, tacked-on arms and legs, and a hat balanced ridiculously square on his head.

In front of him, and facing in the same direction, were a dozen families crosslegged on the grass. He was, in fact, the back row at a Punch and Judy show set up in one corner of a pleasure compound. Past the pink and white striped booth, swings dangled idly and no monkey children hung from the bars. He was comfortable he supposed, but agitated and in a way offended.

"I'm getting old," said Punch, "and everybody thinks I'm stupid and everybody thinks I'm weak because of this hump on my back, so they push me around and laugh at me. But I'll show them." And he threw the baby down violently. The crack of its head was plainly audible.

The man took comfort from a momentary bulging of the canvas below the stage-sill and a sudden foot protruding as the entire stall rocked. It was an ordinary black shoe with toecap and laces coming loose. The audience backed away on the seat of its pants. The figure of Punch vanished for a moment, then his arms poked up in a fit. The mosquitoes began to select their victims. When order was restored it seemed too late. Nevertheless Punch reappeared, this time with Judy. Their falsetto squabbling sketched an eternal inability to understand.

Why am I watching, thought the man. Out came the cudgel. Down went Judy.

Horrible, but I loved it once. Down went the policeman (to a stir of adult approval). Down went the Spanish Inquisition, so much to the delight of the dog Toby that he fell right out of the show and tumbled like a pygmy tiger-rug all head and skin among the smallest children. They let out a scream of fear and delight. Then down went Death and up jumped the Devil with a switch of his red tail and a wag of his black papier-mâché face and a voice the same as Punch's.

"I don't need you," said Punch.

"So I'm not afraid of you," said Punch.

"So I'm going to kill you," said Punch.

The triumphant hunchback gloated over his victories, ogled at the assembled families, lolled out of his box like some sort of malevolent spastic.

I loved it as a child, thought the man.

"I've killed everybody," said Punch, "I always wanted to kill them and now I've done it."

The back row went on sitting there long after the rest of the audience had shut itself in cars and begun the half-hour's drive from the bay to Brisbane. He waited as if to assure himself that it had indeed been make-believe. Even seeing the puppeteers was not enough. Nor the puppets packed in an old suitcase, nor even the dismantling of the booth: he recognized that they were merely the instruments of the moment and were now utterly out of contact with what they had created. Something had been communicated, something for the present unidentifiable. He watched the ritual of stowing away each item in the station wagon. Dead: their meanings lived on in himself. Tyres crunched across shelly sand. The vehicle moved out of reach. Something complete was suddenly endangered by the temptation to go on sitting there too long.

The man stood, looked back at the seat to make sure he had dropped nothing, then set out to walk home. It was a good stretch. He decided not to think about anything. Once clear of the waterfront, the Battery Spit shops and houses, he struck across country. The grass hummed with invisible creatures. He came in sight of the river where it seemed to give up all sense of purpose and, at the point of expected grandeur with its final surrender to the bay, wandered off among nondescript islands and wasted itself in a network of channels. He stopped for a moment to catch his breath. The shrill ratchetting call of a plover spun out a seemingly endless chain, thin, bright, metallic, that locked the whole river to stillness. He determined to do something. There must, after all, be something to do.

Long after he sighed into the cool house, the determination remained in him. In fact it lasted all through that evening, the next day, and the following week —

until even *his* skill at giving up hope could not stand against it and he went under the house, extracted a few rusty garden tools from their cocoon of neglect and carried them out to the front fence.

The soil's warmth was unexpected, rising at each thrust of his spade. It soaked into him, renewed him, so that he kept wondering why he had avoided gardening all these years. He used the blade to slice away a patch of rank kangaroo-grass, enjoying the shock that passed up to his shoulders and chest. "I am here," he said out loud. And turned to peer into the dark recesses of his house.

Mrs. O'Shea had been sorry to sell. Much as he had wanted the place, he couldn't escape a certain guilt at having enough cash to outweigh her need for the past and all its associations. Nice things were said of the Berriwee Home for the Aged and doubtless they were true. But she'd had the house to herself ever since the death of her father, Jamie Douglas (he had built it with the help of two friends, one of whom still lived down the dirt road). Mr. O'Shea, known briefly and only as her husband, had been killed in the Great War well before this.

Probing the land with his spade, he remembered her sharply: having seen the *For Sale* placard tacked to a verandah post, he had gone up the steps. And there she was, dozing in a chair, her face pursed to a spider's web of wrinkles. He had suffered one of his usual bouts of indecision; and this apparently gave him time for noticing a few details because all this while afterwards she could be recalled with uncomfortable precision. Despite old age, her hair still bore traces of its original bright ginger. And she was densely covered with bright ginger freckles, which even spotted her eyelids. This strange opaque complexion, like a pointilliste painting, had an almost non-human look. At any rate it must be tough as pigskin. When he coughed and spoke she raised her head and he withdrew, embarrassed, momentarily in panic for her eyes were dark and brilliant with warmth. It was as if some richly humane person watched him from behind a mask.

On the occasion of this very first meeting she had told him, "I had just the one night with Mr. O'Shea before he set sail. Going to the war. And as true as God, mister, that's the only once a man has ever been to me." He had wondered at this frankness. Indeed it made him squirm. What business was it of his? Now — eight years later — he understood. When he bought the house he had also bought a place among people. It was as necessary to know of the chastity of Mrs. O'Shea, as to know where the roof leaked and where saucepans must be placed to catch the drips. For, even now in her absence, she exerted an influence in the district. To those who belonged there, she was the yardstick of respectability.

He crooked his elbow and leaned on the letterbox where his name was painted in beautifully rounded script: COLLOCOTT. Nice bit of lettering. He allowed his earthy fingers to pass over the red shapes, reading them like a blindman. That's what the postman did the first day the job dried; came free-wheeling down the slope, finely coated with dust, his shirt plastered to him except for a parched singlet pattern, he pulled up and dipped into his bag, the bicycle tyres already settling into the powdered roadside. When he pushed back his hat, Collocott saw a pink stripe of forehead above the ochre face. "Is it dry?" he'd asked as he delivered the single envelope, a faint gritty thumbmark in one corner, the first of all those regular cheques. You could measure the years in cheques. The postman had nodded at the answer, stretched out his hand, tilting his whole body so that Collocott wondered if the bicycle might fall from under him, and fingered the red enamel. "You got a talent there," and he had pedalled away, without a single complaint about the heat, down towards Macy's. Old Macy it was who had helped build the house, and would be sure to be waiting to tell the postie yet again how much better off he would be driving a sulky like the first fellow who delivered in the district, instead of that bike which was little better than convict torture in summer. "Remember when they had convicts out on that island there, I do. Not so long ago, considering my lifetime."

"I did have a bit of a talent," Collocott conceded cautiously as he returned to his digging. That was admission enough, no point in getting further involved; regrets at this failure or that having absorbed his energies for long enough, heaven could witness. "I am here," he said again and the silent house looked out at him. He was answering no one, for no one had spoken, no one else was there. The house contained no secrets — only a small carpet snake, tentative as a trespassing cat, and half a dozen cockroaches making for the fat that had splashed to the kitchen floor round the stove. The lino was of green checks among which some designer had been inspired to wreathe baskets and flowers of the most lurid description, now happily coated a neutral brown. The furniture was small and dark, its varnish scaled and dully-lustrous like the body of the passing snake.

Collocott himself was small, going bald at the age of thirty-seven. Sweat like bubbles stood evenly dispersed over his skull, turning to runnels where the thin hair lay flat. He tugged a handkerchief from his pocket, shook the creases out, wiped his face and neck: remembered how the lettering had taken him three hours. He squinted down towards the river. Macy's two huge iron-barks trembled in the sunlight bouncing off the water. A small figure appeared fuzzily (and surprisingly) at the end of the road, climbing through the sliprail fence on the other side and apparently turning his way. His automatic response was twofold — with one hand he checked his fly buttons, with the other he rubbed his chin (was it two days or three? no matter, this couldn't be a visitor).

As the figure advanced Collocott retreated up the eight steps to his verandah and inside. He hid, watching from the bedroom window, trying to relate the figure to the surrounding landscape, to assimilate the intrusion. She looked so small down beneath the ironbarks, making him realize afresh that Mr. Macy's house must be a good two minutes' walk away. Yet the girl was assertive in her brightness, moving at the point where the soft dull slope of the hill levelled out to become part of a wide river bank. Like successive enlargements of her snapshot-self, at each glimpse she could be seen taking the same step closer and closer. And now, could even be heard.

7

The young person passing his house worked at the dairy. She glanced up; her neighbour was nowhere to be seen. Strange bloke. And Bobbie had heard many a story about him — most of them untrue, as she was in some way aware. You didn't need to believe them, she once explained it, and for a moment seemed on the verge of an extraordinary discovery. But she left it at that. She had even embellished a few of the anecdotes herself. Well, after all, Collocott was part of the mystery of understanding. She couldn't imagine the world without him. She had been nine when he bought the house from her aunt. It was this aunt who had made the bright suggestion of christening her Roberta. Serve the old bitch right if no one *did* go to visit her in that Home.

The curtain hung utterly straight and limp. Collocott cursed himself for having ducked inside. Wanted to talk. Liked Bobbie, though he had never had much to do with her. How could he show himself again now? And let her see he had been hiding, watching from an inner window? She would tell the others up there for certain. Then he had seen her staring hard at the house; pressed himself back against the wardrobe, further out of sight. In time the wood ought to be polished by his clothes. She'd be past by now, her yellow cotton frock touching shin and calf at each step, her bare feet raising little spurts of dust, and dust like particles of light alive in her hair. He'd wait a few moments then go back to the job. Before long (another two minute walk) she would be among her friends at work, giving her just that much time to shape the story and, he could imagine it, suggest an explanation for his odd behaviour.

"I could be rich," he said, sitting on the bed and

noting how limp the springs had become. He pulled back the edge of the matress to look. They were rusty. "If I wanted to be."

A minute later he added: "How embarrassing. Why didn't I stay out in the yard?" As if seized with a fresh urge, he jumped off the bed, "By God I've half a mind . . . " but left it at that. He hung about for another ten minutes before returning to his job in the garden. Digging once more, turning up the red soil, he peered into its heart and said, "Les, I've half a mind . . . "

The sky was heavy with heat, pressing supine against the land, condensing the hills to squat lumps, broadening the shallow valleys between. As if reluctantly, the land inclined towards the river, occasional clumps of scrub blurring the line of erosion. A dirt track cut east-west across the main valley, linking two of the hills, slicing vertically up their sides, so the north-south road (itself a dirt track) along the floor of the valley formed a spindly cross. It led south to the fishing settlement a mile off on the bay; and north straight to the river, terminating in a little wooden jetty. Indeed, from the air, this road appeared to cut adrift the grassy spit that gave the place its name. To anyone landing at the jetty (though in point of fact no one *had* during the eleven years since a platoon of Americans disembarked there in 1944) Macy's house stood fifty yards up on the right; another hundred yards away on the opposite side of the road was Collocott's. The only other building in sight, the dairy, was further along, further left and higher up on East Hill — being just above the crossroads.

The sky was oppressive. No leaf could move in so

resistant an element, the dust was kept from rising along the roads. Cows stood or lay scattered about the paddocks like conscious details of a design. Everything was perfectly still in the early afternoon except Collocott, a small dark irritation picking at the earth, opening minute wounds for inspection. He was remembering. As a child the shelves had seemed intimidatingly high, and so densely packed with bottles, phials, packets, and boxes. Three great blobs of coloured light swam from one side of the shop floor to the other so slowly they took half a day for the journey. How often he had checked himself, practised the discipline of refusing to allow his eyes to follow the shafts of light to their source, to those stupendous bottles in the window, their long necks, pointed glass stoppers. Violet. Yellow. Blood.

What really frightened him most was that one day he had asked his father why he couldn't help in the shop.

"Because it's dangerous, son. All these cabinets are full of poisons; tons and tons of poison," adjusting his rimless spectacles with a plump red hand that looked like raw beef in a roll of white paper.

"But I thought you gave people medicines to make them well?"

"One thing you'll learn when you're older is that all medicines worth the name are poisons."

He had learnt it right then.

His fear of policemen became obsessive, he still had it. Once to a schoolmate he had whispered that his dad was poisoning all the town. "Jesus, you lucky bugger!" said Frank in a voice that almost trailed off into tears.

He was remembering: at twelve he had been allowed

to stay up for an adult party to hand round the peanuts and savouries for, as his father put it — A boy has to learn how to conduct himself, he has to find out what life is like. And proudly he had circulated, bearing dishes and salvers, and everyone had remarked on how tall he'd grown and how his hair was cut. The later it got, the less people ate and the more noisy their conversation grew. But he couldn't remember how or when he left the smoke-filled room and crawled into bed. The bed-end, wooden with an arched top — that came back clearly — and how he'd once stolen a cigarette and burnt a hole in the timber and had to open the windows to let the smoke out.

He stopped work and straightened his spine. Blood whirled crazily in his head. It was pretty depressing to be able to remember back twenty-five years, for a man who still occasionally spoke of himself as young. He shaded his eyes and inspected the valley. Cows stood or lay where they'd always been, utterly fixed. Only the ironbarks jumped about between him and the dazzling water. "There can't be any harm in it," he said and peeled off his shirt, hung it on the mailbox. Immediately the great wet map of South America began to dry round the coast. For a while he kept his arms tightly at his sides, the hot immovable air even then seeming to touch him coolly, impudently. He took courage from the lifeless landscape, picked up the spade and extended the new flower bed a further eighteen inches.

Inside the house the dark scaly furniture stood absolutely motionless on the grease-glossy floor, a blue enamel jug fixed to the tabletop. An alarm clock that had lost one leg lolled on its back, silent — four days since being wound — its paralyzed arms stretched wide as a drowning man's. Dust particles, motes, hung suspended mid-air, glowing with light from the pale dead grass outside. One last assiduous cockroach worked at the patch of fat.

Collocott gritted his teeth and dug methodically.

The brown air in the public bar was easily ten degrees cooler than the clear air outside, despite the crush of sweltering bodies. The noise was tremendous now the fish market across the road had closed. Who would have thought so many men had business in Battery Spit? The world outside presented itself to the drinkers as blinding blanks of open doors and windows. Most of the men wore singlets and shorts, no shirts or shoes. Thick limbs and shoulders jostled. Only one drink was being served. So ingrained was the assumption that this was exclusively a beer house, the customers simply called "Two please," or "Six," or "Five, sweetheart." Tap handles flicked on and off and the beer foamed alive through the pipes. There was a general release of cheerful wellbeing. The need for communication was strong, as with Chick ("I'd rather you use me real name") Charlton and Knobby ("It's all the same to me") Clark discussing the possibility of moving up to the city.

"And live there? With all that bloody noise? Must be mad," Chick roared over the hubbub, "Give me the mornings afloat on the bay with the water clear as it comes from the tap — just losing that touch of pink," he screwed up his eyes till he had the scene living before him, "and making the old boat rock just that little bit ... and me," he smiled as he found himself, "sitting

12

back there grinning like one of them Irish whatdya-callems, looking down at me catch, full to the bloody coaming."

"You, or the boat?"

"The both of us. And old Bert at the wheel too."

"Gerroutavit. No, me, I've often thought of Brisbane — a neat little place in the suburbs, shops handy for the wife."

"By the living Jesus!" Chick nodded in the direction of a newcomer heading for the bar, "that's a lairy rig-out isn't it?" Most of the other drinkers also stopped to take account of the light grey suit, white shirt, the tie, the face saying, "Gin and tonic please," and the barmaid looking helplessly at his tall nose. A profound hush fell on the place. Then Chick was heard to whisper, "'S what'll come of you, mate, up in that flash suburb. Fate worse than death."

In the barber's shop next to the pub, that moment of silence was clear as a gunshot.

"Fight, do you reckon?" said an old fellow in the chair by the window. Then the din resumed.

"No. Wasn't long enough," from Arnold Thompson the barber, who was spinning out his day's work, dreading the domestic tensions that awaited him at home. The customer shifted discontentedly under the blue and white striped sheet. Several clumps of grey hair rolled into a ball in his lap, another slid to the floor.

"Too late now, but I should have liked to have been there for that, whatever it was."

"Shave Harry?"

"Suppose so. Do your worst."

Arnold Thompson adjusted the back of the chair, his

customer reclined. "Comfortable?"

"Good as I could expect." Harry lit a cigarette while the barber systematically laid out his razor, shaving soap, brush, towels, and filled a thick mug with hot water. Once the soap was on, smoking became impossible. The cigarette remained in one hand, smouldering away.

A customer in the second chair was acutely aware of this burning cigarette. Though he didn't turn to watch, in his side-vision he could see a thread of smoke wavering up, dissolving at about head-height. The old man, Harry, is going to hold it till he feels the heat then he'll have to ask for an ashtray. The apprentice reached for his electric clippers again.

"Hey, not too much of that, sonny," said Arnold in genuine alarm, "do you want to leave Mr. Collocott like a plucked chook?" His tone changed for the client, "Get carried away with the marvels of modern science, these young fellows," he apologized; then added briskly, "if it's a final trim round the edges, use your fine hand-clippers. Anything else, use the scissors. Okay?" No answer. Snip snip. He waited. Sni-ip. Then returned to his own job, vigorously re-stropping the cut-throat. A little column of ash tumbled from Harry's cigarette and broke on his knee. "And now, Harry, about those oleanders you promised me." Grunt, from the chair. "No hurry, of course." Must be half burnt away, thought Collocott as the lad pulled his ear and pecked a bit more hair.

They've settled down in there now," said Collocott — fluent after several silent rehearsals. Grunt, from Harry.

"You're right, they have," from the amiable Arnold,

as if he hadn't noticed.

One last snip and the lad flicked a towel across the back of his neck so the tip of it stung, his hand already out for the money. Collocott, as always, fumbled. The butt was dropped on the floor; an acrid smell of singed hair cut through the vague aroma of brilliantine and talcum. "Thanks," and the customer escaped. Someone at the pub window remarked: "That Collocott's a queer joker."

"Just been shorn by young Jonesy, by the look of things. Cripes that kid'll make a good sawmill hand — got the bloody style to a T." Collocott walked up the two steps and into the bar: it was like a dark negative held close against his eyes, gradually assuming defini-tion. He found himself looking at a man's back — im-maculately dressed, shoes well-heeled and polished. Hat. In every detail, familiar. And a vast flood of unreasoning fear passed through him. He bolted out into the street again and up towards the shops. The stranger, sipping his gin and tonic had not turned round.

The hunted man feels safer in a crowd. But where could you find a crowd in Battery Spit, apart from the pub? Collocott peered in butchers' and grocers', looking for the busiest. Never deciding. Whipping out of sight round corners, a cold blade in the small of his back. Knowing himself, knowing his cowardice, unable to protect himself from that brutal awareness by any trick or sophistry. He was scared; and inwardly laughing with hurt; now and again tears drowned him. At the Post Office he leaned against the wall, voices inside said, "Here comes Collocott . . . Where? . . . Who? . . . Collocott, everyone's heard of him . . . Him? . . . Is he coming in, or what? ... Drunk? Never! ... Not that he hasn't got the lolly." He lurched away from the door, collided with a tall weighing machine, cold, silver-painted, ornamental, it struck him in the face. He clutched it, stood on the plate, dug in his pocket, produced a penny and stuffed it in the slot. Black and white disc spun round, spun back, like a ratchet in his head, round, back, dazzle, back. "Collocott ... Collo ... Ollocott." came the voices. Clunk, and the machine delivered into its metal dish a small card. He took it. *Your personal weight.* 9 St. 10 Oz. *For health, weigh yourself every week.* Have to think clearly. Walk with steady even tread. Buy something, speak to shopkeeper. He entered the first shop, his name whispered ceaselessly in his brain.

"Goodday, Mr. Collocott, what can we do for you?" He sent the spinning disc back — unwind — then the words began to happen as if some ventriloquist were using him. Brisk and polite (in a tone so reminiscent of his father) he detailed the goods he wanted.

"Have you had yourself weighed, then?" asked the wife, "What's your fortune?" She laughed a happy, token laugh, "Only thing to get me on that machine — having my fortune told. Though in the old days you used to get it in poetry. Reckon I could believe it more, that way." He looked at the card in his hand, turned it over:

"Your life will be simple and filled with happiness. Don't expect wealth, you must make do with love."

She tidied the pile of wrapping paper on the counter, "Well, there you are, then," she said with satisfaction.

Collocott finished his shopping as quickly as he

could, and set out for home. It was a good half-hour's walk; even so, he chose to take an indirect route that brought him first to the top of West Hill. He was shaking from nervous exhaustion by the time he had the house in sight. Then with astonishing nimbleness he sprang sideways off the track and crouched behind a clump of lantana. Below, like some great jewel fixed to his fence, a green car glittered in the sun. A visitor was standing on the verandah. No need to wonder who. "You —" said Collocott threateningly, impotently, "You — " the choice of an adequate word remained beyond him. However he was enjoying a moment of self-satisfaction, for he was evidently keeping one jump ahead and he would never be spotted through such a bush. He was surprised to notice that the appalling emptiness inside him, his fear of the unexpected, was not wholly unpleasant. The house was locked, he had food in his shopping bag, let the test of staying-power begin.

In the car the temperature crept higher — soon a clear fifteen degrees above the blazing day outside. The visitor, already tired of standing, looked round the verandah then settled himself in an old deckchair. Collocott squatted on the dry spiny grass. The timeless clarity of the scene delighted him. Insects hovered as if suspended, preserved. Birds whistled each other the occasional, lazy reassurance. One of the cows that had been standing, lay down, abruptly, as if this were the solution to some long-deliberated problem. To the south-east an attenuated island enclosed the bay with its arms. The still water, banded blue and buff, was broken here and there by tiny humps of land thick with mangroves. From this particular vantage point, the skyline was interrupted by East Hill, then reappeared on the far side of the river mouth, embraced by another, matching island. And further north, led to a spectacular outcrop of mountains, a distant jumble of volcanic cones, individual, sharp pointed — a shock to the eye, like turquoise icebergs defying summer's heat. It was here, on this hill at Battery Spit, that the Colonial authorities built a defensive gun position to command the river entry. On the seaward slope several courses of stonework could be found, legacy of convict labour. The local School of Arts library actually displayed a dozen iron cannonballs that had been found half-buried in the soil there.

The visitor lit a cigarette, snapping his lighter shut in a single expression of the impatience he was controlling so admirably.

Grass pricked through Collocott's socks. His legs had begun to feel cramped in that squatting position, so he sat instead, and eased them out straight. The ironbarks looked somewhat thin and scruffy seen from higher ground, and Macy's lay flat as a collapsed cardhouse. The convicts, of course, has suffered appallingly under the respected Captain Logan; gifted as an explorer, he may have been, but that in no way affected the issue, the savagery of a perfect military mind. He was still a hated man in these parts a hundred years after his death by violence. So was Governor Darling; the very stones of the battery enclosure had been witness to the inhumanity condoned by that cold aristocrat. It is right for such a man to have such a name, said Collocott who had thought of compiling a short history of the district

— a monograph rather than a book — but finally felt it might be an intrusion.

The side door of the dairy opened, its clank carried across the valley, and three girls came out on the step. They sat there companionably under the corrugated metal awning. The distance was too great for recognition. The preservative got them and sealed them beautifully whole. The door remained precisely two-thirds open. It was just this immobility which brought so many motorists from the city to such bayside settlements on weekends. And the prawns and mudcrabs were famous. A hawk circled high over the point, was enveloped and there suspended, wings spread.

The visitor stood. Went to the rail. Looked out. Remained standing. Collocott watched the shadow of his lantana bush lengthening down the hill. But, he thought with pleasure, it'll be a long time before that car begins to cool. Suddenly the cohesive element of the whole scene dissolved: cows began to move slowly towards the dairy. The girls shook the creases from their frocks and went back inside. A little shiver of hot air disturbed the ironbark leaves. The man walked down the steps, opened his car door, recoiled for a moment (to Collocott's immense satisfaction), took something from the glovebox and returned to the verandah, leaving the passenger door open. He sat and was busy for a few minutes, bending over. He went to the front door, stooped down. Stood, slipped something in his inside pocket. Marched back down the steps and slammed himself inside the car.

The sound of the motor pulsed through the whole valley of dusty grass. Kicking up a spurt of dust the green jewel glittered forward, made slow headway south up the long arm of the cross in the direction of the settlement. Then, to the watcher's despair, swung off along the dairy road, climbed right to the gate and stopped. Engine off. The insects rejoiced. Door clunked. Grey suit vanished into the dark building, to reappear with one of the girls. They stood a moment shading their eyes against the oblique sunrays. Even from behind a lantana on the opposite hill, it was obvious that the stranger was being charming, nodding, raising his hat, no doubt smiling and laying on the gratitude pretty thickly. Collocott, who had half-risen when the motor first started, now crouched smaller than before. He was utterly insignificant, a tide of fear and excitement (yes) passing through him. He didn't relax until he saw the car turn back and proceed towards the Battery Spit shops. He could see it for almost half a mile, on and off.

A long time after the dust had settled, he stood, picked up his bag of groceries, and stepped out into the open again. This side of the hill was already in total shadow which even now lapped at the stumps of his own house and would soon flow over it. The cows were already inside the dairy shed. Doubtless, Bobbie was milking one of them at that very moment. The hawk was no longer anywhere to be seen.

His boots crunched down the hill, small stones cracking and rolling under them. The noise drew too much attention to him; walking on the grass verge was more pleasant anyway. The shopping bag knocked against his leg rhythmically. At the crossroads he looked about in fear . . . no, no worry, not a car in sight. Reached the fence. Red letters COLLOCOTT. Talent there. Gate

Missing. Began to climb the steps. Suddenly he surfaced from the shadow and the sun placed a warm hand on the back of his neck. Again he looked round. There was a faint rustle as the front door swung open. Like a ridiculously small mat — one single sheet of paper, folded. He stared at it, till it seemed a white well of infinite depth, till it grew fuzzy at the edges and was pure light, till it was a mirror burning his eyes with its reflection of the sun's final moments. A tinge of blue spread across it, abruptly brown, and the shadow crept in across the floor, in from the verandah to the passage-way. He stepped over the paper, then banged the door with one backward flip of his right hand.

Arnold Thompson reconciled himself to the fact that no more customers were going to come into the shop that afternoon. He shut the glass door with a sharp clack: the crepe-paper decorations in the window trembled. Already he had half-forgotten what life was like when he and Dulcie cut those trimmings — sitting on the floor folding the stuff and comparing work to make sure the scissor patterns were even. The bright yellow and the blue looked gay together when they were festooned round the glass. Now they were bleached beige and grey, dusty; with reminders of the original colours showing in the folds. But who wants to be reminded? A lot can happen in three years. After all, his *old* shop hadn't been so bad and Dulcie was happier in those days. "It makes you bloody wonder," he commented and took the broom himself tonight, because he had sent the boy home earlier. "A man's a mug," he added, still spinning out the day's work.

A different crowd had gathered in the pub next door. The new neon strip lights were switched on and flickered pink and blue against the smoke-bloom of the high ceiling. These were men from the abattoirs and shops and a few truckdrivers. The small group of fishermen still there had gathered in a corner, on the fringe. One man dominated the others by sheer bulk. His enormous bare feet, hard as the floor, had probably never been inside a boot in their lives. "No one makes them big enough," as he himself put it once. This was Bert, talking quietly, frankly, drunkenly to his cousin the railway employee: "That's about the strength of it, Nev. I suppose there's nothing else I'd want to do. Even with the storms."

"But that one last year, you must have wondered if you'd ever come back." His tone changed, "And when you walked in here, the whole bang lot of yous stood round crying in your beer that there was no fish into the bargain, and how you couldn't even make enough to rake up a feed." Bert chuckled at the courtesy, then acknowledged the main drift of the conversation:

"Look it's . . . Let's have another beer." They stood drinking, contemplating the tidemarks of froth above the beer line, a deep understanding flowed between them, the knowledge of hardship, the knowledge of danger. "Tell you what though, when there's nothing you can do but hang on and ride it out, you get a . . . feeling . . . " he set down his empty glass, "you might say to yourself — so that's what it all adds up to." A touch of embarrassment intruded. "Me and young Chick Charlton has faced a few storms I can tell you. And the sharks attacking. There's a good few shark's teeth in the hull of that old boat. You get used to things." They lapsed into silence, open to the complex meanings of death, silence made bearable by the background roar of conversation.

Chick's wife at that moment was clanging saucepans about on the stove, made violent by a sense of injury. Suddenly the whole kitchen swam a great distance from her. She peered at the dinner through a lens of tears. The two boys began squabbling again in the back yard. She clamped her teeth and darted for the door, "I'll kill them, so help me if I don't."

And Dulcie Thompson next door watched her burst into the garden, her hair flying loose, watched her with considerable satisfaction as she swooped on the boys, her hands flailing — drove them left and right. "She's looking a bit old these days," Dulcie commented without so much as a glance over her shoulder at her teenage daughter who leaned, sullen and lumpish, against the ice-box. She experienced her own flash of anger — turned with ladylike dignity and added, conscious of her superior accent, "I was speaking to you, darling."

"That so?" replied Tricia and stood there. A little dart came into her mind, she aimed it: "Better keep looking, you might miss something."

Arnold tested all the locks and bolts painstakingly. Yes, the shop was secure. He set off for home out along the road that passed the boarding school (a quaint old-fashioned institution privately run for the daughters of rich country people within a radius of five hundred miles). He was close enough to hear the delicious shrilling of girls at play when, for some reason, he decided to turn back and take the other route. Arnold hurried up the hill. As he crossed the Parade, Bert spotted him and called out through the pub window: "Come and have a drink and show us the scalps you took today." With a ridiculous sensation of irresponsibility and relief Arnold stepped in and was immediately swamped, drowned in the noise, abandoned, hanging on to his individuality as if he could suddenly set a limit to his life, see its shape and say to himself — So that's what it all adds up to.

Collocott's house remained in darkness. He had locked himself inside and was just stepping under the shower. He let the cool water trickle across his shoulders and down his back, regretting that it never came out cold in summer. Then he turned the tap hard on, so the spray pelted against his skin, almost stinging. He washed away the peppering of cut hairs from neck and shoulders. There was a prickly sensation where the razor had been used to trim the edges at the back — none too sharp, that lad never put enough work into stropping.

Collocott applied the soap assiduously, foaming it in among the thick hairs. Stopped abruptly. Turned off the tap. Strained his ears, cursing the gurgle of escaping water. Would it never drain out? At last there was silence. He listened. No one was knocking. Even so, he decided not to risk the shower any more. Too much noise, a dead give-away. He scrubbed himself with a grimy towel, but left his back wet so it stuck to the shirt he put on. He always did that in hot weather; refreshing. It was a trick his brother taught him years ago. He crept out along the passageway and eased himself into a chair in the front room, where he could see out on to the verandah through Mrs. O'Shea's old lace curtains —

curtains exactly like the ones she had made for Mrs. Fennell the bank manager's wife, that important woman, who only last Tuesday had questioned her husband about Collocott:

"He's so *very* peculiar," she said, waving her soup spoon for attention, "would you consider him a typical Australian type, of any description?" Mrs. Fennell was English.

"How would I know?" Her husband was a Queenslander. She returned to her meal composedly:

"It's a mystery. That cheque, regular as clockwork." She rose, collected the empty bowls and returned to the table a minute later with a joint of beef. For a brief instant, real expression transformed Fennell, gathering his features into a face.

"Nothing to match our beef," he said appreciatively, "eat lamb in Victoria, beef in Queensland." Then gradually he sank out of reach again.

"Who sends them though?"

"You know I can't discuss matters like that. It's more than my job's worth." Yes, he was well out of reach. She pursed her lips and looked round the room, through the archway into the lounge. A house any woman might envy, she assured herself, and popped a ladle of peas on her plate. The dark furniture (mock cedar) in carved antique shapes, standing so elegantly on the biscuit coloured Axminster. There's nothing like wall-to-wall carpets, even if they are a touch hot in summer. She'd liked the colour of the Wilton a little more, but there's a great deal in a name. The radiogram flashed its gilded teeth at her and lamplight twinkled on the big crystal ashtray. She admired the beautiful hang of her new brocade curtains; the furnishers had fitted them to perfection. And that's what she always demanded. A slight frown flickered across her face as she noticed the old lace curtains behind.

"Aubrey, I think it's about time we bought some fresh lace for the front windows. It makes the whole place look shabby."

"Just as you like, my dear."

"Do you know, I believe it's fully seven years . . . no, eight, since that old woman made them up. What was her name?"

"O'Shea."

"That's right, yes. And I've always suspected her. It's my belief she helped herself to a few yards of that lace. She took me for a fool, but I knew."

"Why didn't you tell her then?" he asked, thinking about a weekend fishing trip.

"Well, the poor thing wasn't very well off, was she? It would have seemed cruel. And besides, she made an excellent job of the curtains, upstairs and down. I've always been lucky with curtains." She prepared herself for the task of going out to fetch the dessert. And sighed, "Oh dear, it would have been nice to have had children, they could do so many little jobs for one." She smiled bravely. A rush of anger flooded through him, up from somewhere so deep he had almost forgotten. Even his hands turned a darker red. His eyes bulged at her, tongue stuck to the back of his mouth. She saw nothing as she added, "Thank you, darling, I think I might try some of that nylon net for a change."

The lace, heavy with dust, turned its stiff flowers

obliquely from Collocott; they were dark against the pale evening sky. The other side of the wall, in the passage a matter of six feet away, one folded piece of paper remained just inside the front door. "What made him come himself," said Collocott, "all this way?" The room itself gave so many connotations to his thoughts. The years were quite enough for gathering memories, even if so little happened. The very lack of what other people might call events created acute awareness of those things they seldom notice at all. And, brilliant through this accumulation of tiny changes and movements, his image of Mrs. O'Shea gave depth and meaning to his thoughts. She had sat in his chair, long braids of hair wound round her head; hair that shone so white and wispy in the dim room, touched by the glare from outside. Her thin old face appeared black by contrast, yet not enough so for him to miss the trembling of her chin. The tremblings of insect wings. Palpitation of the lizards that visited him daily; the vase on the cabinet when someone let off gelignite in the bay; that long quiver passing through the girl's body at each step she took, leaning forward, pressing against the distance between her and wherever she was going. An old lady's hand signing papers. His own hand now on the chair arm.

Collocott had sensed a kind of wisdom growing in himself. It arose from his need to be accepted at Battery Spit, beginning with Mrs. O'Shea — how well he understood her fear and the injury to her sentimentality — continuing when he took his first walk to the village, bought a few things at the shops, then loitered past the pub trying to muster courage enough to go in, and a cheerful fellow at the window had spoken:

"You the new cove at O'Shea's?" He nodded. "Then come in and meet the boys." He had gone in. And, courteous in a most discreet way, they had treated him nonchalantly, as if he always drank with them, asking him nothing, in no way condescending, till with a burst of warmth he recognized that in some small measure he did share the qualities of these men (that they might help him "understand himself", for he was a victim of this twentieth century plague).

Cicadas chirred incessantly. Curious how almost everyone likes the sound, perhaps as a hangover from some cold-climate romanticism about the south seas and hot summers, certainly Mrs. Fennell had the distinct feeling that it added glamour to her home. Anywhere you walked outside, the noise remained constant, not seeming to move with you like the seductive moon, but utterly reliable and impersonal. Is it a mating-call? Collocott wondered. Bobbie heard it too and, by some unaccountable association, began telling the family how that strange person had ducked out of sight the moment she came near his house and how she'd been sure he was peeping from some hiding place.

The moon rose brilliantly, decorating the floor with fine lace from the curtains and thick lace from the cast-iron verandah. It was like a stage prepared for some magical night scene. And Collocott, the audience, hoped nothing would happen. He still hadn't eaten, didn't feel hungry. "Yet we survive," he murmured at 9.50 p.m. The moon patterns moved with smooth imperceptible slowness, those large circles at the centre of the design like full clear bottles; each detail snaked its way through subtle mutations as the unbroken design advanced entire across the floor, lapping on virgin boards, letting others drop into oblivion. It all became somewhat hazy. He must have dozed for he realized with a sudden jolt that there was no longer any light. The cicadas were silent — had gone? An enormous black void of fear imprisoned him; he could sense it pressing against the house like water. "How frail," he said at the still core of his cyclone panic. There was nothing he could do but hang on to his nerve and ride it out. Yet some satisfaction was to be found in completing a pattern, contemplating death, looking back over his life and thinking: So that's what it all adds up to. He lolled, hot and panting, his back and limbs aching; decided not to go to bed. "Yet man survives," he added at 1.25 a.m.

In the soft toneless light just before dawn, he stood up and made his way awkwardly to the kitchen. Gulped down a glass of water. "Still not cold," he muttered. It occurred to him that thoughts of death are too melo-dramatic. He was aware of the difficulty of being unself-conscious. Some of this was doubtless due to a univer-sity education. The phrase startled him, he felt its im-pressiveness. But his mouth sneered against the rim of the tumbler; he knew how little it had meant for him, that in all the past fifteen years he had not yet been able to relate it to his life, find meanings or security through it. Yet he was the one who had chosen a course designed to open a wider understanding of meanings, the one *not* to have taken Pharmacy, the one to break out of his father's clutches. He settled himself back in his chair. The hill opposite was a perfect colour, like a luminous green peach with a cleft of rose. One might well ask

29

what meanings were needed, at what point explanation must stop in order to save experience being impaired. "Or missed altogether," he said, loosening his belt one notch. He had passed his exams creditably. But facts are not necessarily knowledge, let alone understanding. The sun rose. In a blaze of fierce light the hill was suddenly blinding. "The only one to turn out a failure."

Bobbie was up already, dressing perfunctorily, a knife of light slicing her in half. One arm, one shoulder, a stick of brilliant green material. Suddenly a face. No face. A brief play of fingers. A girl half-realized, catching sight of her incomplete self in the mirror, giggling for a second — then sighing as if something unthought moved in her mind. "Bloody work," she said, slapping her hips with more than a hint of cheerfulness. Her father's market garden lay behind West Hill, on the opposite side to Macy's. There was a track running inland away from the river, roughly parallel to Collocott's place, veering left into the valley and so to the dairy. But this morning, for the second time in as many days, she decided to have a change, to take the other way round the hill, through the paddock, and up along Culver's Road. Mrs. O'Shea had explained to Collocott that she'd never heard of anyone called Culver in the district, "Still, you've got to have a name for your street, haven't you? And it's not what you'd call a confusing word." So she had prattled to keep her chin from trembling.

Her red hair fluffed in bold waves, her dress sensuously loose (allowing anyone to see the free movement of her body inside), Bobbie came to the old sliprail fence, climbed through, and set off up the road. Was it involuntarily that she slowed her pace as she approached the mailbox with its red lettering? In his prison of lace Collocott stood up, the folds hung in his clothes, he turned towards the side window just in time to catch a glimpse of green. Yesterday was instantly in his mind. He rushed for the door; was stopped short by a white blob on the floor; raced for the back way; round the side; abruptly cutting back his speed. She was past. Collocott looked at her as she walked on. Yes, he was relieved, and newly aware of his shabby appearance. Good thing, the way it had worked out. Then Bobbie glanced back. His hand went up. "What am I doing? What am I doing?" he whispered almost afraid.

"Hullo," she said, "you must get lonely here I suppose."

"I've got plenty of thinking to do." She came back and touched the fence with her hand.

"And you've begun on the garden — at last." Such pleasure that little rebuke gave him.

"Yes, after eight years' idleness." His fingers traced the upside-down letters as he reached across the mailbox. He stared at the soft roundness of her neck. She could sense his gentleness — something her father had never had, something he had never given her.

"You know, Mr. Collocott, yesterday's the first time I ever saw anyone come visiting your place. Such a flash bloke too. Latest model car." She saw the colour drain from his face, and added hurriedly, "I wasn't sticky-beaking. I'd never have known except that he called up at the dairy. Asked after you, if you was well, working, if you had many friends. You should have seen old Molly making up to him. She was mooning about all afternoon when he'd gone."

"What did you tell him?" came the strangled question. His hurt and his terror; were clear to her. She replied too loudly, but with simple dignity:

"I told him if he wanted to know about your business, he'd best go down and ask you himself. Well," she said almost defensively, "we don't want strangers come nosing around our affairs in Battery Spit, do we!" But Collocott dared not be comforted:

"Did he say who he was?"

"He was going to. But I didn't like the way he gave himself out to be the great I Am. So I said — It's got nothing to do with me what you want or who you are, *that's* Mr. Collocott's house down there along Culver's, and now I've got work to do — then he lifted his hat and smiled and called me a charming young lady. And I thought: I could give you a shock or two, you oily bugger . . . " she bit her tongue as the word slipped out. But that odd man was beaming, looking foolishly happy as a matter of fact.

"I'm in a mess," he explained, indicating his rumpled clothes, "no sleep."

"You are too," she laughed. Then, immensely satisfied with herself, she swung off up the road, still a child, her breasts high and firm, a quiver passing through her at each step. Her mind racing. Already she began to suspect she was perplexed at her own pleasure.

He went back indoors and changed into clean shirt and trousers, not to be caught out again. For the first time in seventeen hours his fear lifted. Collocott unpacked his shopping bag, putting the goods away methodically, each thing where it belonged in the cupboards, and the squelchy butter in the refrigerator (comforted by the metallic pu-chunk as its door closed).

"Perhaps I ought to start drinking milk again," he commented as he soaked some breakfast cereal in water and heaped the sugar on. He had an egg (no, two) and some weak black tea; then took himself into the backyard and flopped down, "To spine-bash," he murmured experimentally, under the gumtree. He had three jobs vaguely in mind: to dig the front garden, to clear the scrub from around the fence, and to begin work inside the house. Looking at it now, from the ground up, the old gum seemed to have struggled to its present size; its limbs ragged and knotted, some atrophied, some like a swirl of pure energy and sinuous as water. He supposed it must be a pretty poor specimen, with scruffy stunted leaves, irregular branch formations — but at no stage did he give any thought to the possiblity of calling it ridiculous. Ridiculous it most certainly was not: the element of effort being all too clear for that. There was an achievement for this tree in the basic fact of survival. "You couldn't say a tree like that is a failure." He halfclosed his eyes till it lost all sense of thrust and thickness, till it spread flat as the blue beyond.

Then with an unfamiliar clarity of purpose he went out to the bed he had been digging the day before, and made a new hole. He insinuated one hand into the earth, his spread fingers working further and further in, his wrist a pink stem. Some novel identity all but sweeping the world into another perspective, another set of relationships. Yet the hand did not take root. And, feeling slightly foolish (indeed, glancing about to make sure no one had seen), he withdrew it. All the same, he had enjoyed the warm closeness; and if the earth had not received him into its mysteries, he had at least experienced something that extended him. They had always told him he would never grow up. Well, even if he had been slow about it, this was helping. And he decided it was all a matter of freedom. The aphorism was stored away: growing up is coping with freedom. By no means displeased with himself he reached for the spade again. At each jab and turn, the warmth of the soil rose, soaked into him and renewed his courage. Why had he avoided gardening for so long?

"I found the answer to that yesterday," he told the soil, but couldn't remember what it was. A terrible day, yesterday. One of the terrible days of his life. Collocot' looked anxiously up and down the road, across the side fence at the dairy. Nothing. He tried to shake it off, but fear moved through his blood. Too exposed at the front of the house, he retreated round the side. The bottle-brush in full flower touched him on the shoulder. If you work close enough to the building, he thought, a vegetable garden could be dug without anyone seeing.

"I want such protection, it could almost be death." His father's death came to mind as a possible example. "No," he decided, "not like that," for he remembered saying at the time: I ought to be feeling more, the death of a parent is one of the major tests in life. Was it inescapable, that his expectations had been disappointed? Put it down to youth: he hadn't understood, so he blamed the old man for not managing something more dramatic. It all seemed to slip by. Finally he could single out the apt words, so he spoke:

"I felt I was cheated."

34

2

Sunday was just as hot as the other days had been. And when the three churches at Battery Spit (Roman Catholic, Anglican, and Non-Conformist) opened their doors, air hot as breath escaped. The iron roofs shimmered. Their pale yellow walls stood two-dimensional against the flat blue bay like a stage backdrop. Inside, flowers a mere thirty minutes old wilted in brass vases. One congregation boasted a bell; its repeated note broadcast a message of intolerable monotony that could be heard out on the shoals, several miles inland as far as Jacobs's farm, north to the convict fort and even across the river — alerting one lone figure on unidentified business among the mangroves; he listened to the fitful sound for a moment, till a faint north-easterly breeze set the leaves in motion and the bell was gone.

Throughout the village women emerged, flushed, tightly corseted, swathed in their nylon best and wearing small flowery hats that, to any but the expert eye, were identical. Boys with their hair slicked down, the rebellious ends still dripping water, their blue shirts starched, shorts almost down to the knee, thin brown arms and legs, felt the weekly hatred in their hearts: hatred of formality, of mystification, of the clothes and, above all, the compulsory waste of time and curbing of energy. Girls in fresh print cotton, in gingham, little white or pink bonnets, ribbons and slides in their hair — a trifle fastidious about the dust, for their shoes had been too highly polished and too tightly laced, were inwardly excited, inwardly afraid, and yet bored also — religion was like growing up, it seemed immensely important and although it was worth any amount of discomfort to achieve, this was no guarantee the process wouldn't be tedious. At last, making sure the front door and windows were left open to keep the house as cool as possible, came the men in their blue pin-stripe suits: as astonishingly alike as their wives, baggy trousers with cuffs that almost enveloped the shoe, double-breasted coats, lapels cut to sharp points that soon dog-eared; smelling of brylcreem and cigarette smoke (perhaps letting a final puff rise into the air and trail after them, dropping the butt on the front steps, carefully treading on it leaving black embers in the grain of the weathered wood).

Down by the water below the skeletal remnants of the fort, from a fibro hut, a single woman issued, alone. Flowered hat more battered than most, cotton dress beginning to rot around the bold contours of its leaf-pattern, skin so dark as to be almost black: Daisy Daisy. From the moment she was christened, victim of an arrogant society. She walked firmly if slowly, carrying her large frame well. No one watched from the window of the hut. She turned left along the road at the end of the track, past Sissons's place, on her way to church. Old Sissons himself was in the front garden; a small tough man with a stringy neck and hideous blotched skin (the dark brown of many years' exposure was now peeling to an obscene lolly pink, which in turn had broken into scabrous irritations).

"Good morning, Miss Daisy," he leered at her contemptuously. She turned her terrible eyes on him without hurt or interest. His tongue raked at the gaps between his teeth. Nothing like a bit of fun, as he explained it later to his young mate Mick. "Going to meet God, Miss Daisy? And the sweet Lord Jesus? *He* was a boong too, by all accounts." Miss Daisy walked on. "Or at least a wop," he shouted after her, "Or a wog," and sucked away triumphantly. Returned to the job of watering the lettuces. Grumbled, "Beats me why they let them go free, hanging around the neighbourhood like a bad smell."

There were no other houses for a quarter of a mile. What could he do to her? The thought was hardly in her mind. What could anyone do that would matter now? She remembered the day, she was eleven, when the strange pale men suddenly roared into her village. Their steamboat swooped in with the speed of a bird. They shouted, caused several ear-splitting bangs to happen, rounded up the people. Picked her, like a grub, from among the tree roots. Forced them on the boat — everyone except two men who were still out hunting. And her mother had come fighting through the crowd, her hair wild, tears on her face, the presentiment of a whole nation's pain in her eyes — had scooped her up and spoken her father's name.

They had been taken north along the coast and put into a settlement with people of different tribes; people who spoke other languages and had strange, troubling customs. And, of course, there was nothing sacred or explainable to any of them about those rocks, those hills, that creek. The Bossmen were the Superintendent, who lived there, and the police from a nearby town.

"The policeman is your friend," one young mouse-haired constable had told her. Perhaps he really thought so. Three years later Daisy Daisy had reason to know what this meant: there came a terrific thumping on the wall, the whole shanty rattled. It was about eight o'clock and just dark, her people were out. Apart from her cousin Amy lying beside her confiding secret guilts and excitements, there was just her brother in the next room. He had the hurricane lamp on, against his mother's request, and was whittling at a lump of wood. The shanty rattled, its rusty iron sheets seemed about to give way at each blow.

"Come out of there," bellowed a man's voice. The whittling stopped. The whispering stopped. Faint reverberations trembled through the walls. Again the voice, "Come on out of there, I said." Fear smothered their faces like death. A heavy tread on the three steps, again the place shook. There was no door. Suddenly the footfalls were inside. Joe sprang up, grabbing the old kitchen stool, lunged at the figure in the doorway, smashed the stool at his face and sent him reeling back. He tried to swing it again, but before he could regain his balance another man hurtled in. The impact as they collided made a sharp slapping noise. The girls listened in terror. Joe was flung right to the far wall and fell there with his mouth hanging open, lip bleeding, and hopelessness already clouding his sight. He got up, but the huge policeman swung him round and sent him staggering out into the dust, where the first intruder kicked him in the ribs before re-entering the house. Daisy still caught her breath at the memory of those men striding into the room. One of them dragged Amy next door. The other rearing like a hill, so massive above her — the rough hands — the nausea — his unbearable weight squeezing the breath from her lungs so that she thought (for a moment gladly) she would be crushed to death. That astonishment that pain. Again and again and again and endlessly the same pain. And afterwards the nuzzling and soft love-words that made her vomit all over his shoulder so he struck her across the face and swore at her for being a filthy black slut.

Daisy found she had stopped walking; and fine dust settled in her hair, on her hands. The grass-tips were rustling. She hissed through her teeth. She would be late if she didn't hurry now. She trod the long arm of the cross that stretched south before her. The church was another half-mile on, where the minister was preparing to deliver a sermon on his favourite text, from I Kings 12, "And now whereas my father did lade you with a heavy yoke, I will add to your yoke: my father chastised you with whips, but I will chastise you with scorpions."

Dulcie Thompson hadn't missed going to mass once in fourteen years. She claimed it as a record for the district. And Arnold himself was quite regular at church, as she had frequently pointed out to the Charlton woman next door. Those Charltons were nothing better than atheists. Once — she boiled at the memory — she had accused him of it to his face, in front of everyone at the corner shop, and he had agreed with her! Surely, not even the Lord's infinite mercy could be stretched to include people like that; though on the next occasion she had threatened him that it would be, and that he'd be humbled then. The only response had been a smiling, "Thanks Ma." She stopped at the church gate and found she had been hurrying well ahead of the others. She watched them approach, her expression hardening as she saw how intimately they talked when she was out of earshot. Tricia laughed, so carefree, suddenly breaking from the sullen defences she lived behind, and the sound of it filled Arnold's heart; he stopped for a moment to catch his breath. The pain was so acute and unexpected for Dulcie that she might almost have cried out: I'm not a bad woman! Instead she blundered into the building, her heels rapping sharply on the wooden floor. She knelt in her usual place and began considering thoughts she could cope with.

"Look," said Tricia as they stepped into the shaded doorway. Far down the road an unmistakable figure could be seen, Daisy Daisy.

"Poor things," Arnold commented, rising in self-confidence, "they can't help it. Haven't been blessed with much up here," he tapped his forehead, "they're all the same that way," and he held the door open for her.

In the church opposite, only one person sat, a lad of seventeen or eighteen. He liked to get there early and take his place at the front in one particular corner, so that as few people as possible would see anything of him other than the back of his neck — no pimples there, at least. He gazed up into the steep-pitched ceiling, the mock-gothic windows set in weatherboard walls, at the dark blood tones of the glass. Yes, Clive told himself, he enjoyed Sundays. Actually what gave him the most memorable and disturbing pleasure was a fantasy he had lived through many times: having sex in that building, the girl sprawled on a pew (he knew which one) just the two of them there and the whole vast belly of the church about them, ribs curving high up into the darkness, a fitful light from the lampbrackets, the place locked for the night; and their obscene whispers, grunts and sighs echoing so that they could almost be audience to their own act. Even now he squirmed and shifted to make himself less uncomfortable as the excitement roused him. The small congregation entered in ones and twos. What if they could read his thoughts? He half wished for that too. Just as the service was about to begin, Daisy Daisy crept to the back pew and crouched there, hoping to avoid notice, her chest heaving and an undercurrent of satisfaction bringing something like a smile to her lips — she wasn't late after all. Ah, but she was trembling today and needed to hold on to the seat in front when they stood for the first hymn. Such painful memories. Joe had been sixteen at the time.

The Church of England was prepared to respect any other denomination except the Roman Catholic. Mr. Fennell himself had been known to say: The Second World War is over, but it's my opinion that the world faces two great dangers still — Communism and the Catholic church, and of the two Catholicism constitutes the subtler threat. Mrs. Fennell had argued the point, but was pleased to withdraw in favour of her husband's superior understanding of politics and economic affairs.

"Mind you," he had added urgently, "this is strictly private. I can't afford to have opinions in my job." Mrs.

Fennell had put in a final complaint to the third party:

"In the great centres of commerce, one is not even expected to *have* an opinion, let alone voice it. Here, on the other hand, the villagers appear to be determined to thrash out every issue that ever was. I don't believe they enjoy it, mind you. I'm sure they're as crafty as anyone. They want to sound you out, see if you let slip something you shouldn't."

From the comfort of his back verandah, Eddie could listen to the polytonal discords as rival hymns mixed, beat against each other, destroyed each other, leaving the air disturbed by a distant undulating pulse, not by any means unpleasant — one occasionally trailing a phrase or an Amen longer than the others. The bubbles peacefully rose in his glass. His wife came out and plumped herself beside him, balancing her own glass on a tiny round tray with a packet of cigarettes, a box of matches, and an APC powder. She took a long pull at the beer. He helped himself to one of her cigarettes, they both smoked.

"You'll have to talk to old Chick, you know, Ed."

He contemplated the proposition. His words floated in the still air, individual as bubbles: "That so? Why?"

"I was over at his place yesterday and Vi has just about had it. He's got to do something about them kids. They're driving her fair out of her mind."

"What can he do — off on the boats most of the day, six days a week? Give a man a go."

"I dunno. But he's got to do something. And you've got to think what it is."

"Me? Why me?"

"You're his cousin aren't you?" He sat silent. The singing had stopped.

"Must be on to the prayers."

"Or the ear-bashing," she put in. He grinned.

"Serve em right if you ask me." They shared the pleasure of the same prejudices. Even so, the worry about Vi had spoilt what looked like a beautiful Sunday of nothing.

Down at the waterfront, a creek uncoiled into the bay, having lived briefly in the brilliant reflection of houses perched on stumps, boats, the wooden bridge, and that onion-domed fishmarket everyone found either delightful or ridiculous. Beneath this green corrugated iron dome, on a split-log bench, sat Collocott. And he was not alone. A man was at work on the nearest of five fishing boats moored there — a man of slighter finer build than most others who worked the boats, his movements gave the impression of inexhaustible vitality and resilience. So Chick Charlton, dressed in his old shorts, scrubbed the deck. Although he whistled from time to time, he was not relaxed; although he appeared to be absorbed in his task, he was concentrating on what Collocott had to say; this was, after all, a man of learning. Collocott, for his part, despite appearances to the contrary, hardly gave a thought to his conversation; he was suffering the bitterness of envy as he watched the other man working, as he sensed in the casual turn of the head, the quick play of shoulder muscles, a kind of self-sufficiency and unselfconsciousness that he had never for one minute enjoyed.

"Course, don't know why you should be troubled

with my problems," Chick was saying, "you being single and all that."

"I'm ready to give opinions," the other replied, "as long as you take them with a pinch of scepticism. I mean, they are your problems and as you've made them, so you must have it in you to solve them."

"Yair. You may be right. But that doesn't seem too logical to me. I know plenty of fellas with a talent for getting into trouble, who're complete bloody drongos when it comes to battlin' their way out of the mess." He stood upright and really did laugh with something like his old gaiety. Collocott was thinking: with men like this around, how could she even notice me?

For a moment it became obvious that somehow communication had broken down. The fisherman dropped his brush and took a flying leap on to the wharf. He settled himself, almost shyly, by Collocott and rolled two cigarettes. He licked the gummed flap of one and stuck it down; the other he passed to his companion to lick for himself.

"Go on," he said, "good tobacco this is."

"Well, I don't usually smoke." But the gesture was so unfamiliar to him, in its way so assertive and gratifying, that he took the cigarette, licked it with an oversupply of spittle, and puffed too conscientiously when offered a light. He was careful not to inhale the smoke. Even so he coughed and coloured. There — he had made a fool of himself again. His manhood, even, was in question. But to Chick Charlton this was by no means the case; he accepted it as a compliment that so obvious a non-smoker should see in the offer a necessary token of companionship. Collocott, certain he had bungled even this, could not stop himself stammering and nervously looking the other way. He tried to recollect the main drift of the conversation, but he hadn't been following it closely enough.

"It's your, your, your wife that's worrying you, then?"

"Not when you put it like that. You see, she can't help it. The kids are at her all the time. I don't understand why. They never leave her alone. Or, if they do, they're fighting one another," he leaned back and sucked at the escaped smoke, snatching it from mid-air. Such virtuosity disconcerted Collocott further, yet it was at this point that he suddenly took courage. What he saw for the first time was that all this self-sufficiency did not imply anything beyond a realization in Charlton that his instinctive reactions were acceptable to the people he lived among:

"Perhaps there's one suggestion I could make."

"Fire away."

"Well I'm sure you're good to your children, and so on, kind. But is it possible that you don't give them enough stimulus?" Chick felt the man's apology for what his suggestion might imply. He put his hand on Collocott's shoulder:

"I asked you, didn't I?" They watched the creek water lapping at the wall. Traces of fish-stench hung in the air. Everything was so clear and glittering in the midday sunshine, Collocott's head sang with the triumph of such a friendship.

"I mean to say, youngsters have a tremendous capacity for mental, imaginative stimulation. You work hard on the boat, your wife works hard at home. I just wonder if perhaps they need something they aren't getting."

"So — because they're missing this whatever it is — they try taking it out on Vi by playing up the whole time?"

"That's all I can suggest. Though, of course, how would I know? I'm only guessing."

"It's a damn sight better guess than any I've ever come up with," Chick stood suddenly and once again the sheer force of the man made his companion uneasy, "Come on." They set off. Collocott hoped and hoped he was not being led to the Charlton home. His shoes squelched unhappily among soggy tufts of grass. This was getting out of hand. It was one thing to talk, quite another to lose command of your own movements. It was downright unsafe. Already he was out of contact with his careful defences.

"You never see much water lying about up at our end of Battery Spit," he remarked, "unless there's going to be a flood." He knew it sounded petulant.

"Why not take them off?" came Chick's oblique reply. That put an end to communication for the while. Even companionship seemed to have deserted them.

Collocott's heart was no longer in it, he was rehearsing the possibilities of escape, none of which held up well enough to risk performance. He dreaded meeting the family as much as he resented being obliged to leave that beautiful quiet spot at the water's edge. His mind returned to a train of thought he had dropped before. No — he decided — this man's self-sufficiency is not just a social factor, it must also arise from a certain kind of arrogance or assertiveness . . . even perhaps a partial insensitivity to other people's feelings.

The house was not far away, indeed the sleepout windows looked across to the cooling-tower beside the fishmarket. The other windows on that side were green and purple bubble-glass; nothing could be seen from inside. They even dissipated the direct afternoon sun to a soupy glare. It was a small place, freshly painted eau-de-nil and so meticulously kept that somehow it looked naked.

"Garden's in good trim," Chick remarked cheerfully, the problem no longer depressed him now he was bringing home a solution. Sensing this, Collocott thought: I wish someone would solve mine for *me*.

Dulcie Thompson, although home from church a few hours since, still wore her hat; her dress and her stays were hanging up, and she lounged on the bed in her petticoat. As soon as she heard voices, she lifted the edge of the holland blind, boggled at what she saw, rolled off the bed and stumbled cowlike into the kitchen. "Hey Arn!" she commanded in a whisper; but he wasn't there and anyhow he wouldn't understand. She caught at the dresser and spun around to point herself at the livingroom. Dulcie lunged forward, "Trish," she croaked, "you'll never guess, not in a lifetime, what I just honest to God seen out of my own window."

"Uh-huh?" Trish wagged her head from behind a movie magazine.

"Him" (pointing) "and his new mate."

"What, Mr. Charlton," the girl sneered, "he's old. And anyway everyone's his mate already."

"Including . . . Mr. Collocott?" The strangeness of it

brought a momentary chill to Tricia's fingertips:

"What I don't like is the way you keep spying on people," she commented piously, the little flame of jealousy licking up just enough to make its presence felt again.

"Well, that's the last piece of news I ever bring you!" her mother was already back at her window, stuffing herself into her Sunday stays, "All I can say is, thank God I kept me hat on."

Collocott was in the kitchen, awkward, wondering if his feet looked foolish. Vi stood opposite, fluffing up her hair in some attempt to make amends for being caught "casual". Chick was refusing to feel guilty:

"Course I could have warned you, love. But why should I? If a man can't bring home a mate without making sure the red carpet's down, it's time to pack it in."

"Ah, but Mr. Collocott — "

Chick cut in: "You haven't even let me introduce you yet." Collocott, turning again to the perfect stranger, watched her say the words, "Of course we know each other by sight." Then, with a gesture more studied than natural, she thrust out her hand. He took it. Chick drew a deep breath, never before had he known her so insulting as to shake hands with a visitor.

"Sit down, mate." He dragged a chair from under the table for himself, dropped abruptly on to it, and waved to the position opposite. His mate followed suit. Vi remained standing; for something to do, she tied on a clean apron. In the silence that began to gather like a thunderstorm, the host leapt to his feet as suddenly as he had sat himself down, reached for the fridge door

48

with one hand and for glasses from the sideboard with the other. Collocott noticed the sideboard, slickly enamelled the same green as the house, with sliding glass doors. And it did not escape his notice that this piece of furniture had an indefinable air of the homemade, though at a brief second glance he could see no reason why this had occurred to him.

A deft flip. The cap was off the bottle and Fourex spun into the glasses.

"Here we are then," said Chick, with boyish charm.

"Count me out," Vi contributed.

"Is that one mine?" Collocott took the glass and sipped at it. The delicious cold beer revived him, "Did you make that cabinet?" he asked.

"Gawd no," out of the corner of his eye, Chick noticed Dulcie charge from the neighbouring house in the blazing colours of her Sunday best, "what makes you ask?"

"I don't know. It doesn't have a shop look about it." Maybe he allowed himself the heresy, Chick's boyishness is exactly that.

"Well, you're right there. But I couldn't turn out a professional finish like this. No — Vi's brother gave it to us a couple of Christmases ago. We just repainted it as a matter of fact."

"It's a beautiful job."

"Yair, not bad. Same colour as I used outside."

Collocott fought down the temptation to retire into his shell (my shell, he had often chanted it over to himself instead of welling with tears, my shell, my hell). Now was his chance:

"I didn't mean the painting. I meant the carpenter's

work. Mrs. Charlton's brother . . . " she shot him a questioning look and his attempt dried up altogether. And Chick, for a moment abandoning his special tact towards this odd bloke, slipped in a correction:

"Carpenters build houses, sport. Cabinet-making, this is."

"He *was* a carpenter once though," said Vi.

"Anyhow," her husband announced a new topic, "we came here to tell you something. Round at the boat I was mentioning our kids and how they play up — "

"They aren't so bad," she warned.

"And he come out with a good answer. Here, you tell her."

"It doesn't seem any of my business."

Her expression confirmed this much at least

"But what you said up there — "

"Well?" she demanded, looking only at her husband. Collocott was now acutely embarrassed. He mumbled about his lack of knowledge and experience, his single estate, even a fragment mentioning the university. "Look, what *is* this?" Vi made an effort to sound businesslike yet not antagonistic.

"The long and the short of it is that maybe we don't give them enough to keep their minds busy."

"You mean . . . " she fired this straight at Chick, she could never again bring herself to acknowledge the outsider, "that we're too bloody uneducated and ignorant to keep up with our own kids!"

"It's a matter of finding interesting things for them to do, love."

"I'll find something interesting for you to do before long," there was a break in her voice. And she stormed out to the passage and shut herself in the bathroom, where she bolted the door, then listened hard till she heard the men's voices start up again. Now she was free: she let the sobs heave up in her. Determined not to be discovered, Vi leaned against the wall with her head tilted back, pouring out a long-drawn, silent howl of pain. Everything in her was concentrated at that point, lived only in the hot gusts of breath, came to fruition at the point where she expelled her pent up energies. The whole of her passionate love for the children, together with an admission of failure, burst into the open. She kept bathing and mopping her eyes to keep them from getting too red — for even in the moment of sharpest pain, she was already aware that she would go out again and face them, that there *was* something wrong in the family, that every last grain of pride would not be enough to withstand an appeal for her sons' sake. And much as she recoiled from the thought of the man, she knew that Collocott was desperately embarrassed at having intruded and upset her — that it was he, not the husband she loved, who had foreseen how this would hurt her. The sobs rose again, like vomit. She submitted and let them come; turned the tap full on to cover those little whimpering noises which escaped despite all her efforts.

By this time Dulcie Thompson was round the corner, she had passed the fishmarket and was nearly as far as the pub (on her way heaven knew where) when she met that Ed Charlton and his wife coming the other way. Of course she always avoided them, him especially you couldn't trust, you never knew where you were with the likes of him. And put this together with the fact that he was one of the same atheist clan as the hooligans next door — well! But on this occasion she not only nodded a greeting, she actually stopped to talk.

"Who'd ever have thought," she began, concentrating her smiles on the woman, "I don't suppose your husband will be wanted round our way so often now."

"Eh?" contributed Ed.

"Well, I mean . . . " Mrs. Thompson then conveyed her meaning with rolling eyes and waggling brows.

"What do you mean?"

"Haven't you heard? Oops, I'm not sure I'm supposed to tell. But Mr. Charlton next door has found a new victim for his yarns. Like I said, your husband won't be out so much now, I suppose." Eddie turned to his wife and asked:

"What the hell's this woman talking about? I can't seem to get near to all this yakking about in circles." So Mrs. Elaine Charlton set her pretty face in a sweet blank mask, and invited Dulcie to be more precise.

"Since you ask me: in a single word, it's that queer cove from O'Shea's."

Ed and Elaine roared and screeched with laughter. They leant against each other and hooted into the sweltering unreceptive afternoon. Over the diminutive harbour, up the creek, out into the bay went their laughter, it machine-gunned along the sides of houses and startled two dogs into a nervous frenzy of barking. In Dulcie, this sparked off a succession of feelings: at first they made her jump with shock, then she felt a fool, this gave way to fury. But the laughter continued long enough for her native commonsense to inform her that most people at Battery Spit would react in more or less the same way to the story.

When she left them, she walked a good deal slower than before. Even spared a few minutes to perch on the wall by the bridge, pretending to be puffed, for time to re-think. At last she was ready to set off again: and, oh what a laughing-stock those poor innocents were making of themselves, reduced to that level to find a friend — ah *how* she laughed when she first saw them coming in at the gate *practically* arm-in-arm — goodness how the corsets had pinched and how red in the face she'd been — and wasn't it the best joke to be heard anywhere round the bay for years!

"Why here's Eddie and Elaine," Chick called out in relief. There was no immediate response from the bathroom, "come on in." They greeted Collocott with routine gooddays and made themselves comfortable.

"Where's Vi?" asked Elaine.

"Dunno. Somewhere about."

"Then I'll find her." Chick caught her arm in a way that instantly communicated the urgency and delicacy of the situation.

"Be a love," he croaked.

"We'll see," and she was gone.

He switched his appeal to Ed, "My mate here has a good suggestion about the kids," he then cocked a thumb at the passageway, "went off the deep end."

"Elaine'll cope. Now where's the beer supply in this Temperance den?" he helped himself to a large glass. Later, Elaine's voice called from behind a closed door:

"We're off to Maggie's. Don't you boys drink too

much." And after another silence they heard the neat Yale click of the front door.

"Look," Collocott spoke up for the first time, "I'm sorry for the trouble I've caused."

"What are you trying to make me feel like?" At that moment a second gate opened; and into the meticulous yard, up the dazzling white steps, charged two boys aged five and eight. They tore through the kitchen without a glance at the men there and disappeared further into the house. A resounding bump came from the far bedroom, followed by a howl of fury and pain.

Mick washed his hands with Solvol, pleased by the gritty feel of the soap as his fingers emerged from their extra skin of grease. He pulled at the grimy strip-towel loosely hung over two rollers, but without any expectation of finding a dry patch. Having wiped his hands, he went out front again to call goodbye to the boss who was in the lube shed, then he made off for the lane, jumped into his old bomb and drove out to the main road. At eighteen he was already an expert with cars. He turned at spectacular speed along the Parade, sounded his horn for the couple of high-school girls running hand in hand, boarders late for tea, and headed for the north end of the settlement. Darkness deepening. Soon he was conscious of streetlights passing like bars over his hands. Swimming underwater with your eyes open, the strong sunshine would break through the sea in cloudy green waves. The lights became sparser. The rhythm of rowing. The glide and pull. Taking the strain with thighs and shoulders. Not in the sea — surf rowing was strictly for madmen — on the river. Beautiful calm tidal river.

Sluggish actually. And when he had been a kid, flashes from the lighthouse lit up his bedroom curtains like a blank cinema screen, always to be cut off at the moment they were about to show something urgent with meaning. That girl he had fucked a year ago. Why didn't she leave the district? There had been those sobs afterwards, building up and bursting out of her, a slow violent pulsing, so that he'd become afraid, grabbing her by the shoulders and shaking her. Finally, desperate for something savage enough to stop her, fucked her again. Never taken her out since. Anyhow, once the call-up notice came (it could be any day) life would begin again. A new start. Start. Start.

Mick didn't usually work on Sundays, but this had been a special job and the boss had promised him twenty-five shillings extra for helping. He watched the long black bonnet of his Plymouth nosing through the waves of light, the ship emblem scratching a bright chromium arc round every corner. He drove exactly midway between the white line and the crumbling shoulders of the road. He was a perfectionist and proud of it. Where Spit Avenue (generally known as The Avenue from some niceness of feeling) became Culver's Road, Mick made a U-turn and drew up outside Sissons's. No one in the yard. He took the front steps in a couple of bounds. At the top he called out. Nothing. Mick wandered in among the brackets of tools and work benches on the verandah. The corridor was reduced to a third of its width by stacks of timber propped against either wall, most of it was cedar the old man had salvaged from demolished properties in the district. He called again. This time a reply came from the kitchen.

Two piles of wooden boxes flanked the door, framing the visitor's first glimpse of this room. The lightbulb was encased in a yellow glass globe, somewhat flattened, with a scalloped flange and a painted rose smack in the centre. Eight ironing boards, five hoses, three treadle sewing machines and fifteen electric irons were ranged neatly round the walls; printed plastic had been nailed across the windows; the back door was open, leading to a tiny trelliswork porch at the top of a flight of steps. At the table sat old Sissons with an assortment of small papers in front of him. Behind, a kettle on the stove silently leaked steam. The stove itself gleamed, polished and oiled like a locomotive.

"Now you can be some use to me, lad," he made it sound as if this would mark a new direction in their friendship, "you've got younger eyes than me." With a gesture of exasperation he shuffled the papers together and pushed them across the table. "Sit down why don't you. I'll put some tea on, if you'll make them into two neat piles; receipts on the one, bills on the other." He got up and began to bang about among the pots in the sink. Mick set to work dextrously.

"Any rate, how are you, Pop?" he asked.

"Tell you what," Sissons replied, "had a go at that black gin today: her going off to church with all her bloody airs and graces. Bailed her up proper, I did," he chuckled, "don't know why they let them walk about like other people. Ought to lock them away for their own good. Leave them to die out peaceful like. Riles me to think of her living just down the track there. Anyhow I bailed her up proper today. Nothing like a bit of fun." Mick was disapproving and uncomfortable. Not that he cared about Aborigines one way or the other. But this was the fiery relic of a man who had become a kind of hero; and gibing at an old black woman didn't fit with that gallantry expected of soldiers. He concentrated on the sorting. In fact, when the job was done he did it all again to avoid being first to speak.

"Good bit of fun. Now then," the old fellow coughed, "have you finished those?"

"Yes, here are the bills and here are the receipts."

"That's the style. Beaut. Well, I suppose you come round to see my snapshots."

"You promised."

"I know I did. And I always keep my word. Pour out some of that brew and I'll fetch the packet over." They were happy again. The awkwardness evaporated and this friendship, which had begun only a few weeks before, assumed the easy-going intimacy they were now taking for granted. The absorbing interest they shared was the Great War. Mick stood at the gleaming stove and stirred the tea; tapped the spoon on the rim of the pot and waited for the leaves to settle again. It hadn't been a bad day's work. Being overtime, everything was more casual. And the quiet streets and no customers had given the garage a new character. Only the Riley to work on. Beautiful car. Hard to get at that fanbelt though, a real bastard from the mechanic's point of view. But driving it back to the owners was worth doing. Jesus, but (that stuck up woman pressing a tip into his hand) a shilling! Why the hell didn't I give it back or throw it down? Why pocket it . . . feeling guilty? And though she tried to hide it, I saw her — yes — bloody wiping her fingers after contact with me.

Mick jiggled the pannikins. Surely the tea was brewed by now? Began to pour.

"Sit ready?" Sissons challenged him, "brewed proper?"

"Reckon," he went on pouring confidently, savagely.

Collocott and his friend were on their way up to the Parade when the streetlights came on. Charlton's plan was to buy fish and chips, and then lead an expedition round such nightspots as the Bay offered on a Sunday. Collocott was most alarmed, he had to worm his way out of this somehow — tried the diversion of continually worrying that the women had not returned and that poor Eddie was being left behind at the house.

"Don't get excited," came the reply, "this means Vi has given in. The moment we're safely out of the road, she'll be back to get the kid's tea. What's more, she won't expect me till bedtime. It's easier to talk things over in bed, apologize and all that, don't you think?" But the man of learning kept his eyes on the pavement. "This means you and me have got some details to nut out before I get back. But I don't believe in mixing business and pleasure, so we had better get the talking done while we're having a feed." This was more like it; the fisherman felt comfortable again. Troubles over, he could never manage much in the line of reappraising the past to deduce meanings, precedents, guidelines for future behaviour. There was even the time his school-mates (would it be sixteen years before? seventeen?) had locked him in a timber shed to help him remember the gang rules: only to find him as thoughtlessly cheer-ful after three hours' imprisonment as he had been before. He remembered it now and it made him want to laugh, because at last he could see himself with their eyes. Yet he could not see he was dependent still.

They crossed the next street. A large car with blazing headlights swept out at them. Each man dodged for the footpath: Chick going forward, Collocott back. The driver punched his horn, stamped on the brake, and stuck his wooden puppet-head out of the window:

"What the hell! Do you want to get killed?"

Collocott tried turning away to avoid recognition. There was almost a touch of embarrassment in Mr. Fennell's manner as he pulled his head back in and drove on at the same murderous speed.

"Didn't you see?" his wife exclaimed, "It was that peculiar half-witted fellow."

"I saw. And will you understand, he is neither half-witted nor especially peculiar," then added expressionlessly, "compared with some people."

"Even so," she concluded demurely, "one does feel slightly surprised at seeing those two together, him and that larrikin — you know, the one who saved me the time my horse bolted."

Chick stood rubbing his head as he watched the two red lights dwindling rapidly towards the end of the road.

"Not a bad car." But the shock had roused Collocott, who answered:

"Fool of a driver, charging round like that. What a fool!"

As they approached the crest of the rise, they could smell the fish & chip shop and hear the gathering crowd. A few more yards then the bright little building came into view. It was a single-storey weatherboard box on ten-inch stumps; the low iron roof v. as partly masked by a timber facade designed to imitate the stepped stone of Dutch houses. Below this appendage jutted an awning of curved corrugated iron, its frame resting on four tall wooden posts set along the edge of the kerb. Half a dozen pearl lightbulbs had been strung under it, outshining the milkbar (an almost identical structure) on the opposite side of the Parade. Round these two islands of light, groups of people had gathered; and their laughter stuttered up into the salty air.

"Here's your tea," Mick announced to open a new stage in the conversation. He watched the old man settle himself, watched him thrust out his lips and suck at the hot sweet brew. He took his own enamel mug and, for sheer companionship, drank more noisily than usual. Sissons rolled some tobacco in his palm and slipped it into his pipe, all the while working his whitish tongue between gapped teeth.

"Were you as young as me when you enlisted, Pop?" Mick had become shy, tentative, almost wheedling.

"Na. I was a full thirty year old by then. And just about to marry. Beautiful young sheila with blonde hair. Name of Lucy. We got engaged — but that never held anyone to a promise. She shot through while I was over in the trenches."

The black road streaked under her; occasionally headlights bobbed up, approached, dipped, swept past perilously close. And trees swished at the open windows. The Riley was going like a bird: she stole a glance at her husband, you'd never know he was happy, Mrs. Fennell thought. Gives nothing away. There was the same wind — she hadn't wanted the brown horse in the first place and when he got his head down chewing the grass, she couldn't budge him. No matter how hard the reins were tugged, he stubbornly fed himself. Suddenly he gave in (such a relief) only to canter off rather too smartly for her. Well, naturally she'd had a good seat on a horse when she was a child in Berkshire; though this was by no means hacking. With an admirably clear head she recollected those early instructions, relaxed but firm grip on the reins, back straight, making soothing sounds. Yet her knees betrayed her fright and hugged the animal's flanks. Was it true they could smell your fear like a dog? He gathered speed. She was coming up behind the rest of the party. She experienced a fleeting triumph, no one had waited with her back there, no one offered to help; just a few cheery cries of Come on! (over the shoulder). Now she would pass them in style. The gelding headed straight into the group at an even pace, jostled through them, spinning Mrs. Murphy's pony side-on. A thin call of protest faded swiftly in her ears. A patch of scrub lay ahead. Bushes, trees coming. Fast. She forgot the rules, pulled back with all her strength, no coaxing words now — not for this brute. Wwhup! a thin branch whipped across her shoulder. Danger, stop. Another one coming, too big. She lay flat along the horse's neck and the branch swept over her, one broken twig ripping her shirt. He means it. Murder. Another. The horse swerved — not to jump that fence o please o God. Swung alongside it, rubbing against it, barbed wire, streaked by, too many fenceposts this side for it to touch at that speed — luck — but leg bruised. Fence stopped. Road. Cars. O God o God. Skid of hooves for a second. She gathered her courage and looked up, made another effort to control him. Bitumen stretched ahead, gradual rise, shops and petrol pumps at top. Watch out on roads: horse may fall with you underneath, crack head open, car coming, most dangerous. Fool to leave home. What use make-up now? Hoof-sounds harsh, domineering. Doubled: another horse? Daren't look round. Snorting breath — yes, black ears, huge eye right near. Voice: "She'll be right, Mrs. You're doing fine," male hand on reins, "Keep her like that. We'll knock the animal out on this hill." How, but how? Good man, anything you want is yours; friend in need for ever, with money and position, to be an ally worth having. At the final rise, gelding's pace broken. Slowed. Stumbled. Walked. Fellow helping her down, tethering the beast. Even in that state, she had withdrawn her hand from his shoulder at the quick animal movement of him. You could never control a fellow like this, "So grateful," handsome in a way, uncouth, "Saved my life," smell his sweat, "Reward," swimming, hand supporting her, "Tore my clothes. Badly? So ashamed."

"Those mechanics," Mr. Fennell allowed, positive she had been waiting all this time for his considered opinion, "have done a first rate job."

Old Sissons unwrapped the parcel, smoothing out the brown paper, and thumbed through the heap of photographs there: "Now that one is me in me puttees. A hell of a job they were. You ever wound puttees on you? These jokers who went to the last war, they just had them little puttees all down round the ankles. Look at these!" he handed the photo across, "That's what I call puttees — right up to the knee. And have a look at the winding, they were put on perfect, not a hitch anywhere, as even as you could imagine it. Real proud of the way I did my puttees, I was. Now this here," he dealt out another one, "is a postcard. Bought that in France. Have a good close look at this church. Observation test for you. What can you see that makes you surprised, suspicious?" At last, the real thing. Mick took in every detail of the building. But he hunted in vain for the clue that must be there. Sissons puffed away contentedly. He was in no hurry: he watched the head of curly hair bent over his test, watched it jerk up with sudden exasperation and disappointment —

"I give in. All I can find is something missing from the clock on the tower."

"Well, what more do you want?"

"Is that it? Now, it's the face of the clock. The loop of the six is blocked in, black, like a hole."

"You'd never make a soldier, too slow."

"A gun barrel!"

"A gun that size, squeezed into a hidden space in the tower?"

"A peephole then?"

"You got it at last. Caused us a lot of trouble that did, the cove hidden behind that clock face with his spy-glass. Matter of fact he was killed by his own mob. We'd just dropped to his little game, when right that very minute the Huns raided the place and blew the top clean off of the church. Some said it was coincidence. Some said they was keeping one jump ahead of us. Look here, this is a snap I took myself a week or two later.

63

Same church, see how smashed up it was?" The picture changed hands, old memories were planted in a young mind.

"I didn't do so badly then that time, did I?" Mick pleaded.

"You did alright, son. Nothing a bit of training wouldn't fix." The boy smiled. Yet there was something tucked away at the back of his mind that troubled him. Yes, he was uneasy. What had happened?

Night came for Daisy too. It was *her* time; once again she was part of the world. She opened her door and walked out in an old shift, no hat, no shoes. She was herself. The soil's warmth flooded into her. She and the earth breathed together. The mosquitoes were bad, Daisy swatted at them for a while. Then she gave up; what were a few mosquito bites? Consciously she drew the dark air into her and the dark earth; and then set off to wander. She took her own track round the foot of Battery Hill, moving steadily, unfalteringly through the scrub, among lantana bushes and the hulks of old cars abandoned there to rot years before. The moon had not yet risen. She sensed the wrecks, rather than saw them, as alien blocks — but without resentment for they were in the death grip of her country. For a few startling moments the perfect night was scratched across by a small aircraft flying high overhead, its tiny lights eventually flickering out in the distance. Machines! she thought, but machines didn't last long whichever way you looked at them.

She walked on again, the entire universe accompanying her out to the point, every star perfectly suiting its pace to hers. Had this land lost its magic? She couldn't really know. These hills and stones were gods of another people who were driven away many generations ago. Could it be that, with no people to relive their sacred lives, the Gods themselves went away or died? Feeling about her — drawing vibratio..s through her skin perhaps — Daisy could believe it. This was a landscape sucked dry of spirit. It really had become the whiteman's land: they'd created a home, passive soil, meaningless features (one hill = a change of gears; one slope of scrub = a convenient dump). And yet when she thought back to her own home country more than a thousand miles to the north, she understood that nothing short of total destruction could eradicate the sacredness of its meanings.

Insects chirred at her, so that she hummed her own little song in sympathy. The dusty scent of lantana leaves hung about. She was lulled. This could be a home; if people had lived here long enough, continuously enough to love it and bring it alive. She knew it wanted life. How could she fail to have faith as the land received her, absorbed her and was in turn absorbed. She was the living water and the living soil. In her the song-rhythms of the sea and the talk-rhythms of earth were no longer in conflict. She stood still as if to say, We need your love though we are not your own people. No one could touch her now. Gummbula; she received her name from the Gods and knew they lived — knew that by her ultimate humility she had raised them from the lost identity of sleep.

So long she stood. She felt how deeply and intricately her roots had taken in the ground. Upright in an ecstasy of disinvolvement, she was bathed by delicate light — a great yellow triangle poised on the sea's horizon, like a divine nautilus shell with its luminous membrane spread for a sail. Remote waves already purled at its prow. As if the delight of the physical world launched it into a state like the heart of joy, the half-moon rose clear of contact, purified even of its exquisite gold. Beyond experience, all experience was drawn to it. In her pale frock Gummbula's body might have been a block of salt. At last — after forty years of silence — the truth could be spoken. She had seen the wickedness of man, but needed no defences, for she had come home. The two men still out hunting had been left behind when that steamboat swept away from the camp, low in the water, no more than ten minutes after her mother had fought through the crowded bodies, gulping for breath, the tendons of her neck pulled tight with strain, hair stuck to her streaming cheeks, forty thousand years of love and retrenchment dying at the knowledge in her eyes that moment.

"My darling father, how long did you search for us?" Daisy called into the night. Her body whirled in a sudden spasm of movement, flickering among the rocks and undergrowth. Down she spun towards the water, into the mangrove scrub . . . till she was fragmentary as a disturbed leaf.

Battery Hill rose up towards the moon. The bay reared a gleaming column like a plinth to support it, or a tablet of memory. A profound stillness lay upon the place, everything so perfectly at rest like the fixed details of a design. There was no sound until half an hour later a tiny creaking announced that Daisy Daisy had slumped on the bed in her shack.

Across the water, near St. Helena Island, riding-lights could be made out, the prawners were fishing inside the bay. Everyone knew it was illegal, everyone knew they did it and that one night they would be caught. For the moment they were safe, an enormous insulation of black air protecting them. What else could be hoped for, but a moment's security? The whole settlement breathed.

Two thousand feet up in the air a small private monoplane completed the great circle of its climb and headed north along the coastline. The pilot looked down. The brilliant spider's web of Brisbane wheeled at his left; to the right occasional pinpoint warnings flashed their rudimentary code out to sea; below a few pathetic strings of lights linked the bayside villages. He looked with particular interest at the last cluster. Down through countless tons of air, his sight reached the pattern grouped around two bright spots with a single string of streetlamps dotting out a straight line beneath him, leading to the furthest extremity of the point. There he watched for signs of individual houses. But the area presented a blank face. Signs of habitation winked at him from islands enclosing the bay. The enormity of the void into which he was moving rushed to engulf his tiny aircraft; this he did not notice. The machine was working efficiently, what else was there to life? Only the machine. Surely efficiency was the one surviving virtue?

The plane's motor drew a thin rasping thread across the sky. In the eau-de-nil house Vi broke off her monologue on the words, "and he has damp hands — I hate damp — " to listen. The fish shop and the milkbar tipped their raggle taggle clientele out, noses up, into the wide street to watch.

"I'll tell you what," Vonnie explained to her escort, "I've lived here at Battery Spit all my life and that's the first time since the war ended ten years ago that I've heard a plane that small fly over after dark though you sometimes get the big passenger ones coming across this way when the wind's wrong or something but little ones like that never and a good job too sounds like a motorbike to me what do you reckon?" As the sailor steered her into the milkbar without answering, Collocott and Chick crossed the Parade to the shop opposite. There were a few shouts of welcome, a few quick curious glances. But they had no chance to go in because Shareen (the last to care about any plane) was coming out, dabbing the grease from her lips. She slipped her arm through Chick's and the two of them twirled round on the pavement like people stuck too long in revolving glass doors. "We only live three houses up," she said and he nodded. Collocott, who overheard this, was quick to seize his chance:

"Perhaps I had better go home after all."

"Come off it! When are we going to have our talk then? Now look, mate, you get the food, then come and join us, the blue place on the right, that's Mrs. Pascoe's, we'll eat there. Two pieces of fish for me thanks — make it schnapper. There's nothing to beat schnapper."

Shareen began crooning *Silver Dollar*, " . . . a girl never knows what a good man she's got, until she . . . "

Collocott stood where he was until a couple of men, still watching the point where the plane had vanished, switched their long-distance eyes on him. And he felt himself driven to do something normal, unemphatic, casual. He went in and ordered the food. He added: "Make it schnapper. There's nothing to beat schnapper." The young Greek lad showed his beautiful teeth:

"What, nothing at all?" The other customers gave out a burst of hawking laughter, in its way good-natured. But when Collocott reacted defensively and didn't join in, they closed against him, and there was a slight sneer detectable as their brief amusement passed through the transition stage back to conversation. The cook, stripped to shorts and singlet, worked at the great vats of boiling oil, sweat streaming down among the black hairs on his shoulders and arms, he gave no sign of joining the joke against Collocott. And this was a slight comfort to the unfortunate victim, not being aware that the cook spoke only the dialect of his native Cyprus.

As Collocott took the hot packet, fragments of the news already printing themselves on fingers and thumb, he heard Knobby Clark saying to Nev Jeffries, "I tell you he came up the hill with old Chick. I saw them together. And they're going to meet again at Mrs. Pascoe's." The snort of astonishment that followed was enough to make him fairly leap out of the place into the safety of that blaze of light under the awning. Would he go down to the blue house as instructed? Fatalistically he supposed he would, but reserved some rights for his timidity . . . he would go in a minute. When he felt ready. Vonnie and her sailor emerged from the absolute green of the milkbar, went promenading past. Her shift was several sizes too small, rucked up round the waist, the hem scandalously above the knee. He watched her with greedy curiosity (just as he himself was being watched if he had only known it): her breasts swaying and quivering; the tops of her legs rubbing together, flesh catching flesh, easing and stretching the skin so that pulsations of some terrifying joy passed up through him. And, with a sudden urge to action, like the cautious fellow he was, he glanced at her escort who was stripping the cellophane from a packet of Ardath. A sailor, at least eight inches taller than himself. A full-bodied man with damp sandy hair, his square-necked shirt clinging to his sides, trousers so tight round his hips that his arousal, made public, shamed and angered Collocott. The serge defining his thighs then flared out from the knee over the ankles. Like a draft-horse; Collocott was pleased with the aptness of the thought. Yet there was an almost mincing self-satisfaction in the fellow's manner, something bordering on effeminacy he hoped. He was afraid of the sailor, undeniable, yet he dared a few more seconds' watching in case she should turn more directly towards him (she did) and was suffused with dissatisfaction at being granted what little he asked. Nevertheless as they moved away he hungrily revived the casual swing of her shoulders, lingered on the way her breasts were pressed together as they lifted, rehearsed his own part in the scene, touching —

"Got a light?"

Startled out of his daydream he jumped at the voice. A girl of about seventeen stood there, arms straight at sides, dangling a stole in one hand, a plastic handbag in the other, yellowish complexion. Here he could be some help. An instant and unfamiliar protectiveness took possession of him: this was someone weaker than he, who might not despise him.

"I haven't," Collocott apologized. She hesitated a moment, undoubtedly sickly, then leaned on him. For support? Fainting? With a tiny moan — her seductive moan. Good Lord, he thought, this is an emergency. He gripped her firmly and she clung to his arm. A good sign.

"Do you want a go?" she asked.

"How did you guess?" he answered, having wanted to go ever since Chick took him home.

"It's the same with all you blokes." He thought it rather a strange conversation, but willingly yielded to her hint that they might walk.

"Which way?"

"Blue house down there."

"Mrs. Pascoe's, is that where you live?"

"Any objection?" — agressively.

"None whatever" — anxious not to ruffle her.

"Thought you wouldn't have! Come on then." She tugged him almost eagerly. Not, she told herself, that he was much of a catch. But intellectual coves like this were always well lined, and she hadn't done satisfactorily lately — never had in fact — so the old bitch was always at her, bellyaching about the room, the bed, the rent. Collocott was pleased that she seemed better. He walked her cheerfully to the gate, thinking this would ease the awkwardness of going into her mother's house and unwrapping fish and chips just like that, as if it were a common eating house. They mounted the stairs to a verandah latticed-in on three sides. There, in a collapsible aluminium armchair, sagged a paunchy woman of fifty. She wagged one hand in greeting and went on with what she was doing. Collocott stopped respectfully.

"Good evening," he said.

"Well . . . good evening to you," she primped.

"Mrs. Pascoe, isn't it?"

"That's right." touch of suspicion; the cops employed all kinds of people these days.

"I believe my friend Mr. Charlton is here." The girl looked at him sharply, then at Mrs. Pascoe.

"That's correct. It would have been about half an hour ago he came in, yes," beginning to enjoy the touch of ceremony. He noticed she continuously fanned herself with a woven rush heart, unthinkingly as if it were part of her breathing, and she peered from time to time at something on the small table beside her.

"So hot tonight," he commiserated, noting also that she wore only a light housecoat over her milanese slip and must, therefore, be suffering.

"Fair melts you when you get to my fullness of figure," Mrs. Pascoe confessed and stole a glance at the table. He looked closer: it was a jigsaw puzzle.

"If you'll pardon my saying so," he ventured, "I really do think you'll harm your eyesight trying to pick out those little pieces in this light." Most of the globe was, in fact, covered in brown paper.

"I don't mind so much about my eyesight, as long as *everything else* I was born with stays young enough," she began to notice her posture.

"Come on, lovey," urged the girl.

"But what I do believe," Mrs. Pascoe invited, "is that I've mislaid one of the cushions I had here to keep my back straight. Terrible slumping things, these easy-chairs." Collocott darted over, put down his parcel, and rescued a cushion slipping out between the back and the seat of the chair. He plumped it. She obligingly leaned forward, swinging out her bosom, even giving it a lift with one surreptitious hand, thinking — well he *must* notice that. In fact he didn't. Once the cushion was in place he stepped back, a little bashful at his over-friendliness. But it had to be admitted he was handling things pretty well.

"Come on, do," whined the sickly girl. As the bowing figure of Collocott began to be edged in through the front door, Mrs. Pascoe was on her feet. She risked spilling the entire labour of that half-completed five-thousand piece jigsaw, swept up the packet and took the visitor's other arm.

"That's right my little doll, don't let's keep the gentleman loitering about out here." As the packet's heat reached her through the newspaper, she added with a little squawk of delight, "Fish and chips is it?"

"Yes, I'm sorry . . . "

"There's nothing I like better. But you must be a quick one if you thought they wouldn't get cold."

"He's quick alright," said the girl with bitter sarcasm.

"Haven't you had your dinner yet?" Collocott was most concerned.

"Matter of fact I haven't."

"Then you must eat some of these."

"But they're yours."

"I couldn't think of having them," the gallant insisted, "really it's my pleasure. I mean it. If you don't mind though, I shall put aside Mr. Charlton's order." To their astonishment he went straight into the kitchen, unwrapped his package on the table, "Are these the plates?" took two from the cabinet. Seldom had he felt so much at home in a strange house among strangers. Fastidiously he shook the chips from their little grease-proof bags — not to touch them with the fingers — and one piece of fish each. Then he rolled up the rest, printing his palms with yet more news. A rare magnanimity was in him: this should be accomplished with style. He swept out a chair from under the table and motioned the older woman to sit, adjusting it to her satisfaction, then another chair for the young one. And stood smiling expectantly, the perfect waiter.

"Tomato sauce?" They nodded. "Where? Ah, I see." A deep gurgling laugh came to Mrs. Pascoe's throat. There was a knowing twinkle in her eye and she played up to him.

"May I help you to some water, madam?" She spluttered into her meal and nodded vigorously. Water was set on the right side with a flourish, and he didn't omit to wipe the bottom of the glass on his shirt sleeve. Impulsively the girl sprang up, spat a few incomprehensible words at the two of them, and rushed out.

"I do hope I didn't offend her in any way," Collocott was upset.

"No, she's like that. Nervy."

"She doesn't look in the best of health, I thought."

"Perhaps not. Don't you worry about it." Back into the kitchen flung the girl, snatched up her purse and sprang out again, bumping violently into Chick Charlton. She dodged round him with a curse and he continued, unruffled, into the room.

"So you got here okay?"

"He did indeed," Mrs. Pascoe answered, "and very nice fish and chips they are too."

"I kept yours," Collocott put in urgently. Chick eased himself into the vacant chair and reached for the packet, saying:

"Our Mrs. Pascoe is a treasure among women." The unpleasantness caused by that girl could now be forgotten.

"But I think she ought to be more careful."

"What do you mean by that!" the woman pretended to be affronted, perhaps was.

"Your eyes, Mrs. Pascoe."

"Lovely eyes." Chick took her chin in his hand, so that she knew he hated her.

"But she'll ruin her sight doing a jigsaw out on that dark verandah."

They ate in silence for awhile. Then a strange thought crossed Chick's mind. He suddenly saw the situation as it was, glanced at the door where the girl had gone, and opened his mouth, only to find Mrs. Pascoe's finger laid commandingly on his lips.

"Never talk, Mr. Charlton, with your mouth full," she admonished playfully. He swallowed.

"All these years I've thought of you as a hard woman," he saw right into her with the surprise of revelation, "who ever would have thought." Touched by the moment of seriousness, Collocott said,

"That young girl — "

"I'll explain everything to her. And don't you worry." The woman rose, her fleshy form sending shiny quivers through the milanese, "She's been somehow off colour lately. And that hasn't helped. But I will explain to her about tonight."

"You'll be specially nice to her, will you?" said Chick, wrapping the remains of his dinner.

"It's my business to bring pleasure. Nothing is allowed to interfere with that."

"Come along mate," he said, knowing the girl would have to go, Mrs. Pascoe has work to do. There's her jigsaw." They moved out along the corridor, the men waving as they went down to the front gate; but at the last moment the lady of the house was pushed aside by the voluptuous Shareen who hopped down the steps and caught Chick by the arm. She gave him a quick kiss and then, out of good manners, threw her arms round Collocott's neck and hugged him too. It was at this moment that he looked up and saw, no more than six feet away, Bobbie watching him while a youth tugged at her hand.

Old Sissons shuffled his pictures secretively. "Now," he heralded the great event, "I'll let you see my prize. I took this off of a German soldier after I killed him. It was in his shirt pocket. And I've kept it ever since as a special sort of souvenir." Young Mick took it with great care, holding only the very edge. It was a postcard, the back covered with miniature spiky writing utterly incomprehensible to him. The picture showed a mother leaning against her upright piano, the vision of her soldier son floating above; she wore long skirts and high corseted bodice and a choker, her grey hair was piled on top of her head, her hand rested on her heart, and instead of a face she had a bullet-hole.

3

Monday: 5.15 a.m.

The languorous waters of the bay heaved and shifted like a woman in bed. In that light, so clear and delicate, everything seemed transparent and it was hard to believe in any strict demarcation between the elements. One of the last boats to chug out past the Pile Light, creating a caress of air, was *Filly II* with Bert Douglas at the wheel and Bert Douglas's eyes dreaming out of the tiny wheelhouse window. His fingers on the wooden handle were huge, but so stubby they might have been chopped off at the second joint. A bush of white hairs jutted out at the open neck of his shirt and a powdering of stubble led right up to where fleshy red ears jutted at right-angles to his head. The marks of spectacles were on the bridge of his nose though no one except his family had ever seen him wear them. He was humming some innocuous tune, giving emphasis to the end of each verse by blowing out through his pipe — the faint hiss of spittle and a scatter of fine ash. Down by his feet Chick Charlton stooped and shuffled in the tiny cabin, boiling a billy on the primus. That was one luxury they allowed themselves: a mug of tea before they cast the nets. The engine, an old V8 taken from a car, was behaving this morning, though last week it played up so often they'd sworn to get a new one. The prow violated that perfect surface, opening back white chevrons of water, unzipping the satin of the bay.

5.20 a.m.

Mrs. Douglas sank on the bed, seeming to shed her immense weight. The springs groaned impudently. There — she thought with the satisfaction of a morning well begun — he's gone, now for me hour's shut-eye. Wondering what time that girl would call to see her.

8.45 a.m.

Already it was developing into a sweltering day. Vi waved as her son Jim ran into the school, watched his small figure; starched grey shirt and shorts, grey cotton hat with two eyelets each side, bare feet, and the chunky schoolbag strapped on his back. She thought, who would ever imagine he could be so wild and such a strain? Into the cold concrete hall he ran, dumped his things and raced out again to join the line. Vi waited there, leaning on the fence a few moments more. A gramophone on its little table (a tall three-legged cane pot stand, in fact) blared out distorted reminiscences of *Old Comrades*. The whole school gathered in the yard, Headmaster at the flagpole in front. A prefect hoisted the flag. A unison of strident child-voices: I HONOUR MY GOD, I SERVE MY QUEEN, I SALUTE MY FLAG. Headmaster bobbed up and down on his heels because he was a short man and irritated. The gramophone, once more grinding round, wailed out its rhythms. A few teachers hurried about like NCOs making sure the correct lines turned right or left and that the march into the home of light and learning was flawlessly military, every child in step, uniformity preserved. She breathed her relief in a long draining sigh. Then her arm was tugged and Tommie, forgotten for the moment, burst into life, shouting and jumping, pushing and wheedling.

9 a.m.

Collocott appeared in his garden. Looked about for a moment, scratched his head, disappeared round the side of the house. Returned with the spade. Contemplated the work achieved so far. A small drab finch hopped across the grass towards his shoes (stitching rotten already, uppers coming loose) occasionally cocking its head on one side for a better look. What are you running the risk for, he thought, conscious of how enormous he must seem, and his huge round staring eyes like a horse's. "How do you know I'm not standing so still because I'm about to pounce and eat you?" The finch suddenly whirred past his head, so close that it made him jump.

10 a.m.

The postman came freewheeling down the slope. He hesitated at Collocott's, let his bicycle roll just beyond the red-lettered mailbox, then pulled up. Already the cloud of dust registered dark movements in Collocott's mind. He inched back from the fence. The great leather postbag remained shut where it was, strapped to the handlebars. He opened his mouth. Householder and postman both were creatures of the mouth, just the mouth, retching silently at each other. The powdered road settled back, making small flurries at the task of burying the wheels.

"Not here?" Collocott asked in a voice so utterly his own that it sent sudden rage through him.

"First time I ever knew that to happen. I said to them down at the office — have another look, in all the eight years I've been on thus run Mr. Collocott has never missed getting his long white envelope the first Monday of the month, not once. He did look again. Nothing." He banged the saddle, making countless grains of dust jump at the vibrations, "Slight sorting delay perhaps," he offered the comfort cheerfully, hopefully, for the other man looked all-in.

"Thank you for telling me."

"Better luck tomorrow then," and he rolled, silently, down the slope to Macy's. Who writes to Macy? swore Collocott indignantly, he must get a letter a week!

10.20 a.m.

Chick paid out the net, the clear plastic threads instantly lost to the eye as it slipped into the water — round corks twirling, little weights plopping like a distant lame horse. Startled by Bert's voice, "Not a peep out of you all morning," (shook his head and publicly relaxed) "family eh?" The older man rapped his pipe on the gunwale, "Good solid rosewood that is."

"Garn you old skite, lucky if its wormy pine!"

"The pipe I meant," then seeing he'd been tricked, he added, "next time I'll knock it out on your head," he was pleased, "then you'll have trouble sortin' out the woods."

"Yes, family," Chick confessed.

"You've got a bonzer little wife, I'll tell you that. And a couple of fine kids."

"Too right, but they play up so bad. You'd think they didn't know what to do with themselves."

"They don't. Kids never do. People think kids are like us, with no time and more than enough to keep them busy. Not true. Same as they say the youngsters always want to shake things up, revolutionize the world. Not true — never has been in my lifetime at any rate. Kids when they're small are the most bored bloody lazy little whingers on God's earth. And when they get to be adolescents they're the greatest mob of reactionaries. That's true anywhere from Cooktown to Perth. You'll find I'm right. Yours have got a few years to go before they start digging their heels in. Meanwhile, the boredom's on them. And they are going to make you suffer for it."

"Me or Vi?"

"The both of yous if possible."

Chick looked into the broad kindly face and conceded, "It's possible alright."

10.25 a.m.

At a brisk whistle-blast, Dulcie Thompson, her hair

in rollers, went out to the front steps. She stood there watching the postie, that old fat one, jamming a magazine into the ridiculous dinky mailbox the people two doors down had built into their brick wall. Serve them right. As if she and Arnold couldn't afford brick if they wanted it, which they didn't. She worked her toes further into her slippers (the fluffy madonna blue ones) smoothed the creases from the sleeves of her housecoat, but decided there was no point in bothering with whether she looked presentable. Bravely, without either powder or lipstick, looking (she knew it) all her forty-two years, Dulcie padded to the fence, "Thank you."

He always had a bit of a fancy for her as a matter of fact — it was a pleasure to see such legs, such a white, so smooth. He patted her letter as if it were her hand and confessed, "Looks like a bill, Dulce."

She took it with a gay little laugh for his sake, "Not your fault, is it?" and tore it open. *Dear Sir/Madam our records show that you have fallen two payments behind in the instalments due on the purchase of washing machine, brand* Pope *model* 12 *serial no.* B08208. *We regret that if payment is not* . . . She stuffed it back in the envelope, her agitation as thumbs breaking through its clear-paper window.

"I'll do my best for you tomorrow."

"Make sure you do," she admonished him with a wagging finger, "George."

11 a.m.

Collocott walked across the kitchen, crushing crumbs of soil into the lino, took his aluminium jug from the top of the cupboard, rinsed it, sluicing assorted dead insects and accumulated dust down the drain. Peered into it to check the job, the mud-mark of his fingers on the outside. Gathered courage, as he had promised himself he would, and set off into the blazing day. Heat trembled round him like a suit of fur. "Wish my palms didn't get so clammy, don't think people fancy shaking hands on that account, some have quite dry palms. Wear gloves, fix everything. Hot though. Eccentric too." Four minutes later he was climbing the slope to the dairy. Kept swallowing, in case he should have too much saliva, nothing worse than little drops escaping, spraying or dribbling, when you want to face someone. In he stepped, washed with the cool milk-and-tin-smell. Bobbie watched him, bursting with curiosity as she was, she waited till his eyes adjusted to the dim shed. Then went up to him just, he thought with amazement, as if nothing had happened.

"Mr. Collocott!" plainly she wanted the others to hear, "fancy you coming up. First time ever, so far as I know." He handed her the jug, a gag of pure misery plugging his mouth and swelling in his throat. "Pint?" she asked cheerfully and coldly. He nodded, feeling his ears pop as if they had been full of water. Back came the jug half filled with foaming milk. "Got visitors coming?" She hadn't meant to be so cruel and regretted it when she caught a snigger from one of the girls at the separator.

"Yes," he managed to force the word past the obstructions. She took his money and smiled at him. Out he went, positive he must be reeling like a drunk-ard, down he shuffled into the fiery hell of his loneliness, trying not to slop the cool milk, cherishing it like some treasure of priceless fragrance and delicacy.

11.10 a.m.

Mr. Macy went into the hardware shop and bought eight banks of rib-glass louvres and some fibro for enclosing his verandah, "to make it a nice little place to sit out of the draught of a winter's day." Still planning ahead, although he was seventy-eight and had a hare-lip.

Two men, never again to be seen in Battery Spit, arrived in a white Holden station sedan. They cruised round the district looking for properties to buy, stopping now and again to hand out business cards and a pamphlet urging people to move to a modern estate on the other side of Brisbane where all the roads were bitumen and every house sewered, where the bulldozers had levelled each allotment. The high price was accounted for by the cost of removing a forest of untidy eucalypts.

"Every place," Knobby Clark read the leaflet with interest because he was always talking about shifting to the suburbs, "with a view."

"That's right, sir."

At this point his mother, that wiry old battler, stuck her sunglasses up on her forehead like Smithy's goggles, "It's a lot of hooey, if you ask me," she contributed, "a beautiful view I dare say — straight into your neighbour's dunny! I know all about you fellows, call yourselves airy-fairy names, real estate agents or what is it now, developers? We know what you're out to develop, your own fat hoard of black money you've got stashed away in some Yankie-owned bank." She marched off jauntily with a parting shot, "Vote for me at the next election!"

11.30 a.m.

Collocott, digging again, became aware that the wind was rustling grasstops against his fence, became aware that the summer should be over, that the grasses though dry as Egyptian papyrus had managed to push up a few seeds. A head of lantana flowers thrust in through the slats, their tiny red and yellow petals no more than a foot from his eyes, and their sour dusty scent reaching out to him. Collocott had a suspicion they were poisonous. He turned this over in his mind, but finally had to acknowledge ignorance. And he never was quite normal about poisons. Ignorance, like failure, haunted him. I haven't made any impression — he admitted — it's a matter of style, because there are quite ugly people who can make it with the best of them, simply by letting themselves go, releasing themselves into style. The next proposition he debated was: is style acquired or inborn? He felt a tightening of the guts and made a half-hearted attempt to drive his spade up to the hilt in the yielding earth. Half-hearted, even though he was aware of a desire to be savage. This time he spoke out loud: "Do they know what it's all about?" The white veils of the sky were stirring. To his relief, he almost didn't care any longer. The thought of making a cup of tea, irrelevant though it may have seemed, was almost appealing. Out of dust and ashes . . . I mightn't be very strong, he said, but I'm not weak either. Not exactly weak. And I am clever; at least I've got some imagination. And a flicker of bare limbs, dragon's breath, gold teeth, oceanographic maps, and the death pains of crucifixion demonstrated the fact.

It was with some satisfaction that he let the water spurt into the kettle, and the gasflame lick the metal hot. Just time for a piss before getting the cup ready, and after a sit down there'll be the News.

"I have come to the conclusion," said his father, "that the boy is a waster," as he stripped off his white coat and shook the folds out of it with a single percussive thump. Thick starch in that.

"What has he done now?" — his weary mother. The culprit spoke up for once:

"I asked for an asprin."

Big brother, with a smirk behind his hand, shuffled the bottles of T.C.P. remembering his own forecast that Dettol would soon dominate the antiseptics market.

"But surely that's not too much to ask?" she said. He couldn't be sure whether it was kindness, or protection for her own headache that drove her to side with him.

"He lives on them. Which, in my professional opinion, is unhealthy." (Brisk and final like the close of a Haydn symphony *ti—tum* — he used to know the one — *ta tara tum ti Tum.*) The audience at this paternal performance was so delighted he bumped the shelf, a bottle of T.C.P. toppled, he caught it in mid-air. Tossed it up higher than the glass light to reassert his equanimity. Watched it turn, a yellowish gleam. Was aware they all watched. Moment of suspense. He caught it, replaced it.

Collocott poured the boiling water: heard the tea leaves hiss. Yet he admitted that if he had been the one to try such a gesture, he would have fumbled the catch. Les never fumbled catches.

11.40 a.m.

Jimmie Charlton was sent up to the Headmaster for a caning when he disrupted the chanting of tables, deliberately causing the children near him to giggle and lose concentration at 7 x 9 = 63.

At the Post Office a forty-seven word telegram was sent by one Capuchin father to another.

Arnold Thompson finally lost his temper with young Jonesy and lectured him on how an apprentice ought to behave, itemized proof of his slovenliness, offered him a week's probation — time to pull up his socks or get the sack.

Even by 11.43 a.m., Collocott still failed to see how worry had eaten into his family, how they were desperate with fear that he might win his freedom and might force them to believe their values could be challenged. To him freedom had seemed impossibly remote. To them, he had to be held tight, kept down, back.

It was at this time that the barber, having slipped out to buy a paper, returned to find the leather seat of his new adjustable chair slashed. And Jonesy nowhere in sight.

12 noon

Bert Douglas said, "Heard you was drinking with that fellow from O'Shea's."

"I was," Chick closed the subject. The catch wasn't all they had hoped. The fish keeping away for some reason.

The light breeze grew gusty, lifted Molly's skirt as she opened the dairy doors, it puffed some dust in Harry McDonald Snr.'s eye and blew the little pillar of ash from his ever-present cigarette, propelled the fishmarket reek to where Elaine banged her windows shut to keep the house fresh; it blew down a wire cage of the day's headlines and raised a few old newspapers from the dead.

Young Jonesy demanded the keys to Mick's bomb at knife-point. There was a painful blaze of light behind his eyes, then he found himself sprawling on the concrete, one tooth dangling a bloody mess across his chin, Mick's boot crushing his knife-hand, and Mick's exultant growling above him.

1.05 p.m.

Even my idol at school, Collocott mused, had a red nose; I couldn't be compared to him for anything except that he had a red nose and I got better results in English and History. Then a timid knock on the kitchen door brought him out from the bedroom, where he had been picking his toes. He went to answer it without knowing quite how he felt about being visited. It was

Bobbie Douglas. As if he had been expecting her and rehearsing his speech, his grasp of the issues was clear and his delivery fluent:

"You've come for an explanation. Well, she just did that on the spur of the moment, it was all a mistake. I don't even know Mrs. Pascoe let alone *her*. I had been wanting to explain to you before I came up for the milk, but somehow the opportunity didn't arise." Bobbie shrugged unbelievingly and, it might have been thought, without interest.

"I came to see if you want a hand," having been unable to adjust to his wavelength, "you know; before your visitors get here," she grew red in the face. It was really an awful insult.

The thought of anyone actually stepping in had not really presented itself. No, his immediate reaction said, this is an intrusion.

"I'm sorry," she backed down two stairs, "I just thought."

And it dawned on him that Mrs. Charlton would come to this very same door all eyes, that every impression the house made would be summed up and put in the balance; that — good God — he would be judged, judged here in the one sanctuary there was, the sanctuary itself would be judged. Have I been keeping people out, he questioned himself, have I made even the house alien here?

"You could advise me," Collocott begged, "I don't know what she would see in the place. How she would see it, I mean." Bobbie advanced again, her spirits rising.

"Depends on who the visitors are," she was conscious of prying and the anticipated pleasure of surprise.

"Mrs. Charlton is bringing her two boys. I'm going to be a kind of — well, a tutor to them." Her eyes watched him in amazement. Her tongue was like dry grass on the roof of her mouth.

"Tutor?" she managed.

"Not exactly. But I offered to try to find something for them to do, keep them out of mischief."

"So *that's* what your work is," discovery sweetening the collapse of a whole lifetime's extravagant conjectures.

"Perhaps. I was a teacher once, ten years ago," in a wooden bush school built round the old chimneypiece of a homestead ruined long before, and square windows, and immense blobs of meat facing him, challenging him to pierce their overgrown stupidity. And the president of the parents' committee (membership: 18) initiating his cross-examination as a newcomer — you vote Country Party of course, Mr. Collocott? And he answered — no. Adding — not yet. Adding — I mean, I haven't tried. Seeing in their faces generations of embattled ambition set hard against him.

"Well," she came in with a rush of practicality, "she'll first of all think it looks dim. But tidy. Why," she realized, "you've kept it exactly as Aunt Zoe had it. Well now we've got something to work with!" She marched into the living room, "curtains could do with a good wash. It's all a bit, well, older I suppose than it was. Still, not bad, but. You give me the broom and a duster, polish if you've got any, a cloth for the windows, and I'll be ready to set to work."

"But," no no, please don't make it any different — I'm settled, "you can't work, you must be tired," watching her with admiration as she already began to destroy his life. She opened the lace curtains and his secrecies flowed out. Windows banged up, dust wafted out, refusing to be hurried by the snapping duster. Bobbie began singing. And a kind of jubilation was in Collocott as he surrendered the defences of eight years.

"She'll think, he does well for a single man," Bobbie called, then took up her song again, till she fired the word "Books!" at him.

"Have I left some lying around? It doesn't matter."

"No, that's it, I can't see any. Teachers have books, you know." He followed her about, understanding. She was happy this way.

"I shall get some out, there's a heap in the bedroom."

"She'll think ... hmm, let's see ... cripes the cobwebs." The girl bounced happily into the kitchen, remembering the place. Childhood was so remote. And here she was, mistress where she had once been told to mind her manners and every few moments warned of the threat she represented to some precious object or another. She bounced back with the millet broom and took to swishing it about in corners. Her singing became intense.

"That's a hymn," Collocott ventured, edging in through the door, all elbows and corners, with a double pile of books in his arms.

"Is it?" she took up the tune afresh, waving towards the table. Obediently he stacked them there and went out for more. She propped the broom against the wall and tiptoed over to spy on the titles, to run her finger down the spines like a stick along the corrugated sides of the garage. Heard him coming. Back to the cobwebs. He edged two new piles on the corner of the table and eased them off his forearms, then patted the corners to square them off.

"How do you say X—avier?"

"Xavier."

"Uh-huh."

"You've been looking at them," he accused joyously. She dropped the broom and she knew he wasn't strange at all, "Xavier Herbert."

"And I bet you can't get your tongue around this," she said returning to the pile and slipping out a tiny volume. He took it. "Microcosmographia Academica," he read. Bobbie clapped her hands. She felt such a woman.

"That's what the chooks say before I feed them," she crowed and Collocott laughed. Laughed outright. And yet he already believed no cheque would come, not this one, nor the next.

1.23 p.m.

Mrs. Douglas hoisted up her sleeves to where the bags of fat overhung her elbows. This was her vanity, to wear long sleeves in hot weather. She stuck her arms in the sink. Soap suds clasped her in their bracelets of glass beads. She had a way of easing a couple of extra inches of dress over her huge breasts by heaving up her shoulders. It was a signal that she meant business. The water swirled after her mop. She found herself thinking about that shack at the bottom of Battery Hill. "I might go and visit," she told the dish as she plunged its clean face back for a second dose of rubbing.

Jonesy was out on the main road by this time, trying to thumb a lift; the good side of his face to the oncoming cars, ashamed of the swollen cheek and broken lip, the throbbing bone. A rattly green truck pulled up.

"Jump in Jonesy," said the truck. And he found himself beside Nev Jeffries.

"What happened to Queensland Railways then?" Jonesy sneered.

"Nothing. This is a private carrying job. My off-day. Looks like yours too." Poisoned blood was in the boy's eyes.

The Capuchin father receiving the telegram, slit the envelope with a horn knife and extracted the forty-seven words. He read them with a sigh. And remembered his seminary days; the cosmopolitan glitter of his conversation. But this was a time of change. He would get used to the country he supposed.

"Was I ever plain Bernard Tolley?" he asked the hall mirror as he went out. With blatant materialism that object evaded the issue: showed him instead how old he was getting and two grease spots down his front.

1.30 p.m.

"I'm going to town this week," Collocott decided.

"Do you go there much?" Bobbie said.

"No." This new possessiveness burst in flower, "Shall I bring you something back?"

"Maybe," the implications were not altogether comfortable to her.

"Some small gift, to thank you for helping," he took in the whole house with his gesture — almost as if it still belonged in her family.

"Now before I go, there's one thing more," she set her face determinedly at the back garden, "the little house," he seemed uncomprehending, "the dunny," she had raised her voice at the delicacy of the suggestion.

"Yes?" no no, not that, his intimacies his shame touched raw. Obstructively: "Yes?"

"Chips?" she said, "are there enough chips?"

"I'll look."

"And don't forget to check the paper," she commanded his back. He went to the outdoor lavatory, unlatched it, looked in, glad not to face her in that burning humility, hoping she would go, get out forever, discouraged that he had let her meddle with his house.

"I hope they don't come," he prayed. Yes, enough toilet roll was there. But hardly any wood shavings lay in the box. He remembered the sackful he'd had under the house for a year or more, and remembered getting them from the sawmill by the railway station, as well as the coarse joke of the workman who brought them out to him. He lifted the seat flap and peered in at the tar-black can. Not even half-full. The sanitary clearance truck came around on Wednesdays in this area. He shovelled the rest of the shavings in, took a bottle from the ledge and emptied 8 fl. oz. of pine scented disinfectant over them. Lowered the flap soundlessly. Waited to see if his feelings would let him, then faced the house and fetched the sack. After he had refilled the box, he took a broom and spun out the job of clearing up the spilt sawdust, till at last Bobbie emerged. She hurried down the steps —

"Got to go. Expected." And left without his thanks. He went back into the kitchen. He would have to begin all over again.

Daisy waded out into the water, mud as soft as rabbit fur curling among her toes. Her skirt trailed in the wet and she liked the tentative clinging of it. She moved with purpose, half a mile of lowtide flats stretched in soggy undulations behind her. She stooped to the horizontal universe. Floating like oil on the bay were long blobs of green an exact match for her dress. She stooped and her arm reached down, the shiny black watermark moving up to her elbow. She drew out a wicker and wire basket with a funnel opening, then turned to wade home again. She scarcely seemed to notice the crab rattling inside. Better to catch your own tucker than join a queue — thinking of her old mission days; sent by her mother to the grub queue; finally lethargically reaching the front when all the good cuts of meat had gone, feeling the tug at her wrists as he dropped a hunk of bone and fat (to the correct statutory weight) into her sugarbag; moving to the other end of the store for sugar and flour (poison enough for her people). This hand-out and that. Take your turn. What are you growling about, it's free isn't it? No. No males in the female dormitory — till she was old enough to get out and have her letters opened and destroyed, till she fell in love with Tony, till his wife reported them. The law, Daisy recalled, is just. Tony was deported as a troublemaker to another settlement, popularly known as Prison Island, three hundred miles away. So the wife had come oone night with a handful of bottle-glass, sat outside the dormitory where Daisy slept, and hacked at her wrists, terrified in case her body let out some sound. The crab scrabbled to escape, reached its pincers toward her. And, as if obeying some law of expiation, Daisy had been first to step out in the morning, step in the blood, first to begin wailing for that poor woman. Crab eyes stood up stiff and wary on their stalks. She quickened her pace. Going back there, back on a reserve, that was the only thing she really feared. And they could put her back, she knew it. Just by looking at her they could condemn her to a confined area, to a bookful of rules, they could make her subject to their will, make her accept their hand-outs. It would only need the local policeman to recommend her case to the Department, for her to come under their protection again: her heart went cold. She heard the animal clicking now. And she foamed on through the muddy water.

2 p.m.

Mr. Fennell had begun to watch through the glass partition for Collocott. They expected him punctually at 11 a.m. Indeed, the teller had glanced at the clock then turned empty-handed to the manager. A thing he never did: make unasked-for communications, nor often communications that were so immediately intelligible. And when Mr. Fennell had returned from lunch three hours later, so intense had the absence of Collocott become that the man had actually called, "Not yet, sir." Naturally, a manager can't afford to seem put out by anything. So he had stared with blank disgust at the fellow making such an exhibition of himself. It was, though, extraordinary. Once before — was it four years ago, yes in the winter — there had been a similar irregularity; it turned out the postman was ill and that fat old one had taken an extra two hours to complete the run. Collocott himself had never been ill on the first Monday of the month. At least, not ill enough to keep him from the bank. Twice or perhaps three times he had come in sniffing and tried to hide the thick-headedness of his consonants. The teller made yet another despairing display of his incapacity to understand what was going on, only to find the managerial head firmly down, the managerial concentration exclusively on the job of paring large coarse nails with a nailclipper not quite wide enough to shape each one with a single snip. Tiny insensitive particles of the man lay scattered on the glass desk-top.

Arnold Thompson received a visit from the old ironmonger next door.

"Getting bored in there."

"Quiet here too, Harry."

Harry continued to chainsmoke his profits: "Only spot of interest was this morning when Macy came in looking as if he wouldn't make it home."

"One foot in the grave and the other on a banana skin?" the barber said. Barbers used to have music instead of jokes, pretty lousy music it probably was too.

"Bought eight banks of louvres. That's not a bad sale. Plus a good few sheets of fibro."

"What's he doing, building another house or something?" Arnold busied himself dusting the wooden hat-stand, its curly steam-bent branches.

"Tells me he wants to enclose that verandah of his. It faces north-east, you see, so he'd get the winter sun in there. Not a bad idea."

"But who's he going to pay to do it?" only two hours ago there was the shock of that slashed leather; the cops would catch Jonesy without any difficulty, of course.

"Himself, by all accounts. It's all for that grand-daughter of his, who won a Beach Girl beauty contest last week. Ready for her to come and stay — which she never will." A young man entered the shop in that slightly apprehensive way men do have at a strange barber's. He jerked his head at the empty waiting-bench.

"Free?" he asked.

"Not here mate," Harry coughed, "he's too bloody scotch."

"Hark at McDonald of the Glen!" Arnold dusted the good leather seat, indicating that it was clear, inviting the customer to sit. "How would you like it cut?" his heart sinking at the duck's bum style oozing with oil.

"Just a trim. Modern, if you know what I mean."

"See yous." Harry left.

"That's amazing," the barber included his customer in the conversation he himself hadn't cared about, "what would you think of an old man building a new front on his house, by himself? A man aged, well, eighty at a guess?"

"He's off his bleeding head." Work began with comb and clippers.

"Yes, and I agree. As I was saying to my friend next

door — the cove you just saw going — "

"Look, how about the job, uh?" the stranger attended to his image, quietly stroking himself under the sheet.

3.10 p.m.

Two bangs of the front door knocker rang through the house. Collocott hurried into the passage. Halted. At the far end, subtly sprinkled with the dust of three days, lay the square of white paper. He backed away, rushed out through the kitchen and round the side.

The boys stood silent and demure, clutching their mother's hands. She herself was, in that moment, determined never to let them go in. She set her face, so that he would see her steely distrust the instant he opened his door. After that — well she was stubborn but persuadable. Her strength would lie in the first impression. She glared at the front door.

"Excuse me." From the garden below.

She spun round. The sprung trap bit on thin air. As she faced him, Vi had nothing left to do but smile slightly, foolishly, and push the boys forward as if they were the ones to be caught out.

"You brought them then," said Collocott, "please come in," her meekness gave him confidence, "I'm sorry I can't let you in by the front door. It's jammed." He led the captives to the kitchen. Go straight in to the books, Bobbie had instructed him. He walked ahead of them, encouraging them to follow. Vi swam into the brown world.

"It's dim," she said, "but tidy." Having given in so

far as to enter the kitchen, there she stopped. The boys went on, following the piper, only her hands fluttered after them. A few seconds later, Tommie ran back,

"Mum!" alarm in his eyes; and buried his head in her skirt.

"What is it son?" already urging him into the living room where her other child was. He circled her, still with her dress in his fist, to keep his distance from the piles of books stacked along one entire wall. She laughed with the piercing hurt: took a novel to prove it harmless, opened it at the frontispiece of the author. Her child instantly dropped to the floor with a scornful laugh, scrambled up again and returned to examine Anthony Trollope's comical whiskers and spectacles.

"More funny pictures," he demanded.

"Ssh," said his mother.

"There are plenty here," Collocott was delighted, "and would you like to draw some of them." He was really afraid of children, they were animals of another species.

"*I* would," Jim said without raising his eyes from a book of old warplanes.

"Do you know anything about children?" said Vi, rallying.

"A little."

"Shall I stay here then?"

"If you want to," he hoped she wouldn't.

"Thanks, I will." She sat in agonizing awareness of each limb, of her expression, of her short breath, of her hemline and worn shoeleather. Everything became an extension of her inner state, an exhibition of inadequacy. The boys, totally indifferent to her suffering.

scrambled about the floor opening book after book: comparing pictures, or snapping the covers shut if there were none. Jim, with his great experience of the world's values, constantly lectured his small brother on handling the books with care.

"I know," he shouted, "we'll put the good ones here. And make a heap of the bad ones there!" it was a question to Collocott and at the same time a command to Tommie. Both consented. So everything without illustration was consigned to a stack behind the door.

"Should I make tea?" said Vi for something to get her fingers on.

"No," chorused her young. She was about to tell them off when Collocott added his voice to theirs:

"Thank you all the same, Mrs. Charlton."

"Then," she got up in sudden revenge, "I'll go out." The host went to the door with her. "If you need me," she stated, "I shall be around at the market garden saying hello to Philly Douglas." Then, as she finally cast herself off and knew her babies were in his care, pleaded, "I hope they're good, for your sake."

"It'll give me something to do."

Although she understood that he would be kind, she went away with anger in her heart. He watched her walk energetically down Culver's Road past Macy's, climb through the sliprail fence, and march round the foot of the hill out of sight.

"Look at him!" Tommie offered a book of ancient art and Collocott shared the joys of admiring a lion with its fangs deep in the flank of a horse, its own flanks in turn pierced by the long spear of a feathered Assyrian prince. "Here Jimmie, the lion's got him."

"Can I draw that?" Jim said.

"Yes. I'll find paper and pens."

"I'm the girl sticking that into him," said Tommie.

3.20 p.m.

Philly Douglas had the tea poured out: "And it's been long enough too," she complained, squinting.

"Yes, I keep meaning to call round on you."

"Now you can, then."

"You mean when I bring them. Don't know if I shall again. I can't say I like it, Philly, he's a peculiar cove. And what does he know about kids?"

"They settled down okay, didn't they?"

"Just as if they was at home," she bit the word off, not able to add — but happier.

"And him being a schoolteacher."

"Who says?"

"Do you mean to say you didn't know? Our Bobbie told me."

"And how does *she* come to find out?"

"He asked her to help tidy up. Well, she passes his place of a morning and waves at him over the fence on account of him being so lonely."

"I *thought* that house was a bit too spick and span to be his doing."

"At any rate, he told her he was a schoolteacher."

"Wonder why he left?" Vi said, a cold tube drawing the blood out of her.

"Search me."

Vi took refuge in her cup, the tea scalded her wet mouth and sent bitter fire through her: "I'll give him an hour, no more."

3.45 p.m.

Two fishermen stood in the shallows. Being brothers
in such a place meant a surrender of independence. So
they were swearing at each other as usual. Where the
great curve of their net ended they had rolled it into a
funnel and were feeding the catch up through this,
lifting the fish straight into their small boat.

"Wind's against us," one grumbled at the meagre
haul.

"And you'll have us booked again," came the quick
retort, "with this tunnel," he shook the offending net as
he spoke, precipitating a few more fish out of their
paradisal existence into the clarity of death by air.

"What do you want to do, go out with your flamin'
rod and a worm on your hook?" But he had already
been convicted eight times of 'staking' and there were
fines still to be paid, "One day," he continued, "they'll
listen to my explanation."

The brother joined him in reviling the common
enemy, "One day they'll find out what they're bloody
talking about. If this is staking, I'm a prawner," as if no
more traumatic fate could be wished on anyone. As
usual they were reconciled — their disagreements never
came to anything. They themselves were caught; family,
legends, knowledge, the very limitations of their experience, all were ties that held them captive. Even their
quality as men partly depended on some romantic idea
they held in common, that because their ancestors came
originally from Holland they were somehow destined

for the sea.

4 p.m.

The afternoon heat congealed into a figure, floated dark and hazy through his gate, rang the bell, till Mr. Macy rose from his bed — the action stiff as raising a telegraph pole. His arms ropes. The weight of many years in him. He panted and croaked acknowledgement. The open door was a glass tank in which a single figure swam.

"Ah, Mr. Macy," she called into the gloom. He knew from the voice that it was Mrs. Murphy in the tank. He wasn't going to save her. Why, he could remember her as a skinny brat who stole his apples — when there had been an appletree.

"What is it?"

"I just called round to see how you are."

"I'll survive." Must be thirty years ago he had to chop out that old apple.

"Well how are you Mr. Macy?" she said, emerging from the tank.

"I'll survive."

"You certainly have, for a long time now." And she felt old at forty-five.

"I'll see you lot out," he threatened gleefully.

"Nothing would surprise me." She could barely move.

"What is it?" he said.

"I was passing — on my way to dear Philly Douglas — when I thought, never pass a friend by. So I rang the bell," she controlled her wide thin helpless mouth, it had a habit of revealing too much gum. Especially now they were those glossy pink acrylics, "And while I was coming I said to myself I said, he's a good Christian so he'll buy a ticket off me."

"Ticket? What are you selling now?"

"Look at this, Mr. Macy. You can win a luxury house for yourself, three bedrooms, beautifully furnished, wall to wall, hot and cold, two car ports . . . "

"To put me two cars in, is it?" the old man stared at her in fury. They were lowering the telegraph pole.

"Mr. Macy," she supported him. He groaned as he sank back in a cane chair and rested. She sat and flapped her bag as a fan for his face, hunting for soothing words. "I do hope those monks won't be a disturbance to you."

"Monks?"

"The ones who are coming to live up the back there."

"On the hill?"

"Yes. Haven't you heard? It's all over town." He sniffed at the word town. "The building's to begin right away. I *am* surprised no one has warned you. Apparently the Church bought land up there years and years ago."

"They pegged it out before the war," he conceded.

"Now that I didn't know." His eyelids bore down with irresistible weight. She went on, "At least it'll be company for you. You'll know there's someone within cooee if you're in trouble."

"There's Collocott," he spoke through hollow chambers.

"Oh, that Collocott!" she dismissed the suggestion without malice, "Just think what a luxury modern home would mean to that lovely grand-daughter of yours. As I said to Mrs. Baker, the judges were *quite* right to give her the prize." He stuck one fist a hundred yards down into his pocket and dredged up two shillings. He raised his three-ton arm and, in an unexpected wave of clear energy, banged the coin on the windowsill. She wrote his name, detaching the ticket from the butt. "I simply knew," the flimsy thing fluttered between them, "you wouldn't refuse a good cause," she smiled, genuinely moved at the thought of the sick.

"Is there a cause?" he fell asleep.

After a swift glance round, she re-entered her element, disintegrating in the haze.

4.05 p.m.

Vi was in the dim kitchen while still wondering how to approach the matter of collecting the boys. They catapulted against her.

"Mum mum, he let me look through his binoculars," Jim shouted.

"And he let me too," from Tom.

"And he told me about thunder and lightning."

"And me all about thunder-lightning."

"He let me help make paper planes."

"And me help."

"I've got a beaut one here. Just you watch. I'll go and get it."

"I drawed a monster. And Jimmie did too. And both of us drawed the lion that got him."

She would never forgive. Would she never forgive? "Thank you very much Mr. Collocott," she said as he returned with her son, "it was more than kind of you —" to have hurt me like this. I was driven mad, but at least I knew where I was going then. At least I was sure it was their fault.

"They've been no trouble at all."

That's it: a bit to the left. Then steal them from me.

"In fact I hadn't realized how lonely I was becoming."

"I suppose not. Well boys, say thank you, and then we must go."

"Can we come again?"

"Of course, Jim, if your mother would like you to."

"And me," admiring his Assyrian drawing: the tacked-on arms and legs.

"Yes, me can come!" Collocott joked, handing them their paper planes. Relief swept through him as they clattered down the steps. They were company, yes. But a strain too. His house was less his own. As their competitive accounts of the past hour faded off his property, he caught one last clear sentence: "Ouch! You're holding too tight, Mum."

5 p.m.

"It'll teach you a lesson," Sissons concluded, "you never know. In this life, you never know. I mean to say, cripes, I watched that Jones kid grow right from the time he was a baby. His mother was great cobbers with the old lady who used to live down Culver's."

"Mrs. O'Shea?"

"Yes — Zoe. And in them days me and Zoe was like that," he crossed his first and second fingers, like two old sticks covered with pink fungus.

"Yeah?" Mick understood that his own heroism was about to be bypassed, "Had a blade that long," he explained with his hands. The old man didn't even bother to look, but that was his privilege.

"She was a beauty, old Zoe. You're always hearing stories of how straight-laced she was. Never with me. Mind you, we had a special way with us. A — " he gazed right out through the house, "relationship."

Mick gave in: "You and her?"

"Well you don't think a fellow like me could live round the corner from a widow like her for the best part of forty years and have nothing happen!"

"I suppose not."

"A perfect secret it was. No one ever guessed. And now to think of her in a Home. Fair breaks my heart, I can tell you. She was a beauty. Only about twenty-three or four when her old man's name came through on the missing list. Course, I wasn't here then, I was in the trenches. Battle of the Somme was on at that stage."

"There has been no news of my call-up."

"Don't you worry. They'll catch up with you. You'll be sorry."

Not a minute early, Aubrey Fennell snapped his brief-case shut, took his hat from behind the door, and strode out. Nobody in the office was favoured with a glance, let alone a goodbye, yet none escaped notice. With the practice of years his side-vision assured him that everything was in order. Except — he recalled the moment he was outside — that fool of a teller had his mouth wide open. One expected something of the sort, it had been a most unsettling day for some reason. He walked over to thepub. He penetrated the saloon bar, like an impermeable object in water.

6 p.m.

Just as a few hundred radio sets pealed with the News fanfare, a great mushroom cloud began scattering pellets about and uttering a succession of rumbles.

"I thought this heat would have to come to something," said Mrs. Douglas as she answered a ring at the door, "Gawd, Bobbie, you haven't taken to coming round the front now, have you?"

"You never know," the girl replied, in kind, "between here and the back I might get drowned in this weather."

"Yes, it's brewing up for a real bottler."

"Is Uncle Bert out in it?"

"No and I'm glad. I'd rather have him under the weather round at the pub than out fishing. Least he can't drown himself in beer," she laughed, "much as he might like to."

"Sorry I'm so late, auntie."

"I did expect you before, but who's to worry, you're here now. I just ate up your share of me new fruit cake, that's all. Serve you right, you damn scamp," giving her a huge fleshy kiss. They went through and settled themselves in the kitchen.

"Brought you this," Bobbie passed over a paper bag, "a little present from me."

"Ta love. Cake is it?"

"Yes, and come to think of it, I might keep a slice for

myself — since you've eaten my share of the other one."
They eyes met, a warm understanding flowed between
them. On an impulse, the older woman reached out her
hand,

"I always did wish you were mine. Four boys, but no
one can say I wasn't warned. Any amount of sticky-
beaks piled on the advice so thick I could hardly
breathe. You know, I think I married Bert on the spot
just to get rid of all that mob of experts. If you can't
beat 'em, join 'em, I say." A pot of tea was already on
the way. Outside, a blinding flash crackled through the
air. Their hearts jumped. As if the whole world were an
egg just dropped, the thunderclap seemed to split their
lives.

"And what about you, Bobbie, when are you going to
settle down?"

The girl shrugged.

"Ah well, you're too young yet. Take your time."

6.03 p.m.

Mr. and Mrs. Strutt in the third carriage, second class,
decided they had reached their destination. Soon the
train would squeal and rock into their station, past the
station master's drowned attempt at establishing
geranium beds along the centre of the platform. They
stood, dusted soot from their clothes, rustled into rain-
wear and shook out their umbrellas. They were ready,
ready for the world. On the seat they placed, as they
always did, the *When you are in desperate need turn to
the Almighty* pamphlet rubber-stamped with their tele-
phone number and the branch address. The engine

ahead hooted and hooted again into the needles of rain. They were ready.

6.04 p.m.

A slight figure carrying a vanity case dashed out of the blue house on the Parade. Vertical rain made her appear even thinner than she was, made the tarmac sprout feathers under her feet. She hopped and dodged round the worst puddles and the tide of water sweeping across the road near the estate agent's; for a moment she took refuge in the sawmill office doorway. But there was no time to spare, she raced on, the bag banging at her legs, rain streaming in at the neck of her plastic coat, dribbling into her sodden shoes, her hair glued flat, her lower lip a weir, eyelashes stuck into tiny horns, her sobbing utterly inaudible in the din. She stumbled across the railway siding tracks, turning her ankle on a worn sleeper. Lightning passed into her eyes, thunder clubbed her brain. Like a rabbit washed out of the creek, she tried crawling up on to the station platform, thin fingers hooked at the stippled concrete. No time for the footbridge. She heaved — not strong enough. A locomotive blew two long blasts down the line. And she decided on suicide. The headlamp swung round the last bend, glittering on the twin ribbons of steel and the steel shreds in the air, and the wet rag of a figure rolling up over the edge of the platform. As the huge machine rumbled past her, someone shouted a single word, she didn't catch it. She forced herself to her feet, balanced the appalling boulder of her head, caught at an open door as two people got out, clung to it, propelled herself into the compartment. She left the job of sealing her fate to the guard who slammed the door shut, and the driver who released a fountain of steam, and the sly creaking of the wooden carriage.

"My God we've been hit," Mrs. Douglas cried, giving way to her fear at last, creeping to the window expecting the glare of flames. The kitchen light, only just switched on, had gone out. That whipcrack still rang in her ears. Bobbie was reaching a hand out to her waist — a comfort. They peered at the back yard. "Tell you what," she shivered, "I give the Lord thanks they aren't out on the boat."

"There you are, auntie; you see, the house hasn't been touched. It was that old tree. Nothing that matters." They stood together, the warmth of contact holding them awhile, looking at the great Moreton Bay Fig. All down one side the leaves had been scorched brown. On the grass a large branch lay trembling like a severed limb.

"It's been there since I was a baby," said Mrs. Douglas, "nothing can last long really. It'll all be different from now on."

4

After two days of solid rain, Thursday broke in a web of silver trails crisscrossing the countryside; and then sunlight blazed off the dazzling mirrors lying in every gutter and depression. Collocott walked out, the spongy ground giving under him, so that he enjoyed an invigorating sensation of weight and power. He made up his mind to dig the garden in earnest the moment it drained. His blue eyes borrowed a touch of intensity from the sky. He waited by the fence, water seeping in through the welts of his shoes.

"Something has happened," he said as he walked round the house, soles squelching. The martins were already revelling in the warmth. Three magpies (yes he would notice the birds today) strutted along Culver's, occasionally fluttering up and swooping on each other, wing-tips curled upward like a Kandy-dancer's. They squabbled, teased and gave vent to rich patterns of song, listening with a touch of vanity as the pure notes carried up the hillslopes on either side.

He had combed his hair and was turned out in a clean shirt and trousers with some evidence of having been pressed at one time. There would be no disappointment, he knew nothing could go wrong now — except that this whole life was doomed. The very fact that no cheque had come, that it was three days late, that he need not tell himself it would never come, this was partly responsible for the relief he experienced. Insecurity was in his blood. He responded, not with pleasure as such, but with competence: when I see myself failing, he reasoned, I see myself. Yet there was something else, for he faced the river and would not take his eyes off the distant sliprail fence.

"The great question is — " as he put it, feeling water in his socks.

"There's something I must understand," he began a few moments later, "if I am to stay here." Behind this lay the knowledge that he was on the verge of parting with his old ways; he could begin to fit himself into the Battery Spit jigsaw. Till recently it had been a jumble of five thousand coloured pieces very few of which seemed to have the least connection, apart from evincing in him a common bafflement. Till at last he held one piece up to his mind and saw his own image on it; and all his recollections told him he had begun, that he had enough matching shapes to fill out the immediate area around it.

"To the game," he enjoyed the image, "my first piece goes on the table." Yet despite the strength of his feelings, despite the energy to start again, he suspected that someone else could perhaps, at a single stroke, clarify his position far more completely than he could himself. Then there would be no holding him.

"I am here," he said. Since last Friday his voice had gained a touch of authority. Yet he expected no one to answer, for no one was there. The silent house looked out at him, he knew it was so, but he would make no return. He had eyes only for the end of the road. A surprising gurgle of laughter and he spun round, shocked, sweating, cold, embarrassed.

"So am I," said Bobbie.

"You came the other way," he said angrily.

"It's a free country," in her turn feeling let down and impatient at his timidity.

"You made me jump."

"I saw."

"I've been watching. Must have daydreamed."

"Anyway, you're here," she joked slyly and was rewarded with his blush of mortification. The magpies gave a few tuneless shrieks and beat off for the monastery site.

"I talk to myself."

"That's because you don't get out enough," this, surely, was going too far.

"There's no denying it."

"Do you need a hand today?"

"It's ever so kind of you. But I don't think so." The speech of a child invaded him.

"Isn't she bringing the boys? Mum will be disappointed, she likes her yarn with Mrs. Charlton."

"Tomorrow. If she decides to bring them at all."

"Good-oh. Shall I call round then?"

"You know there really isn't any need," seeing her shrink at his cold voice (damn it, it went its own way, always at the worst possible moment), he added, "but maybe I'm just not particular enough about the place."

"I'll come then."

He knew now who possessed the key to the puzzle. Everything would fit into place. She only needed to say the word, as she surely would when asked. He must ask her, this was imperative —

"I'm going to town this morning," he told Bobbie, the plan growing clear, "to visit Mrs. O'Shea." That was undoubtedly the answer. He had seen her eyes, after all, and her trembling hand. He knew her capacity for understanding and feeling.

"Whatever for?" she burst out guiltily.

"No reason. Except that I'll be up that way."

"Well don't tell Mum, or she'll explode."

"Shall I bring you something back?"

"You asked me that the other day," she said, pleased. He knew she would accept, if only he could find something she wanted . . . and that he could afford. "I'm going to be late," she flapped her arms against her sides to indicate helplessness, "bye."

"Goodbye."

The hours folded down about him like three sides of a card-house.

He barely had time to change into dry shoes and socks, grab his raincoat in one hand and his umbrella in the other, check his flies and his purse, before running down the road to catch the 9.30 to South Brisbane. But evidently this was a miscalculation as well: steaming up to the line, he found North Spit station deserted. Hoping he was early rather than late, Collocott sat in the wooden shelter watching two immense clouds converge on the last remaining channel of blue sky. Would he never have his breathing under control, nor his heart working less energetically? The effort was too great. He was foolish to have tried. Surely his timing couldn't have been far wrong? Maybe the train didn't stop at this little station; admittedly he had never caught one here before. He blinked out into the darkening day, having finished inspecting the initials on the seat and walls around him. A movement further along the platform caught his eye. A woman was peering at him, standing twenty yards away, arms akimbo. She was diminutive in her bright old frock and a butcher's apron. Her wide hat had been pulled far forward to protect her eyes, so that its shadow swallowed her face and left it like a black hole in the landscape of dusty browns and yellows.

"You got a ticket, mate?" she called, jingling a few keys.

"No," he jumped up as if caught thieving, "I didn't see anyone in the office."

"That's because no one *was* in there," she observed with satisfaction.

"In fact it looked shut."

"In fact it *was* shut." Now he was close enough to see, he found himself confronted by a tough little person, skimpy white hair hanging behind her ears, and a narrow concave face.

"Have I got time to buy one now?"

"You'd better have." She unlocked the door, went to the ticket window, opened that and took his money.

"Is the train late?"

"No. You're early."

"Ah. Thank you. You see I don't have a watch and I ran all the way."

"Do you good!" She shut the window briskly and reappeared at the door, which she locked again. "Can't take any risks," she suspected him, plainly, "and I've got to push that blamed level-crossing gate meself now it's gone on the blink." She gave him a searching look and made as if to double-lock the office. Then grumbled off to the next chore.

As the engine approached, drawing wind like a cloak around it, grass at each side of the cutting lay back and rustled against the stony soil. Soot peppered the station and a line of somewhat ricketty carriages drew up at the platform. Collocott chose an empty one. The buffers let off a *feu de joie* and the whole train jerked forward. Inertia, he decided, was as terrible as momentum. What a waste of time, he added as he slid past the hat at the long white gate, all this theorizing is. I must learn to discipline myself, set myself a task, something concrete, nothing speculative, something that leads nowhere. Let it be an end in itself: observation for the sake of observation. This carriage, for instance. Long and narrow — wood on a steel base — chassis (would that be the word?) — no corridor — brown lino on the floor — seats running the full width with a pair of doors for each "compartment" — must have that "compartment" in inverted commas because it is only as high as the seat-back so you have a clear view of everyone in the carriage (had there been anyone) clear enough to play dominoes with backs of heads and faces. He perched on the edge of the long bench seat and placed his hands flat behind him feeling gritty soot on the black leather; leaned back putting his weight on them, stared at the ceiling of curved iron stamped with an all-over floral pattern and painted coffee-cream. From their cast metal fittings, glass domes hung upside down, each containing two small light bulbs. Now I'm making a success of it, he said. Stiff little luggage racks stuck out at intervals along the walls. He did not fail to note the heavy-framed windows, each fitted with a push-up venetian. Design for a hot climate. The doors, he concluded, have no inside handles — you have to drop the window and reach out — could be hard — possibility of being stuck and the train pulling out again Help Help, no good have to walk back, a mile would it be? There I go again, that's what I mean, he complained. All the wooden frames painted dark brown. And slap in the centre of the blank tongue-and-groove end walls the bold black number 1109.

The effort had been salutory. He lolled back, contemplating these concrete facts, till the abattoirs and meat cannery pumped their nauseating stench in at him. He decided there was no point in shutting the three windows in reach; philosophically turned his attention to the poems he had read about trains. They missed the point somehow. Yes, they recreated a sense of rhythm and movement, a pulsing drive. But the essential experience was that of being inside something tubular. This was not like the world of 360° — but like a logical argument with beginning, middle, more middle, yet more middle, then an abrupt silence, the suspicion that perhaps a hole had been left in the air if you could but see it. There! (Collocott caught himself red-handed again) that's precisely the kind of thing to be avoided.

A few minutes later he added, aloud, "But is it so very bad a thing?" Still no one got in. Between Morningside and Norman Park he began to sing, safe in the tremendous racket; for a moment he achieved, after a long crescendo, a sublimely physical expression. It wasn't so much that he heard himself singing, as that he felt the vibrations of his throat coincide with those of the train. His was the core in that cylinder of pure sound. At Coorparoo he stopped with the locomotive — and found he had attained limbo. After this, the houses were closer together, the inner suburbs swirled round him, a vast whirlpool of fragmented colour-meanings. Something deeply important was happening, he had suspected it ever since leaving the Bay, something involving such a complex of responses that he was compelled to inactivity, to being the passive medium for suffering them. He had only travelled on this line once before in his life: the day he went down to Battery Spit with the intention of buying a house. Now the memory of that journey was taking possession of him more brilliantly than the present. He found he was on a journey in which the past unwound. It had the effect of restoring him to a relationship with the future — as if a permanent present (flowing but indivisible as a river) had continued there, unseen during the time he had taken refuge in the country. He was refreshed by eight years of mental convalescence, this could not be denied, indeed it was gratefully admitted. But how real was it? He had been living untouched by the present. Is it, Collocott asked himself fascinated, that only the past is present — that I have no present at Battery Spit because nothing of my past is there? He believed it. I begin to understand, he prayed, perhaps I have strength after all.

The station came gliding in like a ship. He stepped out and banged the heavy wooden door behind him (the door with no handle on the inside), fed a caged man his ticket, proceeded down some steps with black iron banisters and into the booming tiled tunnel. So familiar, another tube, another subterranean passage — and would this one lead him at last, up from below an ocean of drugged immobility to some paradise of flowers? As he reached the end, he found it closed off by a curtain of rain.

Three men and two women stood there, silhouetted against the brilliant aluminium light. Another man charged in from the street, causing them to sidestep. He flicked his dripping hat and stamped the water from his shoes, then grinned at his fellow-sufferers.

"Only a shower," he said, "it'll pass." They turned their eyes his way — assenting, dissenting, hoping — but some spell held them dumb. Collocott heaved his rain-coat on and released the catch of his umbrella, opening it as he stepped forward, nervous yet glad, into the heaven of metals and plastics. The umbrella trembled as its drumskin thrust up a column of shelter. In a modest way I'm privileged, he said, to have even this much pro-tection. He could have caught a tram across the bridge to the city. But from sheer cowardice he chose to walk: so many faces in the tram, fixed, and him not knowing if he was on the right one, or how much to pay. To ask, and be taken for a fool — no. When he reached the corner he saw the grotesque triple-hump superstructure of Victoria Bridge. How shall I ever understand anything if I can't understand myself? Your own motives, the voice in his brain agreed, are hidden from you. And this is one of your good days, you feel relaxed. You don't even care about the money. So why shouldn't you understand, or be as close to understanding as you'll ever be? No, don't just evade the issue, begin at the beginning. And you must keep your mind to the point.

121

He waited for the lights to swim their green blots across the wet road, then hurried over, sighed at reaching the safety of the kerb, and strolled on. Just look at yourself; that's where it all begins — spiritual scope is the direct offshoot of physical build and facial features. Will that do? Not altogether; there is always the family to be considered. Though it's not wholly false. Well then, your ignorance begins with being five feet five. That's where it begins. Made worse by baldness. He allowed the warmth of his hat to register its welcome presence. But I haven't always been bald. No, but you've never been more than five feet five. And I'm not a weakling. Yes, you are. Well I don't often get sick. That has to be admitted, you are healthy, and you've a great crop of hairs: see the hand on the umbrella, hairs on the backs of your fingers, hair between the knuckles, and that bush of black curly ones under the cuff. Sometimes got them caught, winding my watch — when I used to have one. There you are then. It's no good pulling down the corners of your mouth like that, people will think you're bad tempered as well. Or about to cry. No, it stops me looking vulnerable and I feel safer with them down, just as I do when I close my eyes to slits. Chinese? Japanese, with this moony face? Ancient prejudices. Lips are quite thick anyhow and someone wrote that this was sensuous. If you had a thinner nose, admittedly, you wouldn't look so bad; there's something brittle and aristocratic about a thin straight nose. Mine's straight enough. Yes, but fatty and always has blackheads in under the creases of the nostrils. Nice to squeeze them — that white stuff, sometimes quite hard. Poison? Everything in the world is poison to something else.

The cars driving by hissing with speed had droplets of water hanging from the back tires. So enclosed; the people inside have no idea I've found a butterfly's wing on the pavement (turquoise brown black) velvet over veins, veins or hair-thin bones perhaps. Those men with veins just under the skin, showing like cords, string, wire, along legs, arms, on feet, hands, necks, on temples — they're the ones who get all the sex. Rubbish. They *were* at uni. I noticed. That's just a superstition, or else you didn't know many people. Why shouldn't it be a fact? Why shouldn't it mean they have finer nerves or something, sharper responses? I know I'd give anything to be like that. Yes, of course I would: one arm, all my education, yes, just for olive skin and veins and sinews. And I wouldn't want much, weightlifters are ridiculous. Useless. Nice to have a few muscles though; but not out of proportion to the bones. Why not? Anything but the way you are would be better. Cripple? Anything but that, of course. Mongoloid? And that. Well I'm not any of these things, better or worse. This is me. And I've got to learn to do something, even being like this. What is it to be? What?

He splashed past the city fishmarket and on to the narrow pedestrian lane of the bridge, where a woman charged straight into him. The pink and the black umbrellas clashed and bounced, he took two steps back apologizing obsequiously: she stared at him from behind her blue tinted lenses, from the halo of her blue tinted hair, while scribblings of blood in her cheeks ("Capillaries, my dear, from too much healthy rubbing with the towel") grew a shade darker.

"Drunk," she spat at him and her face chopped

through the air like a hen's as she passed, and she carried her indignation to an ethereal region where shops and pubs floated among veils of rain. Trams shuttled along the bridge under the steel canopy, he listened to the noisy singing of their electric motors and the weighty contact of smooth metal surfaces. He looked down at the broad river of putty, and a huge cement-barge gliding beneath him. The wind drenched him as its side-sweep drove in along the river from the east. Never mind — he accepted everything, no indignity or inconvenience could plumb the depths of his pliability.

On North Quay he took refuge at the bus terminus, peering through wire-threaded glass at some bedraggled bunting dangling from a pleasure boat. He rehearsed his plans (gift for Bobbie, visit to Mrs. O'Shea) and decided there was the rest of the day for doing what he liked. The shelter exuded a faint smell of urine, the floor was mottled with phlegm marks of a generation of smokers' coughs. The rain stopped. Hot sunshine spilled through a gap in the clouds, roadways offered up a thanksgiving of steam. People thronged out of buildings, sloughing plastic skins. Collocott was dazzled by windshields and chromium. He found himself on the alert for green cars. The bastard will have gone, he said, gone long before this. Nevertheless he was careful of green. He passed the Treasury and, after loitering on the corner for a minute or two, turned along George Street. Two microscopes shone in an optometrist's window, that's something he had always wanted. At a fish shop, a sheet of water streamed down the inner surface of the glass from a dozen nozzles, rucking like fine flounced material, rippling, and distorting the thirty-pound pink and copper gropers and jewfish that hung there with heads hooked back so that an obscene gap opened under the gills. Is there no escape, he asked. A gargoyle faced him from the Government Printer's Office, grinning evilly. He stopped to persuade himself he hadn't been taken by surprise; felt his own teeth with his tongue — not at all like fangs, they were square or rounded, little hills, druid circles of bone. And the druid's building was two blocks away behind him, he had noticed it. What on earth do they do these days? Surely not real druids . . . sickles, religion, symbols, dumb-show, magic trees and all that? King Arthur was not a druid. Nor was King Alfred, he was cook to the Christian navy. Joke. Hee-haw. Druids' Temple that building was called, must be religious. Not like the Order of Buffaloes. Or Odd-fellows. Lord, some people have to work hard to make themselves outsiders. Or more exclusive insiders? Yes, that's it, the lure of the secret society — Mafia etc. — subject for thesis.

As he moved out of reach of shelter the rain began again, but so lightly and gently that his heart rejoiced. With everyone else dashing from awning to awning, it was now a declaration of singularity to walk slowly and with no sense of purpose. Down among the maritime offices and warehouses of a ghost-port he read the brass plates like a man among tombstones, savouring the associations he could conjure up for paper merchants, the bulk spice store, sailmakers, chandlers, a cooper's workshop, offices of a ruined coastal passenger service. The past is without threat, he decided in the perfect calm, wandering lonely and thoughtful.

Suddenly monkeys were screeching behind palms and

banyans, blue faces and red rumps swayed and flickered beyond groves of bamboo. Their cries echoed among the dead buildings. Collocott approached, fascinated, terrified, in through the gates of the Botanical Gardens. Bloody eyes glared at him with personal malice, small fur bodies thumped against the iron bars, others swung inside a towering dome of wire that jingled and thrummed at every movement. Cockatoos in solitary confinement nursed their despair, watching through their knuckling eyelids as branches shuddered beyond their reach and leaves scattered bright green drops. The rain pelted down. And the lush jungle became a frenzy of flickering shapes, gleaming teeth, snake scales, feathered plants. Pythons spiralled on the dead bodies of trees in their allotted traps. A dingo padded round his hutch sniffing for blood.

"Poison," Collocott snarled into that chaos where the untamed pitch of colour, sound and emotion revived the birth of his race. He retreated from the obscene monkeys, his legs jerking as if wholly independent of each other. He seemed incapable of coordination, his body lurched like a shipwreck. The rain exploded against the ground. The drops were so outsized and hurtled down with such force, they burst against his umbrella passing through the fabric as exquisitely fine spray. He could hold out no longer — ran for the nearest tree and cringed against its warm trunk. Why am I like this, o God I'd want to be anything but this, anyone but me, I'm thirty-seven and I can't forget how to cry.

As the storm eased, a light wind drove its ragged dragontails north-west towards the ranges. Then this in turn dissipated itself, and the drizzle seemed to hang motionless in the air. The tenderness of it, the easing and shifting of branches, gave him courage. He set off again, leaving the cages behind him, moving deeper among rare and quaint botanical specimens. I'm not unintelligent, nor without humour. But you are small, by no means handsome; as well as timid, not to say cowardly. Now there's a point: big people actually like little people who are game. A bit of guts can get you a long way. I mean, if I saw her drowning, would I risk my own life . . . Specious example — you can't swim, she can. Well, some lunatic is going to shoot her through the head, will I jump in the way? People don't get shot. Is this age so degenerate you can't even force yourself to be a hero? It's the age of those without sinews and veins. Quite the reverse!

He moved about the park, an awkward figure, carrying his umbrella so high and upright that it became a kind of gesture, and beyond question touching. His hat so square on his head was a grey felt trilby, the brim rather too broad and the crown rather too blocky, giving an impression that he belonged to some earlier period or that he had just arrived from some outpost in the bush a thousand miles away. Collocott attained an element of the unique, reading the lead name-plates of one curious growth after another, gazing with anxiety at a gully, riotous as jungle, with deep dripping recesses and thick undergrowth among the tree-ferns, macaranga, celery wood and rose apple. Are you so immature, he said, that you must always be reassured about yourself? The question was left trailing. He touched a soaking tuft of pampas grass (we used to call it alfalfa) which clung to his fingers. Tamarind Tree — he read — Planted 1858:

in three years' time shall I come for its centenary celebrations? He sat down to rest at the foot of a litchi, but mosquitoes drove him to his feet again. And yet, he said, I cannot believe I would think all this and feel it so strongly if there were not *something* in me to raise me beyond myself. Is it ambition makes me hate the way I am? The very thought! How the family would laugh.

He knew something at last. There had been a party at his parents' house while he was quite young. Two colossal men swinging fists. The sharp slap of impact as chest and face were hit. He would never let himself be hit like that. His mother crying out for someone to stop them. And he (yes, offering a salver of crisps) had dodged, but they blundered his way. He had dropped what he was holding and fled to the door. His mother's voice crying for someone to stop them. She had spoken his father's name. Those violent figures were on him again. Women sprang up from easy chairs. The giants were snorting and gasping, you could hear their bones grating and they stank like frightened reptiles as they crashed against the wall and fell his way — help, the telegraph pole! — knocking him down, so that instead of a mouth he had a glittering blot of blood. That was it. And his mother sponging his face. He smiled, it was over. He was out of the smoke-filled room, burrowing warmly into the blankets, looking up at a cigarette burn he had made on the bedhead. Yes, that was it. I'll carve some potato-cuts for those boys tomorrow, so I'll need to buy a stamp-pad or they'll have nothing to print the designs with. He rehearsed his new list (present for Bobbie, stamp-pad, visit Mrs. O'Shea). Of course the cheque would never come. He took out his fat half-moon purse, shook the change on to its leather tray: 14/5d. Train fare home 1/9d, return tram fare to Berriwee perhaps 1/6d. Hope I find it alright. Stamp-pad say 2/3d. Equals 5/6d, call it 5/5d, that leaves 9/-. Must have a snack soon, allow 3/-. Equals 6/- for Bobbie if I walk back across the bridge, which I will. No the cheque will never come.

Collocott took the path beside the river, discovered a whole avenue of weeping figs, strolled under the giant trees, his shoes deep in soggy fallen leaves, sticks crackling at his weight, rain pattering, all echoing among the trunks. This was the lost world of Beauty and the Beast. He reached the Edward Street gate and walked out, past the Naval Office and the great brick arch of Smellie & Co's machinery warehouse (A.1895.D). Drains roared and muddy torrents coiled along the gutters. His shoes were cardboard. Should he take a little something for Mrs. Pascoe and Shareen? No, perhaps it wouldn't be in order. He turned right, took a street to the left, doubled back, turned again, thoroughly lost, hoping for a restaurant, his legs shaky with tiredness, his whole body deprived by the recent shocks; he had felt the fear sucking at his stomach, consuming every scrap of nourishment in him.

At last he was back among shops; collapsed his umbrella, flicking it, the line of drops arcing out, like a fisherman casting. He crossed the road and caught sight of his reflection in a chemist's window. Adjusted his direction to keep the image in view.

"That fellow's looking at himself," giggled one of the girls inside, calling the attention of her friends to a regular amusement, "now what is he thinking?" But for once their attention was too closely engaged by the man's appearance. They and he, in varying degrees of clarity, saw a shabby figure showing signs of fleshiness, bulbous shoes, wide flapping trouser legs now stiff with water — and a ridiculous expression (yes he too could recognize that) on his face, a willingness to revile himself should this prove the only means to social acceptance. I am with you, the face signalled, in finding this man laughable. I am trapped. I am inside. I am . . . acceptable.

My raincoat has had all the shape hung out of it, he noted. Nothing in fashion. Coat sleeves like bells down round the helpless fists. As he stepped up on the pavement, under the awning and out of the direct light, his reflection vanished and he looked through to where three shop girls covered their mouths with a laugh of nervous incomprehsnion. Hurrying off, Collocott's raincoat billowed clumsily, hugely about him.

And yet I'm not so very small. And yet I have a sense of power. The blind masks bobbed past: lights in water, the sudden turn of a goldfish, of a shark. He paused by a litter can, patting its domed top, the patient faithful animal. Someone banged a packet in, set its jaws clanking and snapping. Is there no rest? Am I to be hounded always? He hovered by the door of a coffee lounge: rather too expensive-looking, yet a refuge. Money was running short. As he stood there, relishing and despising his indecision, he noticed two people approaching, an elderly lady with a young man he had a suspicion he ought to recognize. It was hard to relate them to Brisbane: he in his open shirt looking French, agile, eyes arms hands fingers gesticulating, capered before her stolid advance, persuading, entertaining and perhaps boring her — she with that translucent white skin of Italian or Spanish nobility, fat and scarcely five feet tall, rich in black velvet with a jewelled beret, diamonds playing at her earlobes and round her fingers, watched him with an expression arrogant and sweet. They stopped near Collocott and decided out loud on a cup of coffee with cream cakes, then proceeded to the mock-Tudor doorway. An all-leather waitress swathed in chintz barred their way: "I'm sorry, sir, we cannot serve you without a tie and coat." The young man's display collapsed. But the woman projected her imperious accented speech for the benefit of the patrons inside: "And why not? This isn't a First Class restaurant!" Collocott felt the sharp delight of identifying with these two. As they turned his way again, he offered the lady a half-smile of gratitude. For four seconds she pierced him with her frigid stare; then, indolently graceful, inclined her head to her companion.

Idiot! why had he needed reminding he belonged nowhere? As he walked on in the muggy rain, swearing and shaky, he knew this was the journey he would always make; after eight years' convalescence he recognized his madness again, that cities had no meaning for him, that they simply possessed him, and that in this regard they were all alike. The search could not end nor could it be evaded, this was a continuing experience impossible to confine to a time-slot between leaving Battery Spit that morning and his eventual return there (he supposed) in the evening. Could it be that he ought to take his own fleeting ambitions more seriously — perhaps really settle at the Bay and begin work on that local history, the research alone would bring him in close contact with the old people of the district.

He sat in a tiny cafe and ordered coffee and sandwiches (no he didn't know what filling: mixed yes that sounded best . . . safest and least trouble). The vinyl-covered chairs were so narrow he sagged over both edges of the seat. The table could not have been more than twenty inches wide. Awkward with anyone opposite. But there was no one, as usual. He looked out at the street, rolling the imitation lace tablecloth between finger and thumb. How well he remembered his life ten, fifteen, seventeen years ago; coffee in some Melbourne equivalent of this. I was almost in love. He called to mind the features of a pretty, plump girl. But could not rediscover her name. She and I had such long talks perhaps it could have become love. Garbage: love hits you so your whole existence is physical communication, not just gossip. I know because it is the one thing I've never had. Method — subtraction. Love is our ultimate desire, the single hoop we must pass through to life, a hoop that seems. That seems. That for me has no other side. I know because I haven't found it. It's not so much a hoop as a tunnel. And I know and this I really know because here I am an expert as I ought to be after living surviving so long between one side of the hoop and the other and understanding that I'm here and still here and that there is no end to it and that you'd better sit tight and put up with it because outside there's just another tunnel round this one, tube in tube. That's right: make up something pretentious and literary, a tunnel of no-love, a glazed tiled tunnel under the railway of life, ha ha, with everybody else's trains thundering overhead going somewhere, even somewhere expected. You've done it now, he sneered, you don't have to believe anything. But he remembered another face, a girl with some psychological trouble, a poor lost disturbed creature with perfect skin, a bloom of absolute purity, colour and texture that modelled her face; and her hair, how could he forget, in ridiculous little tufts over her ears that were somehow just right, touching, and made her childlike beyond belief, and tender so that his desire to be masterful starved his need to be protected. And he did to her the cruellest thing of his life. She rang him distraught with tensions, with panic, threatened to take her own life. He talked on the phone, reasoning, pleading, commanding advising advising advising. He who — God knew — understood nothing. Please, she had said, please meet me in town and talk to me. They had named just such a cafe as this.

A group of coarse-faced men walked in and sat a few tables away turning their shut faces to each other, conversing without animation indeed without seeming even to open their mouths except to clamp them like pliers for emphasis or to balance a cigarette in one metallic corner. By this and their white shirts and black-framed glasses Collocott knew them for civil servants. He bit into the cardboard-dry food and sipped his drink.

And he simply hadn't gone. That was the moment he chose to let her down. He said it was self-preservation, that it had to be him or her, that he had saved himself and nothing more. Fear had deepened his ignorance till it became panic. Oh there were excuses, of course there were excuses. Always the apology, the explanation, the whining and guilt. As he thought back, he reduced it to a question of five feet five inches. The waitress stood over him so that he dug in his pocket with trembling hand. She wrote the bill painstakingly, ripped it off the pad (which she snapped shut and dropped into her starched pocket) and banged the sugar pot on top of it before hurrying off to the sibilant invitations of the civil service.

Well, he concluded, if I haven't got it inside me, I must find it outside. I mean, many people no better off than me have become great even legendary (not to mention normal). And why is that? A cause, a belief, some impossible ideal made possible. In short, you mean, by sacrificing what little they were given they were rewarded with greatness. Yes, precisely. Well — any ideas about a cause? You see, you poor fool, if you haven't anything else you must have imagination, originality of concept. The great man *invents* his own destruction. And the difference between him and the suicide is that his destruction touches the universal, triggers off a response. What response? A response to being shown a new form. That is to say, a meaning, a symbol, something grander than an image or a legend. They help to give our lives shape. Their self-destruction is in the cause of society, whereas the suicide's is in his own cause. They die in such a way — whether exploring the Antarctic or murdering themselves with a thousand cuts in print — that another minute fragment of the Great Unknown becomes common property. Without property no one will care, no one will remember, no one will even notice. If you don't steal something or give something, the world won't even know you exist, as it doesn't now. There has to be a cause or a principle or some unique belief. He kept telling himself this for a few minutes more.

As he selected the correct money from his purse, one coin fell to the floor and he went red in the face bending down to grope for it. But there were altogether too many chair legs and table legs. He would have to go down on hands and knees or leave it where it was. Collocott mastered his desire to seem not there at all, and decided he could afford to lose whatever it was. He scraped his chair back till it collided with the one behind, jamming his fingers; reached for the bill to do something that might at least appear rational, but had the misfortune to overturn the sugar pot by pulling the docket too sharply from under it. With the side of one hand he bulldozed as much sugar as he could back into the container. But rather a lot had caught in the lace. So had his little finger. His embarrassment became as intense, as agonizing as anger. With beautiful deliberation he grasped his soggy umbrella, paid the bill and left without even glancing at the floor.

Once outside, he knew his money had been lost forever, that if he went back now, it would be as a thief: it had passed to them as part of their property. He had renounced it — an unknown amount. Money for the stamp-pad or for Bobbie. In the doorway of an office block he counted how much he had left and calculated that it must have been a shilling. But the anger was gone beyond recapture. As usual he would accept the loss, would be calm. I am a pragmatist.

At Penney's he bought a little gilded powder compact. How he could feel it in his trouser pocket, tapping him on the thigh. It will be warm when I give it to her, he thought. The lunchtime crowds moved densely past the shop windows in Adelaide Street. Collocott watched the people approaching, controlled the urge to keep his eyes down in case he met trouble, watched them till the masks became flesh, till the movements became expression. I see what I've always known, he told himself, each one is absolutely distinct, unique. Really they are nothing alike. I wouldn't even want to put them in categories — there would be too many. And yet they are completely unmemorable. If you met one in the street (he smiled at the cliche made real) you'd forget him the moment you took your eyes off him. Now there is something in this I ought to grasp. They are all different, but all ordinary. Is it conceivable that I am in the middle of a complicated game: and here's a whole city full of people playing it professionally every minute of the day? Does that lead me to say their real distinguishing characteristics are of attitudes rather than physical details? It could. But where does that leave the five feet five theory? He thought a moment about the act of thinking, about the nature of his ideas: I was trained, after all. Those years at University may not have been wholly wasted.

The bevelled-glass doors of the Inns of Court swung back and a man stepped out, conspicuous in a white pith-helmet and a cream suit with a red buttonhole. Collocott refreshed his argument. Now, physically, there is an ordinary citizen, ageing, distinguished, cold as marble, features regular. But his arrogant slowness, the swing of his umbrella, his carnation . . . and daring to flaunt the whole history of pith-helmets in a town like this! I hate him, I'm afraid of him, said Collocott, is that what other people think? Is that what happens when you move outside the common denominator of attitudes: create fear? At this point his thoughts returned to himself, but he dared not pursue the idea further. *I wonder if pith-helmets are waterproof?*

He watched the trams sliding past, hoping to see one marked New Farm so that he wouldn't have to bother anyone by asking where to catch it. Kalinga, Grange, Ashgrove, Enoggera, Lutwyche (extraordinary names the suburbs here have). He recalled having seen one earlier with the baffling sign: Bulimba Fry. Stafford, Rainworth and Toowong passed up and down the street, but no New Farm. *Timidity is the foster-mother of invention;* and rather than approach someone, he set off to find out by trial and error. In Queen Street the first tram he saw was the one he wanted.

It was one of those old open-sided trams, the canvas blinds had been pulled down to keep out the rain. They flapped noisily, rattling the metal supports in their sockets. They did not quite reach the floor, so the people outside could see a line of feet enroute for New Farm. Collocott sat in the damp, with warm drafts pressing his sodden trousers against his legs. He didn't like the noise. At both ends of the tram there were enclosed cabins — the "ladies" cabin at the front, the "mens" at the back. This distinction only arose from the fact that smoking was forbidden in the one and allowed in the other. At each stop Collocott listened to the partition doors grating open and shut, and wished he could be there in the dry. *Most people,* he said, *don't even know they have got bodies — simply let them function, take for granted that others will accept them. Never sick,* never clownish.

Next time he looked up at the front cabin, round frog-eyes were staring at him. Behind the square of the window flopped a mongoloid man, puppet head wobbling. Although he was about Collocott's size, he seemed huge and hugely unnatural. As the tram swung crazily into the bend at Petrie Bight, the fellow's head banged against the frame. At the unheard impact, Collocott winced. But it didn't seem to have hurt. You can't kill them, you know. You can never hurt them because their nerves don't function properly. You can never destroy them. The face boggled at him, blankly, interested. Possibly the same age. I am looking at myself, Collocott said. And the white frog hands fixed their sucker pads on the glass. No, he said revolted, no. The eyes would not release him. Had they ever managed such a victory before? But you could perceive no joy in it, no exultation; the jerking mesmeric papier-mâché figure had never been troubled by feelings, at least one was tempted to think not. Shall I ever find Mrs. O'Shea? Something was wrong with the paradise of flowers.

The tram squealed to a halt. The partition door slid open. A tall elderly woman stepped down to the open centre of the tram and then out into the rain. Her hair was bright henna and wound round her head in plaits. She wore clothes thirty years out of date: a long coat with fur collar and cuffs (even in this weather, he thought). Her button-up shoes gave a pre-war clack on the bitumen, lisle stockings wrinkled loosely at the ankles. Thinking of it afterwards, he identified the really memorable thing about her: out from the little hat perched among those fiery coils stretched a net; it was pulled tight across her nose as if someone had been fishing, had caught her from behind, and was pulling her up by her drowned face. And this was a mask of mauve powder with a purple cupid's bow plug for a mouth. Gentle hazel eyes moved behind, seeing him, seeing everything. That was why, for one dreadful moment, he almost called to her, "Mrs. O'Shea!" But she was not Mrs. O'Shea. Her mongoloid son was even then lumbering out after her, making concerned clucking noises with his tongue, peering at the road, terrified it might begin to move before he had his boots firmly placed. Collocott put out his hand to steady the fellow's elbow. But he could not quite bring himself to make the final contact. The mother was already at the kerb waiting, with her back turned, for her prison to claim her. How she must love him! said Collocott.

The girl had really perfect skin. Even those who didn't like her admitted that. Even those who didn't like him either. His father, for instance, sitting at dinner still smelling of the shop (he made me hate clinical cleanliness all my life) remarked: "I should think you would suit each other perfectly. Of course you can't get engaged. Fine mess you'd be in, with a wife as stupid as yourself. It's no good marrying a beautiful complexion. What you need to marry is a genius, a military genius at that." She was genuinely distraught on the phone. Imagine being neurotic at that age. And when I did not go to meet her as promised, I called it self-preservation. Never heard of her, or from her, again. Suppose she survived. He searched back for a newspaper headline: no, she couldn't have done it, the papers would have been on to that. She must have survived.

He found the nursing home without much trouble. It was a large place painted pale green (a restful colour, you know); must have been a fine house in its day, all weatherboard with fretted decorations along the verandahs and under the eaves. Having duly admired the garden and wiped his feet, he rang the bell. Made a mental note to plant salvias by his own front fence. A small nurse answered the door. Could she be only fifteen? In response to his hesitant, deferential enquiry, she waved him into a dark cavern: "She'll be up, yes, somewhere in the sitting room." As he moved forward alone, he noticed with contempt how nervous he was. The room must have been forty feet long and about half as wide. Thirty-one secondhand armchairs (he counted them later) had been lined along the walls. And, as his eyes adjusted to the lack of daylight, he distinguished a heap of crumpled rags in each of them. The immense old carpet lay blank as an ocean: conversation had evidently been impossible right from the start. The house had a subtle mixture of smells, in which neither the disinfectant nor the Woolworths' perfume quite overpowered that of human decay. Does it come from their clothes, their skin or their breath he wondered. Will she tell me what I need to know? Of course she won't — she could never forgive me for living in her house. Then how shall I understand?

"Excuse me," he bent to the ruin of one beautiful girl, it was easier than continuing round the room peering at the faces like an inspecting officer at a parade, "is Mrs. O'Shea here?" A light clicked on in the head, the old lady was instantly animated. She prolonged the exciting moment:

"I beg your pardon, sir, I did not quite catch what you said, being hard of hearing," plainly proud of her finishing-school accent, preening, "and I would so like to be of assistance to you."

"M-M-Mrs. O'Shea. Is she here please?"

"Oh yes, of course. She must be. Now let me see . . . " and the eyes grew visibly sharper, the grey hair crackled with energy. She almost stood up, looking round like an actress on stage projecting the fact of her willingness to oblige, "She will be wearing her maroon dress today because Thursday is washing day for personal items and she wore her green one last week. Oh dear, I really can't see her, you know," the blue eyes flicked back along the line of figures opposite and across to her own side. She sank back, the effort had been tiring, but unmistakably there was an air of satisfaction, of success about her, even of amusement. She smiled up at Collocott like a mischievous child, put out her hand and touched the arm of the chair next to her, patted the bundle of rags till it began muttering. "Mrs. O'Shea, my dear," she coaxed, "you have a visitor," and turned to him again, "it's the first visit ever made on her so far as I can remember, except her priest of course, and the Quakers. When I was younger I would have cried for her. But we have no room for pity now. Not here. Except pity for ourselves, naturally." Tears were welling under Mrs. O'Shea's closed lids, marking snail tracks down her earth-hard cheeks. "She doesn't understand, poor thing," said the ruin, "she hasn't understood for years," taking out her own handkerchief she dabbed her neighbour's tears away, "wake up, my dear, here is a gentleman to see you. He has come all the way here through the rain." There was absolute silence in that room, but it was not the silence of listening. At a further shake of her shoulder, Mrs. O'Shea looked up. The mask was still there: pursed to a spider's web of wrinkles, the dense freckles, the opaque inanimate flesh, even her white hair (though cropped short) still made a wipsy halo. He looked into the brilliant eyes for that warm person he remembered as peeping from behind the mask. The eyes were dead: flat salt-water eyes.

"Mrs. O'Shea. It's me, Collocott. I came to tell you I'm looking after your house. Digging the garden. To bring love to you from Mrs. Douglas and Roberta." She was feeling the strain of looking up, her chin trembled. There was no chair for him, so he knelt by her. The eyes followed him. "Mrs. O'Shea I need help," and the whole cruelty of his hopes smashed into his consciousness. Yet there was something ruthless in his character which he recognized for the first time as his voice went on, "*You* understand about Battery Spit, the people and the place. I want to stay, but I shall have to work now, so I shall have to learn what it is you know. You've left, you can see it whole, you were accepted. You've been cut off from it, how would you go back? Teach me." He was defeated, his words had not penetrated the prison of her loneliness. Still, he tried another method, "Battery Spit," he said, "Mrs. O.Shea, remember Battery Spit? The Bay, Mr. Macy? Mr. Sissons, Mrs. Douglas? The Great War, Mrs. O.Shea," desperation gave him strength, "and that — one night — before he went away?" But she was dead. He could not reach her. The flat jellies looked at him, seeing nothing. He added, "I only came . . . I just came . . . well, to bring love from your family." She was stone and earth. "I was in town and thought why not, why not go to see Mrs. O'Shea? I thought, there's plenty of time for a visit." As if that last word were the sole thread by which she remained in contact with life, it produced an instant response – her eyelids closed and fresh tears ballooned at the corners.

Collocott's own eyes stung with tears as he scrambled to his feet. He felt in his pocket, took out the powder compact and pressed its perfect brightness into her hand. He could not speak. A monstrous swelling had occurred at the base of his throat. He jammed on his hat, as a kind of salute, and saw her fingers close on the mystery. He fought through the jungle of his own deadness, for one heroic moment he broke into clear air: Collocott leaned over and kissed her on the forehead. Then he bolted out into the street, emptied of hope, not even thinking to put up his umbrella.

5

The rain set in. For two weeks it emptied solidly on the land. Hillsides were moved into the valleys, dry gullies filled, creeks spread out as wide as rivers, and the slow rivers swelled till their muddy waters lay still and heavy on miles of paddock and plain. In the upper reaches of the Brisbane River an amazing mass of water-hyacinth was dislodged and floated sedately downstream, here and there catching, gathering, spreading until the clumps packed together and spanned the city reaches from one bank to the other. The plants choked the river right down to the Bay. A few barges ploughed this way or that, cutting temporary channels through the flowers, jamming their screws with pulp. People were out in rowing boats, nudging through the tufts, raking at the roots, photographing each other in the act of sculling across a field. Every bus and tram bristled with gaping people whenever the river came into view. Sightseers gathered on the banks and on the three city bridges. Aldermen spent hours of alarm in the Ipswich area helplessly watching more and more weed break loose from its breeding grounds and sail off towards the capital. Commercial radio stations shrilly demanded to know what was being done about it. The Australian Broadcasting Commission contented itself with announcing the bare fact of the phenomenon.

To the man in the street the miracle was how enough hyacinth could grow up there to be choking so large a river: the feeding of the five thousand came to mind. And almost everyone was delighted. It was so refreshing to see the city transformed, so dramatically changed by something that demanded no decision, no choice, no disturbance of the customary intellectual torpor. The thing had happened.

Below the fort at Battery Spit the estuary was too wide to be completely choked, a passage of moving water remained clear at all times. But still the scene was dramatically reshaped, Culver's Road ending in lush vegetation and the ironbarks shrivelling to obscurity at the loss of their sharp outlines. Large numbers of water-birds and fish had come in from the open sea, and the locals were out in dinghies casting their nets. Pelicans swooped in, rattling their webbed feet against the juicy stems. Even some wild ducks whirred about. And a magnificent white ibis. somewhat south of his usual haunts, went gliding low above the blue flowers.

At breakfast Mr. Fennell was, of course, reading the paper. Such meals were frequently ingested unnoticed, not so the news. As he turned to page two, Mrs. Fennell found herself offered the traditional wife's-view of the main headlines.

"Tsch, tsch," she interrupted, "more floods."

"Umn."

"Far north as . . . where?"

"Umn?"

"Townsville?"

"Umn."

"I don't know how you Australians can be so calm about it all. Cattle and sheep drowned by the thousand. Hundreds of people homeless — whole houses washed away, furniture floating about, cars completely underwater. I'm sure I can't understand. Catastrophes everywhere along the coast and what do they do? Establish a relief fund! I ask you!"

"And what would *you* do?"

"Well, something. More than that."

"Umn."

"Oh! Aubrey, they're going to blow us all up," she said filled with fastidious English outrage.

"Umn?"

"See: testing their H-bombs right here. Horrible. Whoever could think of such a thing?"

"The British Government, my dear, in Westminster."

"Five hundred points of rain at Sarina during the past twelve hours — the poor things. The Flinders River five feet above the flood-level bridge. However do they manage. I should like to send something."

"Umn?"

"What should I send? Advise me Aubrey, you ought to know."

"Woollen socks, perhaps?"

She began collecting the plates and cups noiselessly, her lips puckered in protest. But, it went without saying, she would suffer his sarcasm. Hadn't she done so all these years? As her mother had warned her. Mummy saw through Aubrey's charm (and charm he had, in those long lost days) the moment she set eyes on him.

"Don't worry," he said, crackling the paper shut, "the Federal Government won't let them do it. Mr.

Beale has already rejected the suggestion." He added, "Though you can't stop the French using their Pacific Islands. That's the real danger."

"Oh, the French!" she drowned the threat in scorn, "we found out about *them* during the war — if we didn't already know, which some of us did."

"Then, as you're so sure," he played his little game, "we needn't go on worrying about it. I shall rest easier now." And once again, the sharpest cut went unnoticed.

"He has never been in with that cheque, I take it?" she sang from the kitchen.

"Who's that?"

"Your friend, that odd fellow."

"Umn."

"Has he?"

"Umn?"

"Well?"

"Umn? Umn."

The postman appeared, bouncing in a somewhat un-dignified manner over the crest of the rise from the village and down Culver's Road. He swerved to avoid ruts and holes, scarcely bothering to look at them, so intimate was his knowledge of the stony surface. He was concentrating on making the right kind of impression on that Collocott fellow, repulsing any attempt at com-munication once and for all. However, he had under-estimated the effects of the rain. In the three days since he had last come this way a new channel had developed, cutting diagonally across the road, draining into a hollow just the other side of Collocott's fence. So, with disastrous effect on the mask he was directing stonily at the overgrown river, his front wheel dug hard into the watercourse, his handlebars jerked to the right, his back wheel slewed round raking at grit like a speedway rider's motorcycle, and he found himself jolting in the direction of an expectant Collocott (who, despite his absolute renunciation of hope, at that moment felt a stifling joy rise in him) and slithered across the mud, hands outstretched to help his imperfect balance. The postman with the skill of his kind clapped on his brakes so the machine shuddered for a moment, vertical, paralyzed. And, in the full second before veering off again to deliver Macy's two envelopes, he snarled: "What have you done to the flamin' road?"

You fool you fool, Collocott raged at this fresh evidence of weakness in himself. "No letter is going to come," he shouted at the postie's back, not sure whether he would have heard or not — relieved that it seemed he hadn't. Even so there were real tears of anger. "Who do you think you are?" he went on, recalling how the man's behaviour had changed, from apology to sympathy, to defensiveness, to irritation, to a cold shake of the head on Tuesday. All I hope — said Collocott prophetically, making his way back, feeling mud pack in under the instep — is that he's got good news for *somebody*. (While, jiggling about in one pocket of the leather postbag, there was a brown envelope containing young Mick's call-up notice.)

Collocott squelched round to the kitchen door, banged his shoes sideways against the step, first the left then the right. He dragged himself up. His father had been laid out straight and hard in his coffin, feet pointing too precisely upward, flowers on his belly, hands clasped, neck as relaxed and dead as rubber, jaws locked, lips painted, eyes like a Roman statue, and a little ball of cottonwool in each nostril and nestling among the hairs in each ear. The last months of suffering had improved his features, fined away that meatiness which was so much the man and so hated. Even his skin appeared translucent like a baby's. "And who do you suppose, little brother," Les had said from the other side of the coffin, "is going to take over the business?" They could hear each other breathing and the sobs of their mother in the bedroom. She genuinely loved him in her own way. He had given her an easy affluent life, at least. "He gave her two fine sons," Les remarked. At the door Collocott slipped off his shoes, made conscious of Bobbie's floors — floors no longer his. "Les," he said with an unfamiliar touch of pride, "I was never his son."

When the phone rang, Mrs. Jones of 34 Angela Cres minced over to it, answering with such allure and such elasticity of the facial muscles that her Hello was completely unintelligible. It didn't matter this time as the caller was only Jonesy wanting money. She listened for a while, responding with her whole repertoire of raised eyebrows, smiles and scowls, as if the movie cameras were even then gliding in for a sequence of close-ups. All she said finally was: "It beats me why you didn't keep going out with that Douglas girl. You took her walking, whatever that might have meant, one Sunday night. Three weeks ago, it was, I remember. And though she's a plain little thing, she *is* hard working. And they say she saves. And she looks after her mother. What's more she has been buying quite good quality things for her glory box. I know, she has been in to get them off me at the shop. I notice. Money? Again? Not unless you come back here to collect it." She hung up neatly, before he'd had a chance to reply, and dusted her hands. A well-played scene though rather too short perhaps.

"I've had my eye on you," said Molly to the young girl, who flapped her arms against her sides in a gesture of helpless discomfiture.

"Spy on me all you like," Bobbie replied hotly, "I don't care . . . you're as bad as my Aunt Zoe."

"Well, nor do I care. But I'm watching all the same. I know where you go every lunchtime."

"And I'm going there again!" With this, she set off, her plastic raincoat crackling angrily and her stubby little umbrella twirling with a touch of bravado. Of course she wore nothing on her feet — who would in wet weather? We aren't all nongs, she told herself as she watched her toes splash into a puddle that was just on the verge of being cold. The summer would be over any day now. You could smell the cowdung especially strongly when the ground was saturated: she noticed it on this occasion and quite surprisingly it offended her — only for a moment, true, but enough for Bobbie to wonder what could be coming over her.

She decided this was a day to assert herself, that she had earned the final liberty of using the front door. Accordingly she marched up and applied the knocker smartly. For the second time that day Collocott's reserves of courage were drained. He crept toward the hall. Then he caught the sound of bare feet paddling about on the damp wood. It was alright. He went boldly out, round the side.

"Come on in, you must be soaked."

"You open the front."

"No, don't be silly."

"Aren't I good enough then?"

"It's not that — "

"Well what is it?"

"The door . . . is stuck. It has been stuck for years. Last time I tried forcing it the hinges began to give. I won't open it or they might snap off. And I can't afford repairs. Now come along or you'll catch your death." His mother's expression. She followed him, half-disbelieving, but made freshly aware of her lack of rights.

"You've made tea!" she burst out, injured.

"Surprise. I thought I'd have it ready for you."

"But that's my job. What else is there for me to do?"

"Drink it?"

"Don't go making jokes but," she warned.

"I was thinking of you," he said, "and this was my welcome." Would he never let her relax: she sighed with the burden of understanding.

"No milk and three sugar then," a moment later she added, "and I'll mend that door for you one of these days."

"Of course you will," he smiled with terror. She dipped in her purse and produced a powder compact, she placed it on the table and let it slowly turn on its fat little belly, the gilt gleaming and flashing.

"I love it."

He smiled, remembering that endless walk home; shoes and clothes like wet cardboard (he had thought of this description before, hadn't he?); umbrella awkward, dripping inside; uncertainty at crossroads; traffic spinning past, splashing him with mud; the countless times he had sworn at his stupidity, his sentimentality, at the warm round weight of the second compact in his trouser pocket. It had taken him six hours to reach Battery Spit.

"I wouldn't dare show it to Mum."

Even this pleased him. How far we've come, he thought, in the past fortnight. She takes so much for granted. She really looks after me, cleaning and cooking. He had begun to recognize her mannerisms, her peculiar little ways, her prejudices about housework.

"I'll never teach you, will I?" she broke in cheerfully. He blushed, caught once again adding milk after he had poured his tea. "It has got to go in first."

"But I'd never know how much to take. I go by the colour."

"You've always got an excuse," her spirits were rising, "I don't know where you think them all up."

"I suppose I'm just clever." How young, how desirable she is.

"Yes, you are," she agreed contentedly and sipped her tea. We've come so far, he knew it. "What's that book?" she pointed. He took it down from the top of the fridge where he had planted it ready for just this moment.

"A novel."

"What's it about?"

"A young girl who begins to discover love."

"What's her name?"

"Jane."

Bobbie laughed as she tried to fit herself into the concept of Jane: "Where did she live?"

"In Ireland."

"Ireland." At the romance of it, she pressed her palms together.

"Did you know they were more civilized than the English once?" he said. She nodded, eyes shining. "There was even an Irish Christian Church while most of Europe was still pagan. They had their own special kind of cross — with a circle round the centre."

"I've seen those in the cemetery where they put grandpa."

"And the Irish monks had a terrible argument with the Roman Catholic Church."

"Just lately?"

"No. A thousand years ago." He had all the right answers.

"What was the matter?"

"They had different ways of shaving their heads. The Roman Church said everyone had to have the same, the whole head shaved except a thin band of hair circling it like the crown of thorns. The Irish monks just shaved the front, making a line across the top from one ear to the other."

"And they argued about that!"

"Yes, for years and years."

"That's what comes of having no wives. We've got more to do with our time. And this girl, did she fall in love at the end?"

"Which girl?"

"Jane, of course."

"Not really. She understood that she hadn't ever been

in love with the man, not properly. Harris, that is."

"Was Harris his name?" she stored it.

"She went to the airport to see Harris off on a plane, but she was also there to meet Richard."

"Aha! Who was he?"

"Someone she had never seen before. The cast-off lover of her friend Vesta."

"Don't like the sound of him."

"Well, the moment he stepped off the plane from America, she fell completely in love with him."

"I won't believe it."

"Those are the last words of the book."

"Then they got it wrong. Jane would never do a thing like that."

"They couldn't have got it wrong."

"So nothing happened?" She wondered what sort of book would take all that time to get to the beginning, and then just stop.

"Well, you're left with the idea that something was about to happen."

"It sounds lovely. Who wrote it?"

"Elizabeth Bowen. I read it for the first time last night."

"All in one night!" She skipped, "I'd like to read that book some day."

"So you shall," suddenly his words were perilously full of promises, "or I'll read it to you." She gave him a bang on the shoulder, concealing the tenderness, the anxiety within her. She was so close to something she wanted, Bobbie rushed at her work, and while she bustled about she began teasing him. She gave him the broom and together they cleaned the clean house; she challenged him to dusting and polishing races; she dared him to compete; she ridiculed his incompetence; she demanded that he take her to visit Ireland right away.

What on earth *were* his feelings, he asked, thinking of love, remembering the poor creature with perfect skin. Injury at being forced to confront his own weakness? his incapacity to cope? to love? the surprise (could it be envy) at reading of someone else's experiences. The description of an emotion he knew nothing about?

"You're looking serious again," Bobbie nudged him. Even physical contact could now pass unnoticed, she discovered. Why won't he do whatever it is I expect him to?

The eight banks of new louvres had been delivered three days ago, but Mr. Macy began to have doubts about the whole plan. The verandah, hardly more than a box tacked on to his house, seemed impossibly large. He could not believe he and old Jamie Douglas had built that place up the road. Yet they had and it was his monument. Zoe will come home, he said, she's a good girl, she won't stay away any more. Rainwater trickled like a weir over the lip of the guttering which had been blocked all summer, imprisoning him in a curtain of glass beads. He could no longer move. The recognition of helplessness seeped through the walls of his stomach, bowels, heart, so that he gradually grew into some other kind of matter: mineral perhaps. It was now inconceivable that he had ever been able to move. Could that age of heroes even be remembered? Imagination faltered. The raindrops set to work digging an oblong of flat nail-holes round his house. I am never going to leave, he thought, sensing the threat of a wooden universe. He squinted out, his myopia like an obsession. The jungle of paspalum and crucifix lilies wove a stifling pall. As if the fabric already lay too close to his eyes, light came to him through large blobs of orange, grey, sap.

A brace of prawning trawlers edged into the bay from the north. The rain had lifted temporarily and from Vi's window on the waterfront they stood out black against the horizon. She went on with her work. Chick, she knew, was at the river mouth. Anyway, she could recognize the prawners however far out they were. The boys wanted to go walking on the hyacinth when they first heard about it. She had promised to ask Mr. Collocott to take them down to the jetty so they could at least have a look, weather permitting. I still don't like him, she said. Five minutes later, when the clouds darkened, the prawners were no closer.

"Think of a game," Bobbie demanded, pouting.

"Not for you. I have enough trouble getting ideas to keep those boys out of mischief." Like a handful of gravel scattered across the iron roof, the rain made an attempt to begin again.

Bert Douglas was out at the river. His wife, on her way to the shops, was explaining to Elaine Charlton how she had gone to visit poor Daisy at her shack: "Took her a cake, I did."

"You and your cakes. A bit of something nourishing might have been more use."

"I don't know, she always seems pretty well fed to

look at. Anyhow, I did take a piece of steak too, and some eggs and a bunch of those crysanths — the mauve ones — from the front."

"Was she home?"

"Yes."

"I suppose she accepted."

"Sort of. I couldn't get her to talk though, nor to ask me in. She acted more embarrassed than anything. But pleased, Elaine. I'm sure she was pleased," said Mrs. Douglas who believed that a bit of open affection and generosity would break down any shyness, given time.

Looking after Collocott had already become a habit. And Bobbie found ample repayment in those treasured glimpses he gave her of strange places and strange people. She belonged at Battery Spit, of course. But now she had a link with the world outside, beyond Brisbane, beyond Queensland even. Battery Spit could never hold him, or own him, she knew this. Naturally. He had begun with freedom, and this couldn't be taken from him. Freedom: she knew exactly what it meant, the word rang in her brain with its aching note, the lure was intolerable. He was her hope, that was it! So she found herself needling him on this afternoon. And he could not remain wholly indifferent; it was, after all, most irritating. Her childishness was upsetting enough, but the affront to his dignity was worse — suddenly to be jumped at, poked or slapped. Gradually, anger built up inside him. First, she had destroyed his solitude, destroyed his house, his inviolability, then his equilibrium; but all this was made bearable even delectable by her modesty, her naïveté and her fresh beauty. The force that drove her to break out of the tentative manner he so loved now revealed in her what he had perhaps always suspected, a boisterous nature and a kind of physical vulgarity.

Time, time made her frantic, the realization that in a few minutes she would be expected back at work. In one last desperate bid, she came to him laughing, threatening to mend the hinges. When he did not even turn round, she gave him a despairing playful punch in the ribs. A red wave of vexation flowed through him, so he pushed her roughly towards the door. She gave way with a sigh of exhausted gratification. Collocott said nothing, could not manage the apology his instant fear demanded. She was granted the extra joy of being the only one to say she was sorry. And afterwards, how she clung to this flash of male assertiveness in him. Nonetheless, he did go to the steps to see her off. She looked straight into his eyes and momentarily attained full womanhood, putting out her hand to touch his arm, "I don't know what made me do it, but really I'm not sorry at all." As if electric fire struck at his whole tree of bones, he knew he was in love. There was nothing he could say. But he drew away from her fingers: she could never make him beautiful to himself, so he couldn't bear to be touched. The love must be all a matter of giving, he decided as he waved to her.

Collocott remembered the salvias he wanted to plant at the front. He went through the house on to the verandah and tried to visualize the place with her eyes: now suppose she were over that side of the road weighing up her prospects — and the grass cut back, that bed outside running the full length of the fence and, yes, a blaze of red flowers. Nothing like red to set a place off. One lace curtain billowed out and touched him on the shoulder. He noticed it. The lace, whilst it inevitably reminded him of Mrs. O'Shea, had also come to be a symbol for something wider — perhaps for the whole interdependence of circumstances in which he was caught, the delicate linkage of events and people, the impossibility of saying: This unit of the design is isolated and recognizable among all the others. For this reason, though each unit was a flower, it was impossible to speak in the singular, to say: This is a flower. It was already part of another.

He happened to glance up at the real world of the hill opposite, in time to see a chromium grille edging over the skyline, nosing up into the rain. It stopped. Then gowned figures were gathering round it, grouped under large umbrellas. It looked so improbable, Collocott did not hide. I'm being cured, he said. Love, he said. He watched the monks shuffle off peering this way and that, pointing, testing the ground with their sandals, raising their arms as if they had some semaphore message for him. They behaved in straight lines, moving, pointing, calculating, pacing out the limits of this particular security.

The view from the hillcrest was quite delightful, they agreed, not to say impressive. Which it also was. Far away on the north-west horizon lay the smudge of the city: the river wound towards them bearing its lush harvest of hyacinths. As they looked down at the jetty, Douglas's market garden spread neat furrowed mats below them and to the left. It was a mere turn of the

159

sacerdotal head to take in the neighbouring hill at the top of which were walls of an old ruin, and at the bottom a house where a small figure on the verandah tilted its white face searchingly in their direction. One rather breezy fellow, quite the court jester as it happens, raised his hand in salute. There was no response. "There'll be conversions for us in the morning," he announced as the others joined him, "we are in a missionary situation." They all contemplated the valley; marked its whole length and width with a spindly cross of dirt.

"I often wonder about poor old Zoe. She was Bert's eldest sister, you know," said Mrs. Douglas.

"She used to chase us with a stick," Mrs. Murphy confessed, "her and old Pop Macy, as we used to call him."

"I'm not surprised. You and those brothers of yours — well, you were a wild lot."

"Look at me now!" and there stood that empty, insipid, kindly woman revealed to herself, "The things you expect of life!" converting the depths of her grief to a manageable formula. But Mrs. Douglas, true to her great heart, took it at a serious level:

"I often wonder who is responsible. I mean, if they just let us get on with it, I guarantee ninety percent of people would be pretty contented. But no — some smart alec has to begin promising us princes out of frogs, what you'd call lifelong happiness from a deodorant, a luxury house from a two-bob lottery."

Mrs. Murphy flinched but braved it: "I'm guilty there." She produced her book of tickets.

"I'll take two," her friend shrieked a laugh, happy, desperate, courageous.

To everybody's surprise the figure in the barber's shop doorway was Dulcie. These days she wanted nothing to do with her husband the moment she got him out of the house. She nodded at the customers, pleased by their greetings. Quite the lady of the establishment, she felt.

"Just thought I'd look in for a sec, love," she said in a voice that brought to his mind a whole complex of precious memories. I am guilty (he wanted to say) weak and stupid and guilty. I've had what I deserved. "Thought you might like to know, I was just speaking to Mrs. Jones up the Parade, she had a phone call from Jonesy this morning."

"It wouldn't be hard to guess what *he* wants."

"Money."

Nev Jeffries looked up from his *Australasian Post*: "I gave him a lift in the truck some time back. He'd been in a fight by the look of it. That's the last I saw of him. Did you sack him then, Arn?"

"Did I ever! And see this," the barber swept a towel off the seat of his empty chair. The injury was still there.

"Jonesy?"

"That's right."

"He's a case for the johns, that kid. Sorry I helped him get away."

"And they haven't caught up with him yet," said Arnold, "I didn't think it'd take them half an hour."

"According to his mother," said Dulcie, "she told him to give himself up."

"She's a nice little woman," contributed the man under the sheet, "now *there's* a set-back to the broken-home theory: happy family, good solid income and all."

"Where did you put him down, Nev," said Arnold, "that might give the cops a lead." Nev, who drew the line at informing, named a corner on the wrong side of town.

"I hope they get him," came a new voice, its tone so venomous that everyone looked at the speaker, a tall youth last on the waiting-bench.

"What did he do to you then, Clive?"

"Nothing," his face colouring and his pimples all the more painfully obvious, "it's what he did to Mr. Thompson's chair . . . "

Dulcie nodded approval: "That chair! as if it hasn't been struggle enough for Arn and me to set up the business." They sat silent. "Anyhow," she waved, "I thought I'd pop in to let you know about the phone call — it means Jonesy must still be around Brisbane." Conversation started again, the way being opened for Arnold's pet topic, for his inexhaustible diatribe against ingratitude.

"Of course," said Mrs. Douglas, "Zoe had a connection with that Abo woman." Mrs. Murphy was plainly shocked. "Gave her a bit of work now and again. Helped her out that way, by all accounts."

"Really?" she closed the topic. "Look who's coming."

"Now then girls," said Mrs. Clark trotting toward them, "hold on to your hats."

"What has happened now?" smiled Mrs. Douglas.

"Well," she pushed her dark glasses up, the better to see them, "We're about to be invaded — men!" She arranged her face to convey sixty years' experience of the world's pleasures.

"Who?"

"The monks," Mrs. Clark capered in front of them, "the monks are coming, the monks are coming."

"Only monks," they laughed, vaguely uncomfortable at her grotesque antics.

"Leastways," as Mrs. Clark put it, "that'll stop the subdividers. Good on the Church, I say, they're about the only ones who'll hold out against the land sharks."

"So will the Government," said the patriot Murphy.

"But they *are* the land sharks."

"Not the Prime Minister."

"Bloody Bob? You'd be joking. He'd subdivide his grandmother, if he thought she'd sell."

"I don't think that's quite nice," said Mrs. Murphy.

"Neither would his grandma," snorted the rogue.

"He's the only great statesman we've ever had. And that's a fact."

"Well," said Mrs. Clark, letting her glasses drop on to her nose, "in that case, let's hope to Gawd we never have another."

He had the opportunity to notice her appearance afresh before she said, "Here they are," almost cheerfully. But — he recognized as his mind registered the streaks of grey in Vi's short hair and the red hands — it was a cheerfulness from which he was almost excluded, although she was talking to him. What it lacked, as did her smile, was friendliness. She remained closed. She now trusted him not to harm her children, just as she trusted the school, that was all. Her "Here they are" was brisk and (could it be?) exulting. So it means freedom for you, Collocott understood. As the boys jumped in among the boring treasures of a few weeks ago, as Vi stepped lightly out along the road toward Philly Douglas's, he recalled that Chick's attitude had changed too. There had been a couple of sessions in the pub and a couple of meetings on the Parade, all were consistent in one regard: as long as no one else watched them or joined them the man was courteous, almost (how could such a thing be foreseen?) subordinate. But let anyone so much as wave a greeting and Collocott had the distinct feeling he was being treated like a subnormal relative who can neither be thrown out nor ignored.

"I'm sick of those old books," said Jim.

"Good," Collocott answered crossly.

"Mummy said," said Tom, "will you show us the higher-sins."

"In the river," added his superior.

"The river."

"That's not a bad idea," Collocott conceded.

"We'll have to leave our shoes."

"Alright."

"Cause of the wet. It's best in bare feet."

"Best for you, not me," the man became prim. Will I never forget those dreadful years, teaching? Nothing would drive me back to that. I'd rather go to jail. All those heads, those sneaking, sneering, narrow-minded, compulsively stupid, habitually ignorant, treacherous little mammals. But surely you can't hate children as much as that? Yes I can. You were a child once yourself. So much the worse for the grown-ups. You were probably narrower and stupider than other boys. I probably was.

"We're ready now, sir."

They even call me Sir. I'll buy a blackboard and a cane, that'll make them jump. Though it never did in the past. Even wielding the dreadful power of the Head-master by proxy had not made the senior boys jump. Once one huge lout of eighteen had stalked to the front of the class and towered over him, threatening to bash him unconscious. With a flat fatalism Collocott had known it was possible, the fellow was abnormally mus-cular. Yet this was enough to trigger off his automatic father-voice, so with cold fluency he had said: I don't doubt you will, nor that you'll write your exam answers with the same thick fist, nor that it will appear to the examiners you did your thinking with your fist as well, all of which will be of no concern whatever to you until at the age of twenty-five, with half-a-dozen silver cups on the cupboard, half-a-dozen children and a further half-dozen bastards, plus a helpless bashed-up wife, you suddenly find yourself a pick-and-shovel man for the Main Roads Commission, hated for your arrogance and already on the skids; this might be a great and glorious existence for your type, but it's over so soon, before others are even beginning to enjoy success. He had swung on his heel with a parting shot: You should all make up your minds to face facts, on an average your life-expectancy will be about thirty. Victory.

"Come on then," Collocott said kindly. He reached for the umbrella, "We'll have this with us in case it starts raining again." I'd rather be a pick-and-shovel man myself than go back to that, he thought.

"There goes Mum, through the fence to Mrs. Douglas's." Without a backward glance.

Daisy had followed the creek up for about three miles. She was always out trapping birds or catching yabbies. Another mile or two and the suburbs would begin. She kicked at the water contemptuously, it was so dirty, not like a real creek at all. Still, it was cool and companionable and hadn't been wholly abandoned by birds and animals. As always, she had one eye out for food. To think of that fat Douglas woman walking a mile was hard enough, but who could imagine her bringing a bag of tucker as well? And standing there, wanting to be invited in. *You* manage on what I've got, Daisy had thought as she blocked the door; when the gift was offered it had been an insult bitter enough to shock her into her mission manner, to drag her dying flesh into a smile.

She came on a boy fishing with a plastic bag: "What have you caught?" she called.

"These," he held up a large jar, "a mud-sucker, two glassfish, a scat and a couple of others."

She went over to look, handling the wet glass, peering at two silvery fish so frail that their internal organs were clearly visible, at the dull mud-sucker round which swam a gay little fellow with blobs of crimson brown and cream.

"That's the scat," he said proudly while she watched it, adding, "I don't know what those are called," as two drab specimens descended in formation mouthing at the scat.

"Doodies."

"Have you always been that brown?" he said by way of returning her interest.

"Yes."

"So've I always been this — " and found he couldn't describe himself.

"It's nice to be a colour you can put a name to," she said gently, for a moment proudly. He nodded, squinting into the jar.

"Doody," he practised, the friendship sealed.

"What have you caught?" said Jimmie to a stranger on the jetty who stared at the three intruders. Silence.

"Good luck then," said Collocott a moment later, for something to say, not wishing to fail in the eyes of his charges.

"It will be when I'm left alone," growled the sportsman. They walked away along the river bank, stepping over tree roots, slipping in mud, scrambling up glutinous little hummocks. A few yards away the acres of hyacinth plants rustled quietly.

"It's almost as if you could walk on them," said Collocott, immediately winning back their sympathy.

"Tell us about when you were a boy," said Jim.

"When you were a boy," marvelled Tommie.

"Well, the first thing I can remember . . . perhaps I was four or five, was carrying a bottle of milk up from the gate to the house for my mother."

"Is that all?"

"No. I dropped it before I got there."

"And you can remember little things like that? You must be very clever."

"It never occurred to me — that it might be a little thing."

"What else? Tell us another story, Mr. Collocott."

"I was doing exams at school. Maybe I was thirteen or fourteen. And I happened to look up at the window, just in time to catch sight of a tall lady going past. She had blond hair. And I only saw her face for a moment. Then I went back to the examination questions printed on a blue card. Then I went back to the paper where I was writing my answers and it was completely blank. I had no answers."

"But don't you remember anything real?"

"There was the time two boys were talking about me; walking along the street a few yards behind me all the way home. And one of them kept saying to the other: If he looks round that's the signal to thump him in the head. If he looks round that's the signal to thump him in the head. If he looks round that's the signal — and so on."

"Did they?"

"Did they?"

"No."

"Why?" in evident disappointment.

"Because I didn't look round. But it gave me nightmares. Even till the time I went to High School I used to get the same nightmare, wanting to look, to put faces to them. Perhaps," he was no longer talking to the boys, "wanting to end it all, to be able to confront the moment of saying — So this is the shape of my life and this is what it all adds up to! Who knows? There are more kinds of deathwish than wanting to actually die." I've often wondered how I might have been changed if

I'd had the courage to invite that beating. It is possible I would have found I could take it, that a punch isn't unendurably painful. And then what a different person Les would find himself dealing with today. He looked at the boys, but they had gone. In a flash of panic Collocott sprang to the water's edge: O God O God — he peered at the undisturbed plants — would they be heavy enough to hold a child's head under? Would you have the chance to rise three times? No bubbles. Walking the hyacinths! He remembered his words of a few minutes earlier. Then small voices came from the clump of she-oaks ahead. He called. They answered. "Wait," he commanded furiously. And added: I have been poisoned by fear.

"We found some cactus up this way," Jim said.

"I see it. Prickly pear."

"What are them red things on it?"

"The fruit."

"Can you eat it?" asked Jimmie promptly.

"Yes. I'll show you." He led them. "Mind out for spines."

"When dogs lay down," Tommie remarked, "they look like a dead rabbit."

Once they stood near the cactus plant the danger excited them. He showed them how to scrape the fruit on a stone, then peeled it.

"You sure it won't hurt?"

Collocott peered into the broken pear as if he were seeing right into the centre of the earth: the dark magenta flesh shading to a wilder, pinker fuchsia colour the deeper he probed.

"You sure it isn't poisonous?"

169

"Quite sure. I know all about poisons. The only thing to watch out for is the stain — it doesn't matter if you get your hands purple, but we don't want it on your clothes." To his intense satisfaction both boys backed away and refused to touch the pear. He bit into it himself, the taste light like delicate grass-stalks. Nevertheless he was surprised to find it unpleasant after so long. Spat out a couple of small hard pips. "This one isn't so good," he smiled, "perhaps it's the fault of memory." They took his hands when it was time to move on.

On this rainy Friday afternoon Collocott was by no means the only resident of Battery Spit to be thinking back, trying to assimilate the knowledge of failure, to deaden old injuries by reliving them often enough for the nerves to cease registering any response whatever. He definitely wasn't the only one.

"Not children Aubrey! No, not yet. Give me a while to think. The very idea of feeling something alive inside one; as if you'd swallowed some great crab or something, swallowed it whole, and it began moving, swimming, growing. Oh no." Mr. Fennell jerked upright at his desk. She took it upon herself, he said, to cut me off from half my life.

Sissons, shuffling among his treasures, could hear Zoe O'Shea's one scream. He experienced again his own blind incomprehension, till he saw her eyes brilliant with hatred, the carving knife in her hand its butt against her belly, the point twelve inches from his own and held without a tremor. Then his voice saying: But we understand one another.

In the moment she saw that thin little creature jump out into the storm, the pale legs flickering, the girlish leaps round puddles, the utter hopelessness of a child made old by inadequacy, Mrs. Pascoe knew it was unforgivable to remain silent and not call her back. Shareen had exploded: "At least let the poor little bugger stay till the rain's over . . . that's her only pair of shoes you know." They watched her dodge away, fluttering into the road's white blur, the thunder and lightning cracking whips at her back. And Vonnie (who could imagine it?) had run after her, plump thighs rubbing, had run lumpish and staggering, losing ground but plugging on, past the sawmill at the corner and out of sight — too late.

The tram conductor was a New Australian of some sort. A big man with wide jaws, with legs so thick you could see his calves filling out the trousers, and with no hairs on his arms. From the first Daisy Daisy had known the insult in his look. That was five minutes before he came up to them and stood, hanging on the straps, saying: "This one your man? Him and you — you know? How is he like? You make children . . . or fun?" She had glanced quickly at her brother (the shabby jacket, hat, dear old despicable face) and known again the horror of his smile. The stupid, helpless, shameless smile of a man who asks nothing more than permission to exist. So it was she who had to pull the bell-cord and jump off seven stops early.

How are you Charltons going to treat each other when you grow up, Collocott wondered. After all, Les and I played together well enough as boys. There were even times when we were close friends.

"Next time you come," he said, "we'll cut out potato shapes. You can use them like rubber stamps, press them on an ink pad or dip them in some paint and print the design on paper. You could do them as letters of the alphabet perhaps."

"Yes," said Jim, his eyes shining, "we'll print a whole book."

Zoe, Mrs. Douglas reminded herself, was the very opposite of Bert. And while you couldn't help liking the old girl, she was a bit of a trial: being so completely, publicly chaste. I remember her trying to get me to sign the pledge — me! She was too good for this world, as well as a damned sight too frugal. And where did it get her?

The street had been narrow, dingy and wet. Was it always drizzling in Melbourne? Collocott would still be able to find his way anywhere in that part of Prahran. Even now he could list the names of the neighbours — neighbours of thirty years ago. And on Sunday, a dry Sunday, there had been no one in sight: just him and his father inside their shop at the crossroads, stocktaking. Narrow double-doors, set where the two outside walls met, cut off the corner on the ground floor. The blinds were down and a slit of dusty, blinding light sliced in under them. He and the local children had played in tiny backyards, on the brick walls, among heaps of grimy broken glass. They had bounced balls against the sides of houses till the infuriated occupants had chased them off. Yes even me — he said — when I was young enough, they saw nothing wrong in me.

"Rumour has it," said Mrs. Fennell, "that our village idiot is going to leave us."

"I'm sure *I* don't know," said Mrs. Murphy, unable to imagine who this might refer to — and equally unable to bring herself to ask his name.

"That little cottage place could be made to look quite sweet," the great lady continued, "with a quantity of scrubbing, some white paint, chintzes and flowers. You know the kind of thing. That dreadful old swindler, that Mrs. O'Shea, never had enough money, to give her due credit, or she might have had it renovated. But bachelors don't care. So far as I know, they don't even *see*. Especially if they are queer in the head apparently." Mrs. Murphy, whose accent had undergone a metamorphosis during the past five minutes, turned to release her butterfly words at Mrs. Jones:

"Well, fancy him leaving, Annabelle. He has come to be quite part of the local scene."

"One of the local sights, might be a better description," replied Mrs. Jones competitively.

"It won't be the same without him, that's all I mean."

"I wonder what has happened? I was afraid he had settled in forever."

"You may well ask," said Mrs. Fennell, "*And* how he lived so long without doing a tap of honest work."

Daisy had picked up the brown paper bag, once the woman was clear of the place, and hurled it as far as she could, in among the wrecked cars. It had blown apart in mid-air, exploding mauve chrysanthemums the moment it left her hand; then near the height of its trajectory two eggs dropped (one smack on target in the middle of a Willys tourer); the cake shot out through a tear in one side and followed its own curve, landing a yard short of the meat. Leave me alone, she shouted, I've got all I need. Does she go round to a white woman's place with charity — to a stranger?

The boys had gone home and Collocott promised himself he would allow them to come no more than once a week in future. Twice was too great a strain. Then he walked over to the village, carrying an open envelope. At the post office he took out the letter he had written and checked it.

Culver's Road,
Battery Spit,
Queensland

Dear Mother,

I wish you would write to me sometime to let me know how you are these days. My life is quite full, people have begun to accept me more freely and I feel I am growing to understand them better than I used to, and their ways, for some of them are now my friends.

My cheque did not come this month which makes me rather anxious. I blame myself for not letting you know earlier, because of course it could have gone astray and it might be too late now to issue a "stop payment" card. Next month's cheque will be due in a matter of a week or so, I think.

Could both amounts be included on the one cheque I wonder, please? I am now clean out. As you know, I spent every pound of my own savings buying this house — you did approve the plan. And after all, father did make some provision for me in his will.

This is in confidence because I worry about what Les may do. *You* will always be fair, I know, and no-one could imagine you doing anything unjust or in the smallest degree dishonest, but at the risk of offending you I have to say I believe Les is too ambitious for this to be said of him, even though he is your favourite (as I have had every reason to know all my life). Please, Mother, please enquire discreetly on my behalf and see what can be done for me. I am really desperate as a matter of fact *really desperate*.

He sealed it, his illusion of independence at an end. Though, as he told himself, there was no alternative. I'm giving in, I always do. There's nothing so unusual about it, nothing degrading at all, considered in the light of my past. So it was sealed. Collocott did not go to the counter for his stamps, he preferred them from a machine: the thought of dirty thumb traces on the glue for him to lick off — no. And who cares if it amounted to an avoidance of human contact? Should he try to accustom himself to such contact, to like it? Not at the present moment. Out he went to the slot machine, conscious of crimp-lipped old ladies queuing inside, with their gelatinous dim eyes, watching — judging always. Maybe, said Collocott, they need to judge because they don't understand. They are outsiders to understanding, and they feel it. He fixed the clean stamp, dropped the letter in the box, believing for a second that it had slipped out again and might be lying on the ground at his feet. He walked off along the wet pavement, there were showers still. That was it: all these people who belonged to the place as such, were outsiders in other ways. You and you and you, he picked them off like a sniper, and Macy, Chick, Sissons, Thompson, Bobbie — all are outsiders to something, some human feeling, knowledge or experience. And you know it. This is most important. This is the thing I could never credit: you know it and you want it to be otherwise. There are some of you at least who would like what I have got.

Old Sissons inspected his treasures. Yes, he had just about any kind of tool or appliance, timber, glass or wire you could possibly want around a house. He stopped for a moment, satisfied. Feeling slightly giddy, he steadied himself against a doorpost. His life's work (so this was his life's work) turned liquid. He took two lurching steps along the passage, impelled by the knowledge that he must reach the bedroom. Light welled unbearably, a vast flooding lake of light, spilling round the rims of his eyes so that a man might drown in it. Then Mr. Sissons tripped and crashed into a chasm. A mask clapped over nose, mouth and eyes, fitted exactly to his face. He was living inside it. At least he was living inside it. Totally blind, he banged the mask on the floor. He could feel nothing therefore it *was* a mask. With this much knowledge he crawled forward, gratified to be able to hear the rain, each clear ringing drop on his iron roof. The trench walls gradually grew visible, ribbed on either side, wooden supports stacked at an angle. Familiar design. He had, hadn't he, helped build trenches like this one. A black socket surrounded each eye so that he looked out from far within, knowing it was always like this with gasmasks, hearing that familiar soft farting of the rubber cheeks as he breathed out, gas burning into sores, distant field artillery, the whole world a marsh to be swum and dug. He wriggled along. Keep down! No bodies in this trench for a change. Odd that it should be so deserted right in the front line. He struggled uphill to a rim, to open space, and peered out through the mists of rain and gas. Suddenly he was throwing grenades and yelling murder and his whole fighting body was in action — training tells — he was, he had, yes, there was a, a rifle in his hands with, the blade of his bayonet sticking fast in flesh, gristle like a tree, like pulling a knife out of a tree, foot on the enemy's chest, tug, wrench, tug the bastard, stamp him off. Others coming at you. Germans? Turks? He was shouting murder, the yellow spaces flew out wider round him, the universe expanded with a rush, yet the faithful mask clung tightly to his face, sweaty skin squeaking against the rubber. He was shooting, he would kill them single-handed, as in that glorious moment he did, saw the machinegun nest, leapt up out of the trench, the ground spinning underfoot, running in no-man's land, stumbling into pits, out, running to the fame and heroism he never thought would be his, to the certain Victoria Cross, the triumphal bands of the Governor-General's reception. He would carry the War forward, running. He, alone. Faces coming at him, thrown back, stabbed back, blown back. And one face coming again. Again one face, there, a body growing growing clear growing. Out of the poisoned air, a body moving, standing still, clearer, looming, small, dark. He saw the Aboriginal woman watching him from the road, realized the past had been mere images on the blank of the present, realized he had been lying there choking, realized Daisy was the total present, the unforgivable present.

He opened his mouth while his mind shouted: All that glory — just in reach at last — I'll murder you for this. Only afterwards did he realize she was an illusion and the gas began tearing at his lungs again. A sharp pain reached him through the side of his face. Bullet? The waves of a red ocean poured at him so that his head was washed under, came up sodden and streaming. It's the retreat! he yelled. Get a move on, you blokes, into the water! For Chrissake . . . The landing barges were waiting off-shore, an aeroplane came over unbelievably low, firing belts of ammunition into the sea where he floundered. Then it was night and the waves were black. No one could hear him. He had saved the entire army. Yet they sailed without him. So cold. There were specks on the horizon at the entrance to the bay. Cold. The fleet steaming to safety through scarlet blots of shellfire. And the. Tide was. (Sucking the ground away) going. And the tide (sucking). Was (hold on). Going out. Cold. The

Walking back the way he had come, Collocott remembered the flagstone footpaths of his childhood and never treading on the lines or something terrible would happen. He also remembered Les coming home on leave from the war, seeming in his element in R.A.A.F. uniform, bringing a photograph of himself leaning from the cockpit of a Wirraway. And I must have been twenty-three by then: yet he made me feel so much a schoolboy. Unfit for service.

Clive — spruced up, hair raked in furrows, a dusting of powder still on the back of his neck, a trace of brilliantine in the air — presented himself at the dairy.

"I never see you," he said to Bobbie.

"You can see me now."

"Not like this. I mean — " he knew just how he wanted her, on which pew they would sit, lie, with the ribs of the empty building arching above them, "you never come to church."

"That's right."

"What about the pictures tonight?"

"What about them?" said Bobbie pertly.

"Shall we go together?"

"Look Clive, I have been trying to make you understand. There's someone else."

"Jonesy?"

"Not Jonesy."

"Who then? I'll drop him," by sheer overbearing height he tried to intimidate her.

"I shan't tell." And in sour triumph he knew she was afraid for the fellow.

Towards five o'clock the noise in the pub increased steadily. In his usual corner, Knobby Clark was holding forth yet again on the subject of his planned move to the city. Chick, his arm in a sling, enjoyed a quiet beer with Bert:

"I was thinking of the pains of childbirth," he explained, "how big a baby's head is. Little shoulders but enough extra to be like pushing out a mountain ridge. And I was thinking about Vi. Thinking — I don't know a thing about your life really, what you've been through."

"Look mate, that's all okay. And of course you're right. We all think the same about our wives one time or another."

"But is there an answer, Bert?" he gazed in at his trapped hand, at the bandages which were wound on with the precision of puttees.

"Who knows? But I reckon you can do worse than ask yourself another question — what would Vi be doing if she hadn't married you? There's nothing to say she would ever have married. And what would have been the alternative? She'd have to work for a living. Being single isn't all roses either. Is that what it means to be free? Look, there's a lot of people talk about freedom this and freedom that, when they just mean being alone. That's how I understand it anyhow. As for being alone, you can have too much of that as well."

"At any rate, now she'll get a couple of afternoons a week to herself."

"That Collocott?"

"Yes."

"I can't understand you. Put it this way. He fair makes me want to perk, that cove."

Further round the bar Arnold Thompson collared Nev to pump him about Jonesy and ask for a statement to give the police — despite interruptions by the fat postman still in uniform who, for Dulcie's sake, liked to keep on good terms with him. High over the din came a single thread of sound. One head went up, then another, listening. A few conversations remained in suspended animation. But the dominant talk about the races and the coming football season went on. Some illegal off-the-course betting was arranged and money changed hands, small amounts, though naturally they would all be in it. A column of flies twirled on the sticky flypaper hung from the light fittings. Soon there could be no ignoring the steady roar, becoming so strident a man had to shout to be heard.

The whole population was out in the streets, watching the light aircraft as it banked in from the north so low you could recognize the pilot's face if you knew him.

"Must be having a joke," said Chick.

"Or he wants a close look at the handsome natives of Battery Spit," suggested Nev.

"Who're you calling a native?" someone demanded with good-natured offence.

"The stupid cow's winning a bet if you ask me," said George.

"Hey — watch out," yelled Arnold.

"Jesus, he'll crash."

"Look out!"

The Auster dipped, levelled, thundered in just above the trees and telegraph poles. One witness later recalled having seen the chevron-tread of its tyres.

The pilot was permitting himself a contemptuous smile at the bumpkins with their clenched fists. He flew south along the coast as far as Hastings, then turned. He climbed above the vast blue-grey pattern of snaking channels and islands in that sea of mud — the firm land reaching fingers out, with thin hard bones of roads — eventually shading off and disappearing in a low smudge of cloud. He swooped down again and came back along the Bay, setting house frames vibrating, windows rattling, and an instant crowd of high-school girls waving joyously. The treasures at Sissons's place trembled, but the old man did not move. Nor did Collocott, just down the road, crouched under the kitchen table expecting his house to be smashed to matchwood by the impact. Off over the crust of water-hyacinth the Auster climbed as hundreds of frenzied waterbirds took to the air. They rose up after it, spreading out, so it appeared to be pulling an immense net that flickered white, black, brown, white.

Mick was off work early. He drove out along the Avenue with inspired speed, his call-up in his pocket. At last at last, he sang. But when he arrived he slammed on the brakes, sprang from the vehicle not bothering to shut the door after him. At the top of the stairs lay the grey head, face downwards. Within seconds Mick was there, bending over, tapping his friend's cheeks. Just about alive still. Panic held him utterly helpless. He didn't even dare carry the old man into the bedroom, a lesson learnt from First Aid films. He went indoors and found a blanket. Warmth was the thing. Sissons opened his eyes, but only one worked. He flexed the cheek which was not wooden. And the side of his mouth that still had life in it spoke. With intense labour he moulded each word, like a sculptor, gave them out imperfect as they were, each like a unique benefaction. Mick felt the nausea rise inside him.

"That," spoke the corpse, "black woman." and it seemed he would never go on, but he fought for strength, his rage the sole survivor of heart-attack and stroke, "saw me," as the instrument of such rage he must make words, "me fall," he would kill himself to complete this hatred, "would not," his head rolled back, mouth agape. Mick bent closer. Dead? Not yet. The half-face whispered, "not help," another thin sibilant sound came, then expended itself. He lay breathing irregularly. The eye opened again. In a stupendous terrifying display of force, the passion for revenge worked through him, drawing every last fibre to full stretch so that the final words came out clearly, almost loudly, "Left me. Die." Momentarily Mick recognized the lifelong self-pity that lay behind the effort. Then he stood shakily. He knew what had to be done: report the death to a doctor and the police. He was pleased with himself as he got back in the car for having controlled the urge to cry. The fear had always been near the surface that an unforeseen shock might reveal the child in him still. And every man has got to see someone die; important experience. In a way the old coot had taught him a more important lesson during the past five minutes, he told himself, than in all their conversations. This was manhood then. He let in the clutch. He disclosed the truth: the one friend who cared would never know his call-up notice had come.

That night Collocott went to bed early. He fancied he could smell the hyacinth fragrance, even at that distance, and was afraid he might dream they were taking over, creeping up the jetty, along Culver's Road, suffocating him in his house. In fact he fell into a blank sleep undisturbed by thoughts of any kind. Next he was woken by a tremendous hammering on the front door. He sat up in bed, struggling to assemble the last few signals his brain had received during sleep. What was it? A pale light filtered into the room through closed curtains. It must be early morning. The hammering came again. Collocott lay curled under his blanket, his heart's agitation shaking his whole body. He could hear silence hissing round him like rain. The house itself was tensed for the next shock. He would pretend to be out, asleep, dead. Would it never come – the expectation became almost painful, he even put his head out. Again, at last, the hammering. Plainly they were not going to give up easily. Because he was too frightened to remain ignorant, he slipped out of bed and crept into the living-room. His legs weak, flesh palpitating with fear, arms rigid, fingers splayed tensely as if to aid his concentration on making no sound, he stood back from the window, straining to see through. Nothing. Moved closer.

Moved closer.

Craned his neck to see into the doorway. Suddenly the visitor moved right in front of him, stood hardly more than a yard away on the grass – just a face looking up through the bars of the cast-iron railing. Their eyes locked. His turmoil froze. The muscles at the back of his legs were aching. Gratefully he gave in to the soothing sensation of blank incomprehension. It was Daisy out there, backing away from him so that he could now see all but her feet and ankles. The clear pale pattern of her dress appeared to exist on the same surface plane as the mailbox and the road, the hill; however her face was altogether deeper more challenging, a hole, a dark tunnel into which Collocott peered while sleepiness returned. Relaxation possessed him as if he had escaped himself, as if he had passed beyond himself right through into the earth. Yet as she began to approach he grew uneasy — had it been rather the violation of some secret? He waved her round the side.

He opened the kitchen door, thinking: But I don't know you, I don't even set eyes on you more than once a month. She came up the stairs with far greater agility than he could believe himself capable of. Then Collocott was confronted (for the first time in his life) with someone's genuine terror. Immediately he recognized the gulf between this and those petty fears of his own. His whole life was ludicrously insignificant. She stood — curbing the compulsion to act, to run, sob, scream, collapse — till she found words for the question that obsessed her:

"Will you help me, mister?"

Collocott decided to stay clear of trouble, and this was plainly trouble, to avoid getting mixed up in anything, keep her out, play for time, block the doorway, raise conditions and objections:

"Come in," he said. And closed the door after her. What are you doing, what are you doing you fool? "Would you like a comfortable seat in the front room, or a cup of tea out here?" She folded her body on one of the small brown kitchen chairs with a long trembling sigh of gratitude. He filled the kettle. My God you're off your head; she's probably wanted by the police, done something criminal, don't you understand this means danger? The match snapped alight with startling intensity in that room, so Collocott was made to realize how early it must be for the dawn to have scarcely penetrated the house. The gas burned a blue as glorious as the sky. She's probably dirty, bringing in diseases, lice, who knows how she lives or what she lives on, you've got to throw her out this instant before it is too late:

"Tell me what I need to know," he said.

"I'll tell you everything."

"No," he thought it out, "I don't believe talking helps. Some people think it does. But I think it opens old wounds." He took down the tea and two china mugs, his impatient hand tapping on the handle of the tin kettle. He understood something more — went to the table and sat opposite her. In her face he could see how complete was her knowledge. So I do not have to explain anything to such a woman except the areas of my own ignorance. Get her out of the kitchen, soon there will be no going back, speak to her like the man you ought to be at thirty-seven and send her about her business:

"First I must know who you are afraid of."

"The police."

There you are! Now if you haven't had warning enough, you deserve all that's coming to you. He recalled his recent wanderings in the city: and the sign HABIS with its one gigantic painted eye that seemed to follow him up Albert Street, his moment of braving it to read the sign *Household and Business Investigator Service* and the advertisement offering every dirty species of sub-social prying for a fee:

"I see. What are you afraid they might do to you?"

"They want to put me back under the Act," she relaxed, she was in the right hands. He was, in a sense, one of her own people.

"The Act? The Law?"

"The Act for Aboriginals."

Collocott nodded and got up. He stood by the kettle till it boiled. Nothing more was said till they sat again with their mugs of tea, till pearly steam created illusions between them.

"What would they do to you with this Act?"

"Send me back."

"To a mission?"

"To Prison Island."

"I've never heard of it."

"That's our name for it, not theirs. Government say the Act is to protect us, but we know what it is. In those places you can't talk, you can't write a letter, but they know. You don't knuckle under, take their hand-outs, then you starve."

Again he nodded and searched for the next question he must ask. Daisy sat like a patient. She put total faith in him now. Indeed she had anticipated his sympathy. Even the decision to turn to him was not wholly rational; it was "known" to her that this was where she must run. She had not doubted he would help until the moment she first banged the knocker, when there was no answer she knew he was asleep and banged again more urgently. When there was no answer faith gave way to belief. Her hand trembled at Mrs. O'Shea's door. When there was no answer belief turned to doubt as it inevitably must. The third time she knocked with despair. Her people spent their lives learning to face despair, it had become a national characteristic. She turned and walked back down to the sodden grass: noticed the sky's clarity, that the Wet was finished, that the river would soon be back to normal. She had walked right round the house in memory of its previous owner.

"What has happened?" he asked.

"That big fat woman from over the way, she came up last night from town. Now look, she said, they got it in for you so you better hide."

"I understand," said Collocott grasping at hints and the suggestion of connections, "but what happened before?"

"That bugger Sissons dropped dead."

"Were you there?" Look, the police won't be long, this could be murder, just find some polite way to get her out, or get out yourself and leave her here for them to catch.

"I saw him die. But now they say he was not dead. That woman say they tell the police I wouldn't help him."

"And did you help him? He was dying, after all."

"Look mister, lots of people die. And I seen them. I seen more than I could count. Why should that worry me? He has his reward if he deserved it in Heaven. What else can you say? I went up the road and all I could think was: Now I can walk past here in peace and I thank the good Lord Jesus for it."

"Come with me," Collocott said and took her into the livingroom, "let's be comfortable. It may not be true that the police want to catch you. If they do, I suppose they'll come here sooner or later. We might as well be calm."

"Perhaps I better go out now and keep running?"

"Hopeless. They'd have you at the station within five minutes."

"What will you do, mister?"

"I won't know that until I do it."

Daisy looked up at him, a rare and timid smile lighting her face: "I think you're more like us than them," she said so softly he could barely catch the words. Had anything so precious ever happened before?

The sun had risen, earth gave out a delicious fragrance, marshes and flooded fields began to dry. The free channel of the river curled like orange rind flecked with gold. The hyacinth clustered in and back out of the estuary turning brown and rank. Culver's valley was heavy with luxuriant growth. Three bottlebrushes, with their yellow sun of spikes, blossomed against the side window; Collocott was sure there was some literary reference worthy of them. Though in reality his mind was working at two thoughts: What do I want life to be? and This woman and I might be sitting calm at the core of a cyclone.

"Flowers worthy of Paradise," he quoted. And she accepted it.

6

The air, clean and damp, welled up from the panorama like a bubble, too bright to be invisible, and inside there seemed to be no sound. Hard lines and angles had an exquisite sharpness, planes of colour and texture were differentiated with more than ordinary clarity. The light itself concentrated on particulars, glancing brightly from water, nestling into a horse's mane, penetrating rusted car hulks and placing a warm mould on the brown stone ruins overlooking them. There were recesses of darkness and shadows with crisp edges. The outer reaches of the air, at the very skin of the bubble, glowed with traces of the entire spectrum.

The grass had grown tall. A few widely separated houses stood like cattle, wading belly-deep at pasture, eyes down as if browsing. Closer to the bayside beach the gardens became more regular in shape, smaller, a village developed. Tucked away to the south of a long point of land, lines of houses looped round following the indented coast so nearly in a ring that their squared lifeless shapes suggested a rather jumbled druid circle.

As morning grew warmer the bubble expanded. The tiny houses clamped hard round their treasures: the mysteries of washing machine, refrigerator, laminex, and motor mower. Temporary lakes and pools gave back the sun's rays, while on the subjugated river the blue plumes of an unending army nodded sedately. A tiny chapel at the Spit, like a matchbox on one side, gathered up the stone rubble of its hillslope graveyard like a skirt. There were four Gothic windows cut in the weatherboard walls. For a moment it might almost seem that the tiny sound could be heard of its iron roof clicking and cracking as the warm light won miniscule victories over the cold interior.

At the seawall a dinghy lay beached, upside down like some large fish washed ashore; nearby were the rolled nets (one end bristling with corks, the other with lead weights), a bucket and two brushes. One broad stripe of glossy red at the stern showed that work had begun on scrubbing off the incrustations and sluicing away the mud. At the settlement's opposite extremity the horse-breaker's house stood, similarly lifeless, perched on stumps so tall and ricketty they looked like stilts; his large block of land offered evidence of occupation (a few old articles of horse leather, yards, pens and fences) but no horses, no people. Yet one could almost feel the warmed patch of ground where an animal had been resting — and almost scent animal life in the air. The doors were ajar. On the ledge of one open window stood a pannikin of tea still steaming. Had a north-easterly breeze sprung up at that moment it would have carried the babbling of nearly four hundred voices for, although the houses and radial streets appeared deserted, something related to a sacrificial ceremony was in progress on the Parade. Viewed from above, life and movement concentrated at two points: this assemblage of people in three clumps along the Parade, counterpoised by the single tiny figure issuing from Collocott's gateway.

The village responded as a single organism when touched on some tender spot, tightened to consolidate its forces, retracted like a sea-anemone. Such a moment was universally felt, as if by telepathy. Last night when the news spread that Eric Sissons had died there was no such organic retraction. This morning, with the suggestion of foul play involving that Aboriginal woman, the effect was immediate and dramatic. Meatworkers, railwaymen, labourers, and truckdrivers sank their differences to discuss the issue. Fishermen even condescended to recognize prawners. Certain wives, unaccustomed to doing so, spoke to their husbands and their neighbours. Gradually agreement was reached, information and opinion clarified the issues:

Agreed — Sissons was dead

Agreed — Mick had been the last to see him alive

Agreed — Daisy was accused of not fetching help

Agreed — there might have been a chance of saving him

Question — do we want blackfellows among us or don't we?

Collocott walked so quickly he found himself breaking into a trot every now and then, his flesh jogging and trembling. Behind, Daisy lay on the floor of the spare room with strict instructions to make no sound or movement. Ahead of him — help.

A third point of movement suddenly violated the landscape: a police car that had been stationary outside Daisy's shack started forward and sped along Spit

Avenue back to the village.

Collocott ducked between the rails of the old fence and followed the track, a tingling sensation irritated the soles of his feet. In eight years, this was the first time he had ventured into the market garden.

Daisy struggled to understand what was happening to her. Hiding was no new thing. The threat of the law was familiar enough also. But this palpitating excitement she felt — if she had experienced anything similar it must have been too far back to recall. And why should there be excitement? She was powerless. Her people had no rights to challenge the courts, their tradition was to plead guilty. Everyone did it, that was the simplest way, it was the expected plea and the only hope of leniency. Innocence could never have been considered, surely. Then why? Daisy lay there listening to her pounding blood.

The police car pulled up at the tiny station, out jumped a constable and burst into the office with a single word: "Gone!"

The house lay twenty yards ahead. Collocott hesitated. Someone was watching him. He could believe this was his last breath, that he would be shot dead by a sniper's bullet.

Mrs. Jones declared herself absolutely adamant in opposing any leniency to blacks. "Look," she said, "we've tolerated that woman camping by our dump long enough. If you ask me it's a matter for the health authorities anyway."

"Good," the sergeant declared, "at least we can say this gives us a better idea of where we stand," he was not keen on any action that might involve political implications, "if she has cleared out, that's evidence enough of guilt. At least, enough for us to make the next move."

Mr. Douglas blocked the porch. He waited till the visitor was within reach, then he put up one knotted fist and held it menacingly at face height. "She's out," he said. Collocott felt his bones undergoing some chemical change; he was obsequious before that livid, scarred face. "You stay away from her, you lousy poofter. Beats me how she can go near your place without having her flesh crawl. Now just pull your head in or I'll knock it off for you. And get off of my land for a start." As if he *had* been hit, the visitor turned and staggered away; his coat drooping, his trousers trembling, only his hat remaining firm and assertive.

"Then what are the councillors going to do? This is a civic matter as well, you realize," Mr. Fennell felt that here moral obligations, moral leadership, must take precedence over judicial neutrality.

"The other aldermen on the Bayside Shire Council," Alderman Murphy took refuge in the phrase, "warrant consideration. Far be it from me," he continued, "to make any official statement whatever without," he was getting it right, "the correct and proper consultations with those whose concern it is, as much as it is unquestionably mine. Which it is."

"I understand perfectly," said Mr. Fennell crushingly, because he did.

Daisy understood: the new element was the protector, excitement was created by the introduction of doubt, the chance that she might this once *have* a chance. What more could she ask? A chance was as much as ambition had ever led her to pray for.

The door slammed like a rifle report; and Bobbie's father moved heavily through the house, reliving the past. One night, before his wedding, the boys who arranged a stags' party had laced his beer with whisky, laughed to think how they were fooling him, challenged him to drinking contests — till he staggered out to vomit in the yard. He fell over a rubbish bin (he could still react to the sensation), fell like a passenger in a broken lift, down over the back wall, till his face jammed itself into a heap of smashed bottles. Some of them he had thrown there himself after previous parties, it was a game you see. Then he realized the numbness was not his flesh but thick shards of embedded glass.

Arnold fretted at the apathy of his neighbours, their evident unwillingness to become roused at the wrong he had suffered. They were sympathetic, naturally, but that's as far as it went. He set out this Saturday morning meaning to cycle along to the Hastings pub just so he could be free of his own anger. Already the hoped-for lightness of mood touched him.

A train pulled in at North Spit, carriages squeaking and creaking. The station-mistress waited, inscrutable under her wide hat, one twig stuck out from her dress collecting the tickets. Mr. and Mrs. Strutt took possession of the platform.

"It was at the next station we saw her, remember dear?"

Whistle, steam, dragging grinding of old wheels, jostling of buffers: and that procession of Queensland Railways property gathered momentum behind their square backs, dwindling through the cutting.

"It's like an anniversary," Mrs. Strutt agreed.

"Truly a mission."

"The Lord led us to take note of her."

"And it was the Lord who placed her in our path again, don't forget that." As they faced the challenge of the future, satisfaction settled round them like deodorant made visible.

"I'm not standing here just for the sake of me health, you know," said the hat.

All three of them failed to notice that one other passenger had alighted at the station and dodged into the toilet shed. He stood now in the stench of the single cubicle, listening to his heart, straining his ears to catch the sound of Miss O'Brien locking her station master's office.

The entire police force sat in the front seat of the car that returned to Daisy's.

"We should," the sergeant addressed his two subordinates, "be able to pick up some clue if we look hard enough," he sighed with something like pleasure, "at

196

least this is a break from bloody Arnold and all that fuss over nothing."

Mr. Douglas touched his face. Forty-five stitches had been needed to close the wounds. He had not sent a message to Philly. When she saw him in church she wept, a huge aching hollow round her heart. He could hear her whimpering "No no no no no no no . . . ." through much of the ceremony. He had made sure his best man would not forget the ring. As for revenge — what could he do? He was an unconvincing liar: and of course he had realized his drinks were laced right from the first mouthful. So who was to blame?

"I'm sure it was a good idea to begin at this north end and work down that way," said Mr. Strutt, "we should be able to leaflet every place from here to the shops by lunch time."

Before Arnold had pedalled two blocks from home he was hailed by postie George. The two men swung their bicycles to meet in the middle of the road. They talked. A few minutes later when the fat old postman resumed his labours, Arnold's mood was broken. He was without anger. Instead he was filled with energy. But he needed time to think, so he dismounted and pushed his bike back the way he had come, along the Parade.

"He knows what's coming to him now," Mr. Douglas growled, blundering towards the darkness inside, his scarred face rucking like fine material into the remembrance of a smile.

Then the Capuchin father contemplated the mirror itself. I have got used to this furniture, he said, which means we have been here a long time. Some people adapt quickly. Not me. I shall be sentimental when we leave. Just the way I was long ago as a little boy kissing goodbye to the wardrobe the bed the walls, understanding for the first time that they were rented: not mine at all, not even father's. I suppose I was about ten. Ten, would it have been?

Collocott recovered when he was safely through the fence and on the road again, with his house in sight. I can run, he said. It is the end of something, he said. Things do end. No more cheques anyway. Even Les might change. People do change. I've changed. He walked slower, thought deeply about it, opening his mind to the whole span of his eight years at Battery Spit. What he was trying to receive was knowledge of when the turning-point had come. As he said: when was the last day my old self remained untouched? For the moment he was satisfied that the *quality* of change became clear — it was when I lost faith in my own innocence. The thought surprised him, being of a kind he had not expected. Yet it so evidently answered the vague discomforts of intuition that he knew he had hit on the truth. That was how I remained indolent all those years, almost as if in mourning for myself, for the prolonged death suffered during childhood and adolescence. The wronged innocent, he said (his hat a halo), is a most treacherous concept: there remains no will to do anything. Self-pity feeds on self. Excellent, I'm progressing. The shock was wearing off. Now, when was the turning-point? *Was* there any single point? Probably not. He recognized this as an evasion for, curiously enough, one occasion did come to mind: he had been sitting with his back against a split-log wall reliving the childish violence of a Punch and Judy show. But, he said, Punch does what I can never do, Punch is triumphant, brutally hedonistically triumphant.

"But I have at last succeeded," Collocott spoke aloud, "in killing my innocence." There was fresh energy in his manner as he stepped across the muddy ditch and squelched on the verge of his own property. "In killing the baby in me."

As if borne up by a huge flame of indignation, Arnold dominated the discussion.

"Look, we just want to be left to live in peace," he shouted to the one hundred and seventy people gathered outside the school, "we've got our standard of living, we've had to fight hard for that. You have," he pointed to Bert Douglas, "so have you," to Mrs. Murphy and the councillor, "so have I, so has my neighbour," Chick looked uncomfortable, "we've all fought hard and now we're getting on in years we deserve the chance to enjoy what we've made — life as we'd like to see it." Dulcie was there, she had been there well before him, but this was the first moment he caught her eye and found her looking at him with an expression he had forgotten. Her admiration sent him dizzy with fulfilment and words could not fail him, "I've spent all my life at Battery Spit and I have a right to choose who I'm going to live among. That's not asking much, is it?

That's my bloody right. Majority rule is what I stand for. There's all of us to be considered. Why should a place be ruined for so many by one single woman?"

"Yes, we're all being held up to ransom," one of the schoolteachers agreed.

"But she can't help it, Arn," said Bert, "she doesn't know any better."

"Then let her go and live among others who don't know any better. She doesn't belong — that's it, she just doesn't belong here. Let her find people of her own kind. We've found people of our kind. I'm not asking her to do any more than we've done. Am I? Now, am I?" The crowd shuffled uncomfortably.

"Bobbie wasn't home," Collocott told Daisy, "I wanted her to take a message to my friend Mr. Charlton. But she wasn't home." The woman made no comment, he was back, which put an end to a new fear that had begun to press down upon her. She met his eyes and saw there all she needed to know. They were waiting together. Another quarter of an hour slipped by. Then voices drifted in from outside. This is it, he told himself, now you will regret it. He looked out through the lace curtains in time to see a middle-aged couple picking their way among the tufts of kangaroo grass.

"Never seen them in my life," he answered her unspoken question. Of course, they made for the front door. He hurried out through the kitchen. They were already peering in at the french windows when he called up to them from the lawn.

"Ahh," said Mr. Strutt, his tone indicating that a joyful surprise awaited the undeserving Collocott, "good morning." Mrs. Strutt offered him her face, which was fixed to a mask of determined sweetness.

"Yes?"

The husband, an aggressively friendly businessman who had met this type before, flashed a full scale of gold-capped teeth and advanced down the stairs with one open hand extended like some omnivorous creature in reach of food.

"Good morning," he said again.

"Yes?" Collocott spared a glance up the road in case a police car should happen to be coming.

"A very beautiful morning too, is it not? And I'm glad we chose such a fine day to make our visit, because here the glory of the Lord is all about us."

" . . . fell upon them," murmured his wife, correcting the quotation for the benefit of her own soul and the private relationship she enjoyed with the Saviour, for whom things must be just right. She aimed her smile at the stranger. By this time Collocott was sure they were what they seemed, chance callers unconnected with the present crisis. That they were no threat endowed them with positive helpfulness. It was this, coupled with the urgency, the sense of importance rousing his blood, which infused his manner first with gratitude then with impatience. The change was not lost on that seasoned campaigner Strutt, who dropped the pleasantries and came straight to the point:

"You are, I am sure, a believer?"

"If you're so sure . . . " — assent of a kind.

"It is our calling to represent the Lord Jesus Christ and in His name offer help to those in need." Unmistakable as a stab of pain Collocott felt the overpowering presence of his chronic disability — hope. Almost laughing with relief (although a desperate fear cried: No don't don't), "Well, you've come just in time," he said (are you mad!), "I'm expecting the police any minute." Fear stifled him, as if the words might create the event. His flesh turned to ash. "This is serious, you understand." His nervous laugh chilled them. Mrs. Strutt was already at the gate though still, to give her credit, smiling. Her husband wagged his head reassuringly, speechless. "I need someone to take a message to a friend of mine at the village. I think you are people I could trust. You are kind. You have courage. This is really terribly urgent. If you don't help, if, well, if you don't help it'll be the end of everything. There was a bad enough mess already, I was in up to my neck, before this came along." The astounded Mrs. Strutt protected her mouth with one gloved hand. "It has really been too much. Look, you are strangers here, aren't you? You would be able to do it secretly for me. No one would think of stopping you, don't you see? I've got a pen and paper. It's inside. Will you come in — no? I'll print the name and address on the message. It won't take a moment." He held up his hand demanding that they remain exactly where they were, then backed away round the side, and ran indoors. He rummaged, scribbled the note, amended it, folded the paper, held his breath to make Chick Charlton's name and address as clear as possible, so that not even by the exercise of ingenuity could any letter be misread; then he ran out to his deliverers, heart beating with hope, only to find the garden empty. Two portly figures could be seen halfway to Spit Avenue, elbows pumping, handbag and briefcase flapping, as they trotted, ran, staggered to safety, as they frequently glanced back in fear, praying that they might be accorded mercy enough to reach the house ahead (with an undertaker's car parked outside).

Leaving the station lavatory after his long wait, the furtive arrival made off along the rails, ducking from sight at the least noise. He knew exactly where he was going.

"Anyhow," Molly declared, "if it's true, that creepy boyfriend of yours'll be leaving the Spit."

"So what?" Bobbie was angry.

"You don't mean you're going to follow him do you?"

"I'm going somewhere."

"But they say he comes from Melbourne."

"I don't know," she was miserable now.

"Then where are you going?"

"I don't know."

"Alright — if I'm not good enough to tell!"

"It isn't that, Moll, truly. All I know is that I *can* go and I want to go. Somewhere."

"Do you love him then?"

"How can I tell? I expected more than this . . . you know. Yet I do feel *different* about him. More than I feel about other people. Is that love?"

"Do you want to kiss him?"

"Yes."

"Do you want to go to bed with him?"

"I don't mind. He's — gentle."

"Then you aren't in love, my girl. You listen to me

young Bobbie, whatever happens, don't marry. If you go away with him — Melbourne or — that's your business. If you want to look after him, okay. But don't marry or you'll regret it as long as you live. Wait till you find a man you can't keep your hands off — some bloke — so that you're always undoing his shirt or his pants because you can't stand to have him covered, when you miss every minute his skin isn't touching yours. When that happens you've got the man you ought to marry. Not before but. You'll go sour."

"Has that been what you've done with your life?" Bobbie regretted the cut instantly, for there was no mistaking the kindness in Molly's interference.

"Perhaps," her voice began to crack as she drifted into the world of women's magazines, "but Mr. Right just never came along. Still I've had moments — what would you say? — glimpses. Enough to know what it's all about, you might say." At this point, such overwhelming emotions had been bared in each of them that they stood for minutes in the most absolute isolation. Bobbie felt her blood as a mounting cyclone, spinning, tearing about a hollow core. She hung on to her nerve. And waited. Riding it out. At one point, in a flicker of unexpected calm, she heard her inner voice saying: This won't solve anything. She was her own prison, the limitations of body grew till they filled her universe, till she was suffocated, drowning in captivity. She could not bear it and there was no way out, there was no rest, no comfort, till she found her arms were round Molly's tired neck and Molly's cheek was against her wet cheek.

The three policemen locked themselves inside their car

again. As they approached Sissons's place, not only were Grimble & Son there but one of the old man's nephews was standing right out in the roadway flagging them down.

For want of more purposeful employment, Collocott began tidying up, as if this might set his mind in order. Might he not see the whole shape of his life? He began by washing up the cups, putting the milk away, wiping the table and removing the novel from on top of the fridge. He tucked it in the corner stack. She had had perfect skin. Perfect. Someone would have told him if anything had happened. He recalled the exact intonation of her voice on the phone and, more surprisingly, of his voice reassuring her. Emotionally, he remained blank. Or, it was unmistakable, relieved. Yes positively relieved. Perhaps a little pleased. Certainly more at ease. Even gratified. That was the end of her. After so many years.

"Come off it," said Elaine to the astounded Mrs. Fennell, "what are you coming at? The old girl has as much right to live as you and me. Why can't you leave her in peace?" Encouraged by a few murmurs of approval and the impossibility of her ever having to do business with the bank, she pressed home her attack, "What would you Pommies know about it anyway? You come here thinking you own the joint. That old Aboriginal has more right to live here than you. More right even than me. And that's a fact."

"Well! I never thought I'd hear such language!" the lady whined.

"Language?" Mrs. Douglas assembled her vast bulk to preternatural height, "if that's what you call language your old man must leave all the talking to the budgerigar."

"Don't suppose he's ever given the chance to open his mouth," Elaine added. Over the road the total green milkbar had seldom been so quiet on a Saturday morning. It was jammed to the doors with the town's young people, who were taking no part in this debate but reacted to the crisis. Cold jets of malted milk syphoned through straws into their silent mouths, eyes clouded, a sulky respect for their elders leading them to keep out of things. So they all heard Mrs. Jones's mangled syllables cooing round the walls:

"But then, Mrs. Douglas, you can hardly claim to be unbiased. Was it two weeks ago that you paid a visit to the lady in question?" Silence. "Bearing gifts, wasn't it?"

The police banged on the kitchen door so imperiously that the wall shuddered and something rattled in the cabinet. Daisy sprang into the darkest hole she could see, behind heaps of books in the dusty lobby. Silently easing the bolt across, she crouched against the front door. She heard the voices clearly through the house; so he was facing them.

"Do you mind if we come in?" For a moment Collocott could feel himself fainting, even remarked on how everything blacked out, on his pathetic weakness. Then his voice took command, crisp and authoritative, sounding exactly like his father.

"In that case we must observe all the legal formalities

206

— for your protection in the public eye, as well as mine. You will need a warrant."

"Now look, Mr. Collocott," the sergeant's friendly voice came from the bottom of the back steps, "let's not make difficulties," he advanced, "we've got a job to do. And any waste of our time is a waste of the tax-payers' money — yours," though he wondered in that instant if the man did pay taxes, "And," he went on kindly, "we have no quarrel with *you*. It's just we've been told there's a woman here; now I'm sure you wouldn't wish to harbour anyone contrary to the law. No, *you've* done nothing wrong. Why everyone agrees you are behaving like a gentleman."

"What everyone thinks," came the cool voice, "is in the furthest degree immaterial to me. My concern is for legality, not popularity."

"So," the voice knotted hard, the manner was transformed, "so you want to play it tough! You've picked on the right man for that. Now, if you'd please stand out of the road, we'll come in and do our duty. There's a job of work to be finished."

Collocott was aware of the immensity of his terror. It paralyzed him, locked him where he stood so that he knew his body — baldness, the round head, knob of a nose, the staring eyes, the tacked-on arms and legs — stood revealed before them, in every detail contemptible. Yet his voice outlived him:

"I am not accustomed to tolerating insolence from a public servant." An irrational loathing of the fellow outweighed the sergeant's judgement and training:

"Look, sport, you get out of my way, or I'll flatten you."

"And I would remind you this is my private property," a violent shuddering passed from his legs up to his stomach, he knew he would collapse, "so until you can produce a magistrate's warrant for coming here against my will, I advise you to leave with the least possible delay." With one hand he flipped the door shut in their faces, the latchlock clicking home, with the other he clutched the sink, missed, and crumpled on the floor where the lino surrounded him with floral tributes.

Mrs. Pascoe kept well out of the discussion, her position being what it was. She had her opinion, naturally, but her social standing was always a trifle delicate; everything depended on her not presuming. She mingled with one group or another, where she might be received, but contributed nothing more than a nod, plentiful tongue-clicking, and a tactful smile. Then, as she was on the point of returning home, Nev Jeffries's wife pulled her by the arm:

"Come on, ma, there's some people over here who're supposed to have seen the old Abo you'll never guess where." They picked their way among crowds of people, scuffing through litter (it was quite like a holiday).

"What is it?" she asked breathlessly.

"A practical joke, if you ask me." They joined the clump of faces round Mr. and Mrs. Strutt.

"And clear as day," said the evangelist, "we saw a black woman in his house, didn't we Mavis?"

"We did."

"Sitting in an armchair, just as we might, comfortable as you like in the front room."

"Having a bloody good snoop were you?" Mrs. Clark cut in.

"You mind your manners," Arnold threatened, "these are respectable folk."

"Since when did I have to ask your rotten permission to open my mouth?" she retorted. "Hey Eddie," she called as she caught sight of him passing, come over here and meet your Maker, save your soul, it'll do you good. You might even be lucky enough to get elected on to a lynching party." She defied the angry faces, "So this is civilization, is it?"

Daisy helped him to a chair. "I better go," she said, "make a run for it."

"No."

"This means trouble. They get you."

"Don't go. They have no grounds, you can't be touched."

"Cops don't need grounds."

"You've done nothing," he spoke out of tiredness, "they aren't such fools. Stay." She watched him, understanding how much the effort had cost him. Then Daisy filled the kettle and put it on. Light was streaming into the house, the gas flame was scarcely visible.

"There was this," she felt in her pocket, "on the floor." She passed him a scrap of paper. Without thinking what it might be or where she had found it, he accepted and opened the note:

> Mother died last Saturday — I will be in
> Brisbane till tomorrow p.m. — then fly
> to the reef for vacation — if there's
> anything to discuss ring me at the Aero

Club where I'm staying.
        The party is over — you're on your own.
        Les.

A breeze now blew in from the sea. The tiny leaves of a poinciana tree, like a sumptuous shimmering of feathers, cast their freckling shadows on young Mick and the constable as they walked out of the police station.

"It's almost enough," said the uniform, "but we need that little bit more before we can act."

"I've told you everything."

"It's getting her out of that house that's got us stumped. Having to deal with him makes it complicated." Mick didn't reply, he had told the truth, told everything, that was the end of it, there was nothing to add unless he began to invent information. He wouldn't come at that. They walked past the post office and past the little general store run by that woman who referred to Heinz 57 varieties as Heans' Beans. They were hailed by Arnold Thompson, suddenly grown aggressive:

"And what are you going to do?" Arnold said.

"I came along with Mick here to tell yous that we can't act. The sarge is wilder that I've ever seen him. If you can come up with reliable evidence, he'll go there like a shot."

"Otherwise?"

"Otherwise we'll have to wait till one of them leaves the house."

"Someone ought to be watching then." Ever since the police failure in the simple task of tracing Jonesy, a tinge of disrespect spoiled the barber's perfect conservatism.

"We won't be doing that," said the constable, nettled. Arnold turned on his heel and rejoined the expectant crowd in the school grounds.

Two friars in brown habits padded along the river bank with easy energetic strides, as if trying out the district. Occasionally one head would incline toward the other in deference to a brief nutshell of wisdom. They were waiting for someone.

Mrs. Fennell first asked the compound question: "Where did those cheques come from? Who was paying him and why?" then supplied her own solution: "In one word, I believe he could be a blackmailer."

"No!" exclaimed Mrs. Murphy, unable to sort out her feelings.

"Why not? It does happen, you know. It happens all the time."

If only I had opened this note, thought Collocott, the day he wrote it I would have saved myself one humiliation at least. Anyway, he thought further, it's just as well for him to think me completely weak and defenceless, I shall have a better chance of catching him off-guard.

"It's not my business," Daisy replied to a previous question.

"You wouldn't believe it, but I could be rich. I should be rich."

"I believe it." It had never occurred to her that he wasn't rich.

"My father was a chemist, in fact he owned a chain of

pharmacies in Melbourne by the time he died. Well, there was just me, my brother and my mother. He didn't like me, even so he left me a small amount of cash and a percentage of the assets to be paid as an income. He didn't trust me, took me for a fool, and because I was weak he thought he could push me around and laugh at me. In his opinion I knew nothing about money, he expected me to throw it away or something." Collocott began grinding one fist into the other palm, "They paid me my income, but all these years I know they've been cheating me — sending just enough to keep me, and keep me quiet, slipping the rest into their own bank accounts." At long last the injustice began to generate anger. Now, as he saw it for the first time with an outsider's eye, the full insult struck home. "He always called me a child." The memory choked him.

"We all had troubles," she was inscrutable.

"But I bought this house out of my own savings." He stared at the window, hat on his head ready to go out, "And I'm going to sell it." He stared at the floor. "So I can use the money to fight my brother in court." It seemed impossible. He stared at Daisy. She felt hope rising in herself and pointed to the bottlebrush tapping at the side window, saying —

"That is the flower of my country."

Once again stillness had asserted itself: the people on the Parade settled into groups of agreement, the large meeting broke up. The empty houses cooled as they stood open, the Capuchin friars sat by a clump of lantana, even Sissons's place was deserted (the planks, irons, toasters, crankshafts and innertubes released from a personal association). Only the irresponsible ironbarks, jumping about as the river cleared, defied the old order.

"You were a mate of his weren't you Chick?" All eyes were on him. Chick didn't need to think, the reply was readymade —

"Not me," and hugged his injured arm to his side, adjusted the sling where it cut against his neck.

"But you take your kids there," said Harry.

"And you took yours to the school. And now *they* take your grandchildren there. Does that mean you know what the teacher does in his spare time?" He felt the onus of proof still rested on him, "I'm with you."

"Well then," said Arnold, "if we all agree, we had better do something. No good standing round here."

"But there's nothing we can do."

"D'you reckon?" growled the horsebreaker; and yet he felt at a loss.

"What did the johns say — " Harry reminded them, "if either one of them set foot off that property, bang, she'd be in clink. I say if no one else is going to picket the place, why not us?"

"That's right."

"What? You're off your head."

"It's no good standing round saying what we'd like to do. Let's get over there."

"Who does this bloody Collocott think he bloody well is in any bloody case?" one of the fishermen contributed, "He's hardly been here more than a couple of weekends."

Further down the road Mr. and Mrs. Strutt explained

the miraculous circumstances by which they were led to solve the crime.

"Two weeks ago . . . " he said.

"A Thursday it was," she said.

" . . . we were in a train on our way to Hastings to a meeting of the society. They were discussing the possibility of setting up a church somewhere down that way," he said.

"And naturally they needed advice from those with experience," she said.

"We were chosen. But unfortunately we counted the stops wrongly and, what with the heavy storm, the station in darkness and so on, we got out here. As we opened our door, we saw in the light of the carriage this poor — "

"Bedraggled."

" — figure of a girl, wet and wretched. And bedraggled. As she got in, I said: Excuse me, but is this Hastings? There was no reply. She didn't even seem to have seen us. But we had seen her and her face was etched forever on our minds," he said.

"The poor creature, I'll never forget her," she said.

"Well last Tuesday, who do you think phoned us in the city? That same girl."

"She'd picked up our pamphlet," said Mrs. Strutt, "I always knew there would be *somebody* saved by those pamphlets."

"I said to Mother: Do you think we ought to meet her?"

"Of course, I said, of course. It was plain as the nose on your face that she was in trouble and she needed us."

"So," he continued a trifle heavily, "we offered her

our help. And we had her to our own home."

"She was ever so grateful, the poor wee mite."

"But the story she told us — such things in such a little place!"

"It chilled my bones."

"And she begged us to come to Battery Spit to talk to a certain lady, a Mrs. Pascoe." The crowd reacted: smothered laughter, disgust, under-the-breath comments.

"This girl," Mrs. Strutt was suitably moved, "ran away from Battery Spit in *despair*." The word trailed with appalling harshness.

"So now we're here to bring the gospel to the sinner." It was to be a simple case.

"But we want you to think of us as available to you all, to whoever else needs us. The church agreed this was evidently a summons from the Almighty to do His work in the whole area." The locals were struck dumb. Except for Mrs. Clark clutching Mrs. Douglas's fat arm and hissing up at her ear:

"This'll put the monks' noses out of joint. Dare say they think they've got a special licence from up above . . . "

"And we were to go about it systematically," Mr. Strutt had not heard her, "we came with leaflets to distribute — to prepare you for a thorough house to house visit."

"What's this got to do with the black woman?" roared one fisherman at last.

"Well . . . we got off the train as I was saying," Mrs. Strutt spoke demurely, "at North Spit so we could start at the last house and work towards the village here.

215

From top to bottom you might say. Well, at the very second house we came to — "

"Through the window," Mr. Strutt explained, "after a long walk, mind you."

"A very tiring walk! There we saw this black woman," said Mrs. Strutt, "sitting as easy as you please, quite at home, in the front room. In a perfectly normal house! And that criminal, I couldn't *tell* you, actually bribing us to carry a secret message to some accomplice of his who is still at large."

"That's exactly how it was."

"Thank heaven for protecting us."

"And perhaps, Mother, even using us as an instrument of Justice. We took his name naturally. It was on the letterbox, and gave it to the police." Bobbie, who had been listening in a state of indecision (was it unbearably funny or unbearably boring?), now made a connection. O God. She set off along the Avenue. Once past the bend, out of the public eye, she ran — her long legs flashing — ran like a champion, chin up, hair flying, ran with all her strength.

At Sissons's house the corpse lay in its lidless coffin. Three men sat in the kitchen making subdued fragmentary conversation. Flies began to settle.

Mrs. Jones's laundry window slid up and a man climbed in. He opened the louvres to the adjoining kitchen, reached in and unlatched the door. With a sense of achievement he walked in, upright for the first time in several hours.

At Hastings, a tradesman and his apprentice sat in a utility truck (but, because they were also father and son, they were arguing angrily).

"First the farm job, then to Battery Spit," said the father.

"Okay," the son assented in a venomous tone, made less effective by his pleasant features, "have it your way. You always do. Don't blame me if we aren't through in time." He drove too fast, dust kicking up from the shoulders of the road like spray in the wake of a water-skier, his brown elbow jutting out of the window.

Vi considered the news. Apart from the first flush of pleasure that Collocott had been proved as odd as she had always found him, nothing she felt was simple. She had come to trust him with her sons because — she knew it now — his comments which they repeated were evidence of a sound set of values. So this dislike had been . . . physical! She had it. And the injustice of her own actions appeared obvious; and unchanged. Slowly, Vi edged back from the group, leaving a gap beside Mrs. Pascoe, leaving Mr. Strutt's account at the point of transmutation from narrative into piety.

"Next thing," said Mrs. Douglas joining her, "it'll be Pass round the hat dear."

"Are you convinced?" Vi asked thirty yards later.

"No, I am not. And that's honest."

Bobbie trotted in spasms, with a fist dug into her side. Nevertheless the stitch brought her to a halt. She tried touching her toes and then bending over backwards. But that remedy didn't work either; and it wasted precious time. She was so hot too.

The thief in Mrs. Jones's house went through her drawers and cupboards, emptying the housekeeping money from a blue flowered jug by the stove.

The friars stood and faced the hill they were to take possession of. "He should be here soon," said one, "shall we wait up top?" Agreement was signalled by a glance. Together they began the leisurely climb, bindy-eyes bristling on the rough cloth and collecting as thickly round the hem as fur trimming.

"Was he ever plain Bernard Tolley?" said the elder.

"It seems difficult to imagine him other than he is."

"Yet he was. And such a bore with his fashionable chatter. I suppose there were some people who thought it clever and witty." He added as an afterthought, "Though I never met them." They had begun to pant. "Everybody I knew, without exception, came away from those monologues in a state of nervous hysteria."

"At least he has improved then?"

"Yes, give him his due."

"This is   more of a hill   than it looks."

"If the police won't go," declared Arnold Thompson, "then I will. As a duty." Although it was agreed that only a limited course of action lay open to them, a small group of militants decided to form their own picket and wait outside Collocott's.

"As Australians," Dulcie added. Old Harry (everyone knew he was well past his prime and slow to catch on) considered the idea out loud:

218

"As I see it, you reckon we can go up to O'Shea's and wait. No trouble, no breaking in, just wait."

"Right."

"Then if it's the darkie woman who comes out first, we grab her and drive her back to Sergeant Riordan."

"Right," wearily.

"If it's the cove, we let him go where he likes till he's out of sight of the place, then we go in quietly and fetch her."

"That's it."

"And," Clive put in, "tell them she came out of her own accord."

"She'll deny it, though."

"Who would believe her?"

"Exactly," Arnold slapped his hands against his thighs impatiently, "Now we've been over this several times — who's coming with me?"

"Things have gone wrong ever since that bloke of mine got a smashed arm rescuing his useless cousin in that storm," said Vi, "but what the hell — and now this business. It makes me wonder what we've all been doing."

Mrs. Douglas clarified the issue: "You can't just sit back, comfortable like."

"I'm afraid you're right. What's more there's no point in trying to talk sense to the men. The only thing is to go round, ourselves."

"And take some food Vi," the older woman agreed.

"I have never seen people here so stirred up except that once when the American prawning outfit wanted to move into the Bay, remember?"

"They don't care about *him*," said Mrs. Douglas, "it's *her* they are after. The poor thing has little enough, Lord knows, without taking away her right to live here." They began packing a basket. "But I'm hanged," she went on, "if I didn't think you had it in for him too."

"I did," said Vi, her face relaxing so that her friend was shocked into realizing how much younger she was than she generally looked, "He's got damp hands and I can't stand a bar of him."

Suddenly there was someone clumping on the steps, calling, tapping urgently at the back door. Collocott opened it. Bobbie began to come in then checked herself, sensitive to a change in his manner and impressed by the urgency of a situation in which he left his hat on in the house.

"Thank heavens!" he said. But she knew he was afraid for her. He loves me, she thought, I know it now. And she fixed her attention on the hat, so that he might be saved from her consuming eyes.

"What can I do?" she asked.

"I don't want you to be involved, especially after your father said — "

"Has he been round?" startled.

"No." He faced the memory, "I went to your house to find you."

"Jumping saints!" she could see in his face what she feared would have happened.

"And the police have been. So, Bobbie . . . You've been running, you look worn out."

"Just hot. Came from the town."

"Running?" When she nodded, he savoured the moment. He had all the proof he needed. In case he should weaken, Collocott acted precipitately, jabbed his face at her and struck her a glancing kiss on the cheek. He sought her hand. "Now," he said as acknowledged master and in his best man-of-the-world tone, "we have to keep you safe from all this unpleasantness."

"I don't care."

"There is only one thing I need you to do. I have a friend. Please take a message to him. Tell him to come, urgently. He can help."

"But I must stay here, you'll want . . . "

"Honestly this *is* what I want. How else can I get word to him, with no phone nearer than half a mile away?" She knew finally that she would not go inside now. "Will you be a good girl for me?"

"Who is it?" she asked, disappointed.

"Mr. Charlton."

"Ah, of course. Okay, if you're sure it'll help."

"More than anything. But you must go secretly. If they see you they might stop you." She brightened; he added, "How about cutting up over the top of West Hill?"

"Yes," she agreed warming to the subterfuge, "then I can cross the patch of scrub at the back of the cemetery, run over the road and down to the rocks, then along the beach. No one will see me." He let go of her hand and it became a great moment in their lives. "Is it true she's here?"

"Yes."

Bobbie struggled for the confidence to find words: "I'm real proud of you," she said. His eyes filled with tears of love and pride, fear and disillusion.

Mrs. Pascoe decided the time had come to speak. "Now then," she said to the Strutts, "we can show you where to find Mrs. Pascoe, but we've all got a right to know what she has been doing." They shrank from the question, however. To pronounce judgment is a public matter and no offence to decency, whereas details of the actual issues are a case for the conscience — the spiritual advisor's private battle for the soul. Yet Mr. Strutt rather liked the forthright way this plump wholesome country woman was eager to confront the problems of evil (though he was on guard against the brassy young miss beside her).

"These things are confidential between my wife, myself and Mrs. Pascoe," he replied.

"Plenty of men could say that," commented Mrs. Clark drifting among the bystanders; Mrs. Pascoe shrugged good-naturedly at the burst of laughter this provoked, though she could hardly fail to detect a few bitter voices among the amused.

"I'll tell you one thing," Mr. Strutt volunteered, feeling that he was losing their attention, "the poor young girl was refused permission to attend church on a Sunday. Whatever church she belonged to, there's no excuse for that." This much was true Mrs. Pascoe had to admit — trust that little chit, she couldn't even invent an interesting lie.

("It was working time," Vonnie whispered to Shareen, "after all.")

"I'm afraid I cannot say any more here in public. The whole story is a catalogue of evil such as I've never heard before. Unspeakable things."

"Do you," someone was asking Mrs. Pascoe, "believe this about Mrs. Pascoe?"

"Every word," replied the great lady, "they have me convinced."

"Then I think we ought to show these good folk the house, so they can meet the woman in person," Mrs. Clark glanced triumphantly round to see who would make the next move.

"Quite right too," Mrs. Strutt braced herself (being considerably helped by an uplift brassiere). She enjoyed tussling with the Devil.

"I'll point the place out then," Mrs. Pascoe offered, "it's on my way."

"He who hesitates . . . " Mr. Strutt said bravely and philosophically, taking his wife's elbow to give her strength and guidance. They nodded courteous farewells to the assembled natives and, to everyone's huge delight, set off with their guide.

"This I can't miss," said Mrs. Clark and trotted after them.

Sergeant Riordan sat tensely at his desk polishing his horny fingernails on his lapels. He knew the quandary in all its terms: on the one hand public feeling was against Daisy and demanded he should act, the legal instrument for removing her and placing her in the care of the Department was ready at hand; he had never been popular (coming as an outsider from the city and utterly failing to find the Battery Spit wavelength), he was getting the reputation of being weak and brutal (people had their ways of letting him know — even his own subordinates who achieved far closer understanding with the locals), "reasonable" arguments were impossible, public feeling in this case was unreasoning being in the full sense racial prejudice (he knew it, and with this he was in sympathy). On the other hand, there was Mr. Collocott. That was the equation. Collocott alone stood in the way of direct, popular action. Collocott, with his rights, his property, the possibility that his family were rich and influential, the fact that he was inscrutable, eccentric, unreliable, untouched by the desire for popularity, there were the dangers of crossing an educated man, his rights were undeniable, his understanding of them clear, his fluency and control of the situation depressing.

The ladies Murphy, Donnelly, Jones, McGillivray and Jeffries lost interest and went home, as the joke turned down towards the waterfront away from the burning-blue house and the chances of Mrs. Pascoe being unmasked.

Bobbie, head down, hands on her knees to help give her legs extra driving force, trudged up to the top of the hill and collided with the two friars, similarly bowed by their ascent of the north-western slope. She treated them respectfully although she was in the habit of scoffing at church-going.

"My goodness, you are in a hurry," said the senior brother.

"No—o," she decided her responsibility was too great for any hint of it to be allowed to leak out.

"Have you lived here long?" asked the young one.

Heavens! she thought, he looks quite normal — like any young bloke dressed up — even his hair in a modern cut.

"All my life," she answered, then she accused them: "and what about the poor Irish monks?"

"What about them?" they said in surprise.

"The— the— " she found the word he had given her, "tonsure."

"What!"

"Why couldn't they shave their heads the way they wanted, that's what I want to know. Specially as you don't shave yours at all."

The young man went red with embarrassment and confusion.

"I've got it," cried his companion, clapping hands, "My dear boy, far from a missionary situation, we've landed in that impossible utopia where even the most unsophisticated — unspoiled — " (he qualified it quickly, tactfully) "of girls are educated into the proceedings of the Synod at Whitby, anno Domini 663, during which — am I right young lady? — the Roman calculation of the date of Easter was accepted by the English and Irish Churches and the Roman tonsure was preferred to the Irish." She nodded, trying to remember. "Remarkable."

"Now I must go," she said and hurried off.

"In all my years," he went on, "that is the most extraordinary conversation I have ever had."

"And the briefest, I should think," his friend added, driven to a touch of acid by his own show of ignorance.

"There," declared Mrs. Pascoe, "is Mrs. Pascoe's house," and pointed further down the hill, "the one with the two pencil-pines outside," then added apologetically, "this is my turning, so I'll leave you here. All the best."

"Thank you for your help," said Mr. Strutt with a certain apprehension as he followed her finger, "and may God go with you."

Mrs. Pascoe made off out of sight. As for Mrs. Clark, she wouldn't miss this for worlds, she crossed the road so she'd have a clearer view and perched on someone's wall, wheezing with the explosive laughter she dared not release.

"It looks a well-to-do place," Mrs. Strutt observed, "well kept, lace curtains and brocade too by the look of it," she repressed a spasm of envy at *that trade* declaring such evident profits, only to find herself left with a deeper vaguer unease that the moral leper might (to all appearances) be indistinguishable from her social superiors.

"Very well-to-do," her husband murmured. Mrs. Strutt touched his arm with real affection.

"Neither of us knows what we're going into," she said. Giving each other courage they faced the large house like the normal respectable people they were, and unlatched the iron gate.

Two American cars squeaked cautiously over the bumps and came to a halt in Culver's Road; they were those large black high-domed models left over from the mid— 1930s with both the front and back doors opening to the centre. No one got out. The dust settled, drifting away from the house where Collocott, who kept well back from the windows, was peeping out. For Daisy's sake he tried to appear unconcerned.

226

"Just one moment," he excused himself and ducked into the bedroom where the view was better anyway. He pressed his body back against the wardrobe and squinted sideways out at the road. A wavering curtain made it hard to see, but he identified the barber and the hardware man Harry. And that was (wasn't it?) the postman driving the second car. "Never mind," he said as he returned to his guest, "that girl went to bring help. My friend is the most popular man in town. He'll fix everything, you'll see." She sat, following him with her eyes. She made no attempt to see what was going on outside, her total concentration had to be on him, her sole defence was through him, she must be ready to respond to his slightest need or whim: they were partners. Collocott noticed fluff sticking to her dress and patches of white dust on one dark forearm. She'd been in the hallway — yes he hadn't cleaned it since Les's visit. They sat absorbed, staring at each other, free of embarrassment, free of the need to form judgments, free (so it seemed) of the past.

Two hundred yards away, in the purgatory of flatirons and fusewire, Sissons lay in the ultimate dark, his coffin closed, the body's molecules busy adapting to their new condition — centralism reorganizing its mind-free behaviour. And flowers on the lid, juice bubbling at the cut ends of stem, were dying their own soundless active death.

After they had rung the buzzer four times, the evangelists stood back from Mrs. Fennell's doorstep to await her return. They used the time to calm their agitation of mind.

Mr. Macy, for the second time that morning, issued from his house into the bright agreeable world. He peered up the road, shading his eyes although the sun was almost overhead. "I think I can see something," he grumbled. He set off, half-strangled by a starched detachable collar (mother-of-pearl stud) and the stone-hard amateurism of the knot in his tie. His best pin-stripes, fresh from the trunk, stank of naphthalene and were creased laterally as well as vertically, but who would notice or care? It was the expected thing to turn out respectably; leave the details to those young enough to benefit. "Yes, I can see something," he said, setting his face to the south and driving the weight of his aged flesh half a yard at a time up the incline, the long arm of the cross.

At the opposite end of these bayside settlements a utility truck bounced over a rutted stony drive. "Here's your farm," said the driver, thereby dissociating himself from it.

"Look," his father sounded furious, "this is a job for an old mate. You and your jiving no-hopers wouldn't know what mateship is. Get this through your head: I promised Jack a quote and a quote he is getting. Okay?"

"Who cares about Battery Spit!" came the surly response, overloaded with sarcasm, so the father was obliged to recognize his own dead hopes in his son:

"They'll wait. They'll damn well have to."

Mrs. Jones let herself into the house, gave a scream of terror, then a laugh of disgust. She took out a cigarette without offering one to the thief who stood threatening her.

Councillor Murphy and Sergeant Riordon scratched their respective heads. "I have no choice in the matter," the councillor concluded, "responsibility cannot be placed upon my shoulders."

So *that* avenue of hope was closed too: "Nor mine, in that case."

"I told those people as much before they set off for Mr. Collocott's place."

"Before they WHAT!" the policeman was on his feet, buttoning his tunic, wild visions of westerns and lynchings flashed in his mind, "You come with me," he ordered. Then shouted: "John — at the double!" A minute later he was roaring, "Where the hell is that fool?" The veins bulged and lumped in his neck, on his forehead, "Don't tell me he has taken the car! O Jesus no!"

"This must be her," whispered Mr. Strutt as Mrs. Fennell walked in at her gate. He and his wife stepped forward, arms linked, to meet her. Her with her keys.

"The judgment of the Lord is come," Mrs. Strutt declared in her quiet calm voice to that amazed lady.

"Madam," Mr. Strutt said, "we beg you to have proper respect for your immortal soul." He was concerned on her behalf, "Have you thought of the terrors of eternal damnation? Please repent here and now while there may still be time."

"We have been praying for you ever since we heard the . . . description of . . . "

"You see we know everything." He looked down on Mrs. Fennell with infinite pity and compassion, "but it is not for us to judge, that is for the Almighty in His wisdom."

"I cannot imagine," rasped Mrs. Fennell haughtily, "what on *earth* you are talking about." She took a decisive step towards them, which in itself declared that this was her territory, "And now, if you'll kindly leave my front doorstep — " She engineered herself past without the taint of the least physical contact with the low creatures and tried to insert her latchkey in the lock.

"Madam," said Mr. Strutt sadly, "we've found the girl." Mrs. Fennell was fuming, she had the stupid key upside down. (This *would* happen to me!) "We've heard her story. You cannot imagine we as Christians could let the matter drop."

"You must be raving, the both of you," snapped Mrs. Fennell as she wrestled with the stupid door which had chosen this moment above all!

"Oh no," a sudden storm of anger mushroomed through Mrs. Strutt, "not mad. Outraged yes, but not mad. Oh no." She breathed ponderously, no one was going to insult *her*.

"Now my dear," her husband restrained her.

"She's not going to slip through our fingers that easily," said Mrs. Strutt. Driven to desperate action as the door yielded, swung open, offered refuge to the evil Mrs. Pascoe, she bellowed (so that the poor man realized he did not know who he had married): "We know your house is a public brothel."

Mrs. Fennell froze. Mrs. Clark nearly fell off the wall with delight as these, the first words she'd been able to hear, rang across the street. Mrs. Fennell swung round to face them.

"We know it all," Mr. Strutt confirmed, flashed his teeth at her, the metal caps clicked with confidence.

"No use denying . . . " his wife blundered on, "we have information. One of your own victims in person. A poor child you seduced before she even left school," she was out of breath.

"Nevertheless we are here to offer you the chance of salvation though you've reached an advanced stage of wickedness."

"Now. Look. Here," Mrs. Fennell demanded, rallying.

"Don't bother trying to deceive us," the man pleaded, "we know about your — em — employees shall we say," for a moment his courtesy was ridiculous.

"Your prostitutes!" shouted Mrs. Strutt's red face.

"Listen to me," the lady snapped imperiously, hearing windows go up in a few neighbouring houses.

"Not till we're done," insisted the handmaiden of the Lord, "and, having seduced, as I say, young innocent sixteen, *sixteen* year-olds, and initiated them into your vile practices, you cast them off the moment you ceased to make enough profit from the sale of their poor tender bodies."

"Stop. I command you to stop!" Mrs. Fennell was shuddering with fury and shock, her voice hard and resonant as a cornet. The whole street listened, front doors opened, heads poked out, hoses and showers were turned off. Everyone who was not at the Parade, it seemed, heard the banker's wife continue at the same piercing pitch, "MY HOUSE IS *NOT* A BROTHEL." No one dared to breathe. The horror, nausea, frenetic apologies, the laughter and the lawsuit, all were to follow. But for the present a merciful paralysis gripped the forces of life and held them.

"I can't bear lantana," said the late Bernard Tolley, "if there is lantana on the monastery site, kindly instruct the contractors to have it removed before my arrival."

Vi and Mrs. Douglas came to the beginning of Culver's Road. They had a grandstand view of the main action. As they paused for breath, and the basket passed from one to the other, they saw the slow figure of old Macy covering the last few yards to the parked cars, saw all eight doors burst open like wings and ten people leap out.

Mr. Macy realized, pressing forward, that though the black smudge would indeed materialize into motor vehicles, they were too far up Culver's Road to be the ones he expected. It was a pleasant day, not too hot, so he elected to go on rather than back. Then doors opened and people poured out. The visual impression was so explosive that the old fellow remembered newspaper stories of gang violence in Brisbane, youth on the rampage, bashings and knivings. But he recognized the postman, the barber, the butcher, the barber's wife, the ironmonger, two fishermen, a teacher, a meat-worker, and the meatworker's sister.

"Goodday Pop," said the butcher, "how're you going?"

"Pretty good. Is this," Macy planted his walking stick on the first car, "for Eric Sissons — for the funeral?"

"No. It might be for *someone's* funeral," he joked, "but not Eric's."

The old man leaned against the mudguard, "In that case I'll have a blow." They left him resting there and crossed the road to Collocott's. A voice from inside the other car called:

"I'll be with you in a minute."

They lined up by the fence, not really sure what to do, feeling perhaps a little foolish already. But they had waited for other carloads of angry citizens to catch up — sat idle in the vehicles — and now what other choice was there but to get out?

"Did only eleven of us come?" complained the postman peevishly "there must be five hundred living in Battery Spit."

"And I've never seen the Parade so crowded," one fisherman agreed.

"Must have been a fair few there alright."

"Yair, a fair few if you ask me," the meatworker conceded.

"Do we go in?" — from Dulcie.

"Better not," Arnold's caution had begun to reassert itself from the moment it was clear they no longer had mass support, "If only there had been a whole camp of blacks," he put his finger on the explanation, "then every man and woman in town would have come here with us."

"No use crying over that," said Dulcie bitterly.

Two women and a basket began the final hundred and fifty yards of their journey north.

"Come on out of there you rat," shouted the meat-worker.

"Yeah — come on out," they chorused.

Collocott heard them. This was the living nightmare his whole life had prepared for. He sat perfectly still where Mrs. O'Shea had sat after she invited him in to look round. His hand trembled on the chair arm. Control, control, he said, or we speak blood. That's what we live by. I sometimes feel so masterful I could encourage the pain, tempt it to break through. It won't. Who else could I tell such a thing? He watched her. Only you.

"Pain," he said and Daisy listened, "what else is there for us? Sometimes I think we must stand still, take all the air we can hold, and let out a long howl of anguish. On and on." She said nothing. Another shout was heard from the street. "I am often amazed, thinking how long the pain can go on existing just below the surface and never be noticed." There were more shouts. "Howling like dingoes." When she spoke, her voice was so remarkably light and youthful one could believe some other (original) self lay hidden in that bulky body:

"That's why they can't kill us," said the voice, "what pain have they learned?"

It was all he needed. Collocott stood, went to the french windows, the frail curtains brushing unnoticed against the grey felt brim of his hat, slipped the bolts open and stepped out on the verandah.

"*The Spanish Inquisition*," his lips trembled at the joke he murmured. In the no-man's land of surprise his thoughts cohered: so this is the shape of it, this is how things are.

"We don't want to cause trouble," called the old fisherman, "just answer one question — is that Abo woman in your house?"

"Yes," Collocott replied.

"Do you," the schoolteacher inquired mildly, "regard yourself as belonging here?"

"In a way, yes."

234

"In our way?"

"No." His hat, so unlikely and so square on his head, became a kind of gesture beyond question touching.

"Alright then. Do you think we have the right to decide who does belong here?"

"I suppose, in a general sense, you have." (This is unbelievable. If you'd told me about this I'd never have taken it seriously.)

"Then it is up to us, not you, to say?"

"Well I don't think it is up to me to say." The sly joke escaped them.

"So it *is* up to us, it is not up to you. Right?"

"I have to agree."

"But Mr. Collocott, you are taking the decision into your own hands," said the schoolteacher. The others nodded and growled. "She is in there because *you* believe she has a right to live here. *You* believe that, even though you admit it's not your place to have any say in the matter. The fact is that you're trying to force us to accept someone against our will. And," he added, "how long do you think you can hold out?"

"Not long." It was so easy to be perfectly honest.

"And then what?"

"I don't know."

"Well we do!" Dulcie declared.

"We've come to fetch her," said the postman.

"She doesn't want to leave."

"Then that makes an easy job unpleasant," the butcher snarled.

Fear began to drain Collocott's blood. The relaxation he had felt was so far out of reach, he couldn't even remember it.

"Yeah — unpleasant," someone added with emphasis. Just then the eleventh figure climbed out of the car and stood at his full height. For one ecstatic moment Collocott knew he was saved, it was Chick Charlton. Then he knew he never would be saved. His friend was never his friend. So he found the power to talk:

"Perhaps it is my turn to ask a few questions. Do you really believe you are adequate representatives of Battery Spit? I have admitted to being an outsider. Does that mean I have no rights, no conscience? Does that mean I am the only outsider?" The voice was his own. He was there as a whole man; every word was thought out and felt, nothing came automatically, his tone remained soft and fumbling. But they listened. "To judge by the number of you here," and he faced the worst, "eleven of you — there would seem to be hundreds of outsiders still back at the Parade doing their shopping."

"It doesn't alter the fact," yelled the postman, "you're harbouring this woman."

"So I am." In that instant he even considered the heroic generosity of giving her his house. But he knew the gesture would bring him no satisfaction, that the house was necessary to him. "If she has broken the law the police will come with a warrant to arrest her. And of course I would not dream of obstructing them. If she has not broken the law, then you may find yourselves in a delicate position. Perhaps I should warn you right now that I shall interpret one step forward on to my property as evidence of aggression, as a threat of violence, and you may expect to hear from my solicitor." His tone then suggested a plea, "I am not such a stranger: I can put names to most of you." Yet the victory was beginning to reveal its emptiness. I ought to be experiencing more, he told himself, I'm missing something. The crisis was passing and seemed to have left him uninjured. He could not put a name to the sensation. What has gone wrong if I can no longer learn? he asked. The recent troubles must have changed me, am I a stronger man? He envisaged courage like a flowering plant invading, taking over the course of his life, filling him with miraculous possibilities of blue, red, and gold. No, he sneered, much as I might long to believe it, that's not the truth. He recalled Daisy's words of a few vast minutes ago: yes, she had understood. I have completed a discovery of my weakness and my oddness. Now I can face anything. "Whether you like it or not, I have a right to make up my own mind, come to my own independent decision according to my own set of values. I have every right to choose my company and to say that in my opinion you are behaving in a superstitious, hysterical manner."

After a troublesome pause, Chick resigned good-naturedly, "Well, that's that then."

"The fact remains," said the schoolteacher —

"That we won't have blacks at Battery Spit," Arnold cut in.

"Precisely."

It was at this stage that Mr. Macy lurched across the road, the long-forgotten tiger in his eyes, and almost fell among them, waving them aside with his stick.

"Now see here you mob," he said, "the fact is you've got no quarrel with this cove except because he has shown you up. I can remember when the blackfellows were camped all round the bay and out on the islands. Not on St. Helena of course: that was a whiteman's prison. And there's a nice idea for you — shut them away behind stone walls on an island. Tell them about the sharks. It's not so long ago neither, considering my lifetime. What's the matter with the blacks? What are yous afraid of?"

"Of the dirt," said Arnold. Vi, Mrs. Douglas, and the basket sat at the side of the road within earshot.

"The dirt!" Macy spat among the clumps of grass, "You wouldn't have to go out of your own backyards, some of you, for that. Or along to the dump at the end of the beach: enough dirt there. No, don't give me that. It's not dirt you're afraid of. My guess is that you're a lot of cattle and you don't like having to think. That's why you can't forgive the blacks — for making you think!" He put his hand on the letterbox and faced Collocott. "And I've got something to tell you too. You've been here a couple of years and I haven't spoke till now. I've been saying you was queer or — what do you call it — some sort of — here missus what do they call them — the kids who are born nongs?"

"Retarded?"

"Retarded. Well after what you've done," his hare-lip rose to a snarl, "and the way you laid about them with the long words," a wheezing laugh escaped him, "I'm here to say I was wrong. I dip me lid to a fellow like you. You're a man. Glad to have you as a neighbour. Y'never know, perhaps I'll even give you a shout when I need a hand with the alterations to me house." He shoved the fence away, like a man in a dinghy casting off and propelling himself into midstream. Once afloat,

238

he hesitated only to wag his stick at the new mate and growl, "If I last out."

As it happened, Mr. Macy was not destined to walk more than another dozen paces, for just then a hearse with headlights glowing in the brilliant sunshine swung on to the unmade surface, approaching him. Two other cars followed it in close succession.

"It's Eric's coffin," cried the old man in excitement, "what are they doing? Why drive it down here?"

"I'll be blowed," said someone in the picket, seeing a chink of hope, "old Grimble has come good after all." Arnold took Dulcie's elbow and confided:

"He suggested he might pass this way as a protest; as a mark of respect to Mr. Sissons, you might say. I never thought of taking him at his word." The cortège drew nearer. "Course, Grimble was one of the few real friends the old man had," he remembered.

The hearse edged past Mr. Macy who was now in the middle of the road, swerved into the new deep rut outside Collocott's, bonnet dipping and nodding like a ceremonial animal, sedately completed a U-turn with the grass brushing high up inside the mudguards, and paused.

Collocott looked on with the deepest respect. Much as he had disliked the man in the coffin, he was most devout in his beliefs about the soul and his reverence for formal obsequies. The hearse remained stationary. The undertakers, eyes left, rivetted him with their unblinking attention. He stood perfectly motionless, unwilling to move an inch in case it should be misinterpreted as an insult to the occasion. Still they stared, telepathically compelling him to remove his hat, to capitulate. Still he remained frozen, having forgotten it was on his head. In the onlookers, jubilation turned first to outrage, then disbelief, then respect. Plainly he would not be beaten. Eventually Grimble and son set the hearse in motion. The flowers on the coffin joggled and jumped as if the man inside threshed about in fury. The first car of mourners (now including Macy who had taken this time to scramble into the back seat and had missed the drama altogether) had difficulty turning, backed up into the gutter, the engine raced, tyres were set spinning in the dust; when they suddenly gripped, the vehicle set off rather too fast, jerking the stiff figures hard against the seat backs and causing the sister of the deceased to jam a handkerchief in her mouth as if threatened with a fresh vision of death. The third car, Mick's Plymouth, remained for a moment — long enough to seem like a permanent fixture — while the driver stuck his wooden puppet-head out of the window:

"You heathen bastard," he said. Then he negotiated the turn flawlessly. To everyone's surprise it was now found that a fourth vehicle had attached itself to the procession unnoticed. It pulled over to the left behind the two empty cars already parked there and out jumped Sergeant Riordan.

"Break it up," he shouted, "break it up now. All go home." As an afterthought he added, "Please." So great was their surprise they behaved like a well-trained herd. As the Thompsons faced him the policeman grated, "Don't worry I'll get him in my own time . . . slamming the door in my face!" His jaw relaxed, "By the way Arn, we've got Jonesy. He came back to squeeze more money from his mother and she dobbed him in." The dry territory of the barber's face cracked, slowly he began to smile, life came back to him. This was the only news that mattered. With a flash of elation he ran for the nearest car:

"Come on Harry, to the police station. Back to the good old cop shop." He was feeling fine, definitely fine.

Chick stood back while Vi took the basket in and placed it on the bottom step, "Mrs. Douglas and me," she began, "thought you might need some tucker," then explained, "you and her." Collocott mumbled his thanks. Mrs. Douglas had already gone in one of the cars. The other waited, engine revving.

"Don't worry about us," Chick called, "the walk'll do us good." He waved a hand as they drove off. "Let's go, love," he said, laying his good arm like a heavy yoke across her shoulders, "a man begins to feel a fool here."

"That's because he *is* a fool," she answered. We are still in love, Vi thought as she listened to her own words. They sauntered reflectively.

"Just for you," he said at last, aware that neither of them had even glanced back at the house, "I wish I wasn't."

She felt wise: "What'd be the point? Perhaps we're best off the way things are." They began to see with the same eyes, "It's people who can't understand a simple thing like that who're always smashing things."

"Who," he teased, "has been coming to that bloke for lessons, the kids or you?"

"There's worse ways of wasting time. It takes all sorts. And if you ask me," she closed the matter, "he has given us all a lesson." Certainly they saw with the same eyes and both knew the moment had passed. The arm became a burden. Nothing could be solved for long.

The two friars on the hilltop had been scratching their untonsured heads with amazement at such singular happenings, including what must either be a unique funeral formality peculiar to the district or an impious joke at the expense of holy solemnities. The cortège, having circled round in the middle of the road, was now well on its snail's way to the cemetery where a solitary bell had begun hammering out its repertoire of one wrong note.

"This is very annoying," said the young one, "the contractor must be an hour late at least."

"But who would regret it?" came the reply.

"I wonder where that girl was going in such a hurry? It really is the most outlandish place."

"It's where she came from that has me intrigued. The Synod at Whitby!"

In fact, Bobbie had not gone far. When she skidded downhill she found her father waiting at the bottom. In the few seconds left to her, she had all the necessary arguments ready. Independence was worth a fight. But the chance was not offered. Without speaking, he caught hold of her ear, twisting it cruelly, and propelled her sideways along the track, up the steps, across the cool green verandah, and into the house.

"There," he said as he slammed the door with his boot, "now we're going to find out what you're up to." This time even the torture and shame were insufficient to prevent her seeing in his scarred face something that hurt more deeply, and raised half-recognitions from the past. Glimpses of a darkness without definite form clicked into focus. She sprang out of reach like a hunted cat.

"You like doing that!" she discovered, "You — get pleasure from it!" She backed away to the bedroom. "You do, you do, I can tell." And he knew he did not dare follow.

"Children," snorted Mrs. Jones. As she re-entered the house, she recalled the last conversation she had had in it:

Who would ever want children, the way you turn out.

Cut the sentimental stuff, mum, I need more money. Quick. And a place to hide till tonight.

She clapped her hands with a single explosion — If your father, she cursed, could see you now!

"Keep cool son," the builder warned, "there is a speed limit you know." Still the utility hurtled over the patchy bitumen.

"We'll be lucky if those monks are still there," the words escaped from between the boy's clenched teeth.

"Why," (remembering with some guilt the couple of beers and the couple more beers he had just enjoyed with his old mate), "should that be skin off your nose anyhow?"

"God! no wonder the firm only just pays its way. Look dad, you offered to train me so I could be your partner — right? And one day take over the family business — right? Okay. Well I have ambition. This is a big contract. A lot of money for a small outfit like ours. We are not going to foul it up, not if I have any say in the matter." The front tyres turned, dipped off the bitumen and dug into the dust of an unmade road. The youth looked up ahead. "Can't see a sign of them," he wrestled with the wheel, "I only hope they waited, that's all."

Standing at the open grave, Mr. Macy peered in. I shall have a worm's eye view of it one day soon, he joked, then looked round at the mourners. I wonder if there's anyone here who really liked the old skite? He fingered the lottery ticket in his pocket — to be drawn soon. What if he won that luxury home? It would be all hers, he said longingly.

The utility was giving out a hissing noise well before he applied the brakes. As the friars stood up and dusted their robes, one of them pointed to the motor.

"Steam there," he said, "looks as though you might have run dry."

"Thank you, Father," the older man lifted the bonnet, inspected the engine, stood back and looked meaningfully at his son. "Your job isn't it, checking the water and the oil?"

"Lucky she hasn't burnt out," said the other, adding generously, "I'd look a fool then."

"What do you think of the site, Father?" By way of reply, the Capuchin spread his arms, "Pretty good view — eh?" the builder translated as he extracted a pipe from the multiplicity of pockets in his overalls.

"Complete," said the young one, watching the

tobacco packed in and set alight.

"Clint," the builder told his son, "I'll leave you to fix the truck while we get down to details, the facts and figures." An exclamation mark rose from the briar bowl and hung, startlingly blue, in the air.

A plover flew along the river where the hyacinth had washed away, leaving in a line his piercing brass nails of sound. Collocott listened for a while. He had come to a decision. He went back indoors. "What will you do?" he asked Daisy Daisy.

"Go," she announced. The bond between them was weaker. She even added, "Go walkabout," with a touch of sarcasm.

"But you could stay where you are. No one will touch you now. You have friends."

How did I ever come to trust you? — she kept her eyes down — "I will go," she confirmed it.

"Perhaps that would be best," he tried to imagine what it would be like, and failed, "to get away from the memories."

She hated him already. "Why do you people always talk?" It was an accusation, yet behind it he heard her thanks. And this was enough.

Bobbie's one thought was to pack, to escape, leaving nothing of herself that mattered. She heard her father go out. Now was her chance, she must have the job finished before dark. She would run down to the Parade to Clive's place. He was bound to help. Even Clive seemed bearable now, especially as he could drive his father's car — it was only a matter of arranging for him to come at midnight and take her away. Before tea she would call at Collocott's, tell him everything, promise whatever he might demand. It was clear. She smoothed back her hair, watching herself in the mirror. I am beautiful, she said, I am, I am. I want to be. There was a knock at the kitchen door. Swearing to herself, Bobbie took one last farewell of her image and rushed to answer. A boy waited there by the tank stand. When he saw her he held out a large plastic flask. She saw only his boots, his chopped-short bluchers, and two thick downy shafts rising from them. She dared not see anything else.

"You haven't asked me what I want," he said, looking down at the top of her head, even catching a glimpse of the back of her neck, ready and vulnerable.

"I know," still not looking, even his boots hazy. She knew already that the dust was cement powder and that it was in his hair too. She knew this, though she would not check. Lightning flickered in his arm as he risked reaching out for her, as he seemed to breathe into her dress.

"Water," he said in a different voice. "Please," he said in yet another. She took the greasy flask, but did not go inside till he said, "Show me where then? From this tank?" he slapped it, but it was too full to ring. She felt her body tightening. He moved a step closer — was there such a step to be made? — and she withdrew into herself. He struggled to approach her with banter, which was impossible. He has a blue shirt, she was telling herself, with the sleeves torn out at the shoulder and with no buttons. He wears it because he is in love with his own beauty. And she ventured to look up, at the cross of his chest, after which courage failed. "It's for the truck," he said, "our truck. Up there." He waved one arm back at the hillcrest where a truck stood, doors open like a scarecrow stamped into the sky. Stamped into her sight. The shirt was all she could cope with.

"No one ever uses that old road," she said at last, in a way fearful.

"We do," noticing three of her eyelashes glued together by a tear.

"Yes," the syllable rushed out. He was ashamed of those loose boots.

"That's because we have a job on, Dad and me."

"You mean you'll be coming back?" yes come back, no stay away from me.

"We are contractors for the monastery. It's being built there. You'll have monks here," somehow making this sound like a dirty joke . . . Then touching her for fear there was a wound. She looked right into his face now, he into hers. They passed through each other and stayed like that, with just the flask between them like a baby.

"I've got to fill this," she said as she took it to the tap. He watched her movements shyly and greedily. On the hill, three figures stood up by the vehicle. He felt short, squat, movements jerky, neither legs nor arms wholly his.

"Thought I might call round sometime," he hitched up his shorts as if that might ease the burning, a muscle trembled along his thigh.

"While you're down this way," she confirmed, holding the water.

"We live here, or at least just along the Bay at

Hastings."

"That's not far then." He could see her body lift, nipples through the cloth, skin delicate and glowing, her neck so tender he felt his power positive as pain. He took the full flask showing that it weighed less to him, a runnel of water sparkled on his fingers. Walking away, the boots fluttered at his ankles; he felt how stupid they must make him look.

"See you," and his shadow was gone, snapped off at the root.

"See you," the new Bobbie responded. Would she bother to unpack?

Collocott opened the front door. He let the warm scent of countryside flow through his house. Rolls of fluff scurried away among the books. He felt the warmth soak into him. It was a renewal. Then he walked out, down the steps and round the perimeter of his land. Property, he said (the ground was already firm), it is all a matter of property. "Property," he announced the word, launched it like a floating sculpture, in a voice with the exact intonation Les had. Which made him think: indistinguishable.

Of course, leaving was bound to be hard. Some part of myself will be lost, he said. But no, let's cut the romantic pathos. He rummaged underneath the house, collecting an armful of tools. First he tacked the *For Sale* sign on the verandah, selecting the same post, remembering its position, careful to use the original holes.

"I'm ready for you now," he dropped the words quietly, "the last one," he had an allusion ready, "like the labours of Hercules." And after that fight, what about coming back for Bobbie? Yes, he comforted himself, needing comfort because the question hardly seemed to stir any feeling in him at all. When the money is in my bank, it might be a good idea to come back here to settle. But the notion seemed irrelevant and so hopelessly remote. He had, after all, turned his face away from the ideal.

Collocott felt a presentiment that in the moment he welcomed the thought of going back to Melbourne, he had betrayed his long search for meanings — partially betrayed it, at any rate. Or, if not actually betrayed it, relinquished it. When I get my income, he said, it will be unearned. What a comfortable death, one could contemplate it with pleasure. At last, he said, when I am fully despicable it seems I cannot despise myself. He laughed aloud. At least I *hope* I'll get my income. He wavered on the brink of life.

Collocott thought of his father smoking a cigar, never letting the ash drop. Not a single flake fell away, till he laid a complete scroll of ash in the tray (to the young boy this was an object of the most moving beauty). But the achievement itself was all his father cared about, never the contemplation of illusions, and crushed it with his thumb.

Collocott took the small tin of red enamel and a brush out to the mailbox. This is not sentiment, he told himself. He knelt on the soft turned earth and, concentrating all his patience and skill, retouched the lettering.